I0822406

MURDER AT THE PICCADILLY PLAYHOUSE

A CLEOPATRA FOX MYSTERY, BOOK 2

C.J. ARCHER

WWW.CJARCHER.COM

CHAPTER 1

LONDON, JANUARY 1900

"That was marvelous!" Flossy applauded loudly as the lights in the Hippodrome's auditorium came on. "I don't know which act I enjoyed more."

Floyd blinked into the sudden brightness. "I liked the acrobats."

"Of course you did. The girls wore little more than their underthings." Flossy suddenly clasped her mother's elbow and thrust her chin in the direction of two women trying to get their attention. "Oh look, there's Susannah and her mother."

Aunt Lilian had already spotted their friends and begun to move off. "We ought to speak to them. Come along. Everybody follow me, now. Try not to get crushed."

Flossy lost her grip on her mother's arm. "You're going against the crowd," she whined. "We'll never reach them."

"Fiddlesticks. We can make it."

Flossy appealed to her father. Uncle Ronald seemed to agree with his daughter's opinion that it was hopeless. The audience was simply too thick and they were all heading in one direction—out.

"We'll see them in the foyer, my dear," he said to his wife.

Aunt Lilian waved him off and plunged into the stream of people, moving up the aisle. "Excuse me, excuse me," she said as she battled her way to her friends, three rows down.

"I'm not going that way," Floyd said. "See you all in the foyer."

Flossy and I followed him, but Uncle Ronald waited in our row for the tide to deposit his wife back up the aisle to him.

If my hand hadn't been held tightly by Flossy, I might have lost her, but we made it safely to the foyer with Floyd. He ordered us not to move while he fetched our coats from the cloakroom, and we kept an eye out for their parents. While some of the audience left straight away, many remained behind to talk with friends, and the foyer quickly became crowded.

Now that we had a moment to catch our breaths, Flossy wanted to discuss the show again. "I think my favorite part was the polar bears sliding from the stage into the water. What was your favorite, Cleo?"

It was difficult to choose just one item from the evening's program—printed on silk, no less. I'd never seen anything like tonight's performance. Flossy might be one of the most excitable people I knew, but tonight I felt just as giddy after watching London's newest venue's opening night show. Indeed, to call it a show wasn't doing it justice. It was a spectacle. A large area in front of the stage had been left bare with no audience seating. Performers had used both this arena and the stage to full advantage. As with any circus, there were contortionists, acrobats, and high-wire acts, as well as trained dogs, ponies and lions.

But the second half of the show was even more thrilling. The arena floor sank and was flooded with water, streaming from brass nozzles. A theater show was performed on the lake with more circus animals, singing, dancing, comedic routines, and swimmers in figure-hugging costumes. Brightly lit fountains spouted water in time with the music. Boatmen rowed actors from one side to the other, and even deliberately pushed them in, much to the delight of the audience.

The entire production was wonderful, and the brand new venue itself was just as spectacular. I'd grown used to seeing luxury at every turn at the Mayfair Hotel, but the opulence of the Hippodrome's auditorium was more vivid. The gilded trimmings and red, blue and gold ceiling wouldn't have looked out of place in a palace.

"I can't choose," I told Flossy. "I enjoyed it all. Thank you for inviting me."

"Why wouldn't you come along? You're family. We were terribly fortunate to secure five tickets. It's a shame they weren't for the dress circle, but Floyd said Mr. Hobart did his best."

If the Mayfair Hotel's manager couldn't obtain dress circle tickets then I doubted anyone could. According to the staff, Mr. Hobart could get guests and the Bainbridges whatever they desired.

Aunt Lilian and Uncle Ronald found us, dragging a group of friends in their wake liked salvaged flotsam. We ladies waited while the gentlemen fetched coats, chatting about the grand evening we'd had. I recognized some of the group from the New Year's Eve ball, and they claimed they remembered me. Thankfully none knew what I'd got up to that night and the danger I'd faced when a murderer revealed himself as the clock struck midnight. If they ever found out, they would probably never look at me the same way again. It was better this way, with them not knowing, and Aunt Lilian was also being kept in the dark.

I was glad my aunt didn't know. She'd be horrified to learn that I'd been in danger, and even more horrified to learn that I was getting my hands dirty by investigating a murder. Bainbridge women were not supposed to do anything more than look pretty and socialize with the guests.

I'd frequently protested that I was not a Bainbridge woman, I was a Fox, but it had fallen on deaf ears. In truth, I didn't want to push the point and test the boundaries of my aunt and uncle's goodwill. They had set aside old family wounds and given me a home after my grandmother died, when I had no one else in the world. I would always be grateful.

Aunt Lilian was in one of her energetic moods tonight. She was as excitable as Flossy and just as talkative. Her moods seemed to oscillate between highs and terrible lows. During the lows, she remained in her room and did not accept visitors. She also suffered from dreadful headaches. The only thing that helped was her doctor's new medicine.

The men returned and handed out cloaks and other winter accoutrements to the ladies. The audience had thinned, and there was a little more breathing room in the foyer, but we only stayed long enough for Uncle Ronald to invite their friends back to the hotel for a drink.

I eyed Aunt Lilian carefully, worried she might be growing tired, but she seemed enthusiastic to play hostess to a late evening party. Dressed in navy velvet, with cream lace trimmings, she was at her most elegant. When she was happy and well, she reminded me of my mother. My memories of her were some thirteen years old, so it was bittersweet to see her likeness in the form of her sister. Some people mistook me for her daughter, not Flossy, as I'd taken after my mother in appearance and, according to some, her character too.

Even though I only knew my mother while I was a young girl, and I'd only recently met Aunt Lilian, at times like this, when Aunt Lilian held court, I knew she must have been the more vivacious of the two. My mother had a more subdued character. Not serious but not someone who liked to be the center of attention, although she had a witty sense of humor.

We headed into the cold night air and spotted the Mayfair Hotel carriage in the long line of conveyances waiting to collect their masters and mistresses. We five piled inside and headed home. Flossy and Aunt Lilian talked about the show, while Uncle Ronald, Floyd and I found it unnecessary to interject. Uncle Ronald and Floyd stared out of different windows, seemingly distracted by the lights.

Indeed, there were so many lights, it was as bright as day. All the street lamps were on, of course, but light also streamed from the windows of the theaters and concert halls. Powerful lights illuminated advertising signs, and a river of carriage lamps stretched as far as I could see. It made the darkness shrouding the Piccadilly Playhouse seem out of place; a missing tooth ruining a bright smile.

"Was there no show tonight at the Playhouse?" I asked.

Floyd seemed grateful for something to talk about while his sister and mother continued their lively chatter, unaware I'd spoken. "*Cat and Mouse* was supposed to be on." He peered past me to the darkened theater. "How odd that it's not playing. I believe it's been very popular." He sat back as the theater passed out of view. "I'll ask Rumford. He'll know."

"Lord Rumford? Is he a lover of the theater?" His lordship was a guest staying at the hotel. While I didn't know all of the guests by name, I made a point of learning the important ones and making myself known to them.

Floyd's smile looked wicked in the dimness of the cabin. "You could say that."

"Floyd," his father barked, proving he was listening to us, after all.

The sharp tone silenced Aunt Lilian and Flossy and nobody spoke for the remainder of the short journey.

The carriage deposited us at the hotel's front door. The night porter greeted us in order of importance, beginning with Uncle Ronald and ending with me. The chandeliers in the foyer blazed, and a small number of guests passed through on their way to the lift or stairs after an evening out at one of London's theaters.

The new assistant manager said something to the man he was talking to and approached us. Mr. Hirst wasn't nearly as handsome or as young as Harry Armitage, the man he'd replaced, but he was just as charming. He was a quick learner, according to the manager, Mr. Hobart, and had already settled into the Mayfair's way of doing things after ten days. Having worked as assistant manager at another of London's luxury hotels, he was familiar with the role and expectations. No doubt Mr. Hobart and Uncle Ronald had chosen him for that very reason, to ensure the transition was as smooth as possible. With the hotel being only half full, now was the best time to hire new staff and train them, so Floyd told me. That way there would be no hiccups when spring saw society flock to the city for the opening of parliament and the many entertainments the social season brought.

"Good evening, Sir Ronald, Lady Bainbridge," Mr. Hirst said.

"Who is that fellow you were talking to?" Uncle Ronald asked, squinting at the other man. He had his back to us now as he walked quickly to the staircase, but I'd caught a glimpse of his beak-nosed profile before he turned.

"A guest," Mr. Hirst said as the man disappeared up the stairs.

"Who?"

"Mr. Clitheroe."

Uncle Ronald's frown cleared. "Didn't look like him."

Aunt Lilian patted her husband's arm. "Your eyesight's not what it used to be, Dear."

Mr. Hirst signaled to the night porter to help us with our coats. "How was the show?" Mr. Hirst asked as we handed them over.

"Marvelous," Aunt Lilian said on a breath. "Simply wonderful."

"Were the seats in the stalls adequate?"

"Adequate, yes." Uncle Ronald all but grunted. "The dress circle would have been better."

Mr. Hirst looked pained. "I'm sure Mr. Hobart did his best and would be deeply upset to hear you were disappointed."

I frowned. He was twisting Uncle Ronald's words. Not that Uncle Ronald leapt to Mr. Hobart's defense. He must still harbor some anger towards the hotel manager and what he saw as a betrayal for hiring his nephew, Mr. Armitage, years ago, despite knowing Mr. Armitage had been a thief in his childhood. It had been my fault my uncle discovered the truth, and it was my fault that Mr. Armitage subsequently lost his job. My heart still pinched every time I thought about it.

"We weren't disappointed at all," I felt compelled to say. "The seats were perfect. We were very close to the arena, but not too close."

Mr. Hirst bowed his head in acknowledgement. Uncle Ronald and the others didn't seem to have heard me. They were welcoming their friends to the hotel.

Once coats were taken away and evening finery was again on display, Uncle Ronald suggested the gentlemen disperse to the billiards room, while the women enjoy the comfort of the small sitting room. While both sitting rooms were located in the left wing of the hotel, the larger one was reserved for afternoon tea, whereas the smaller one offered intimacy for more private functions.

"Once we're settled, you may retire," Uncle Ronald said to Mr. Hirst.

Mr. Hirst bowed. "Thank you, sir. And goodnight."

Mr. Hirst lived in the hotel, as did the other unmarried senior staff. The only married one among them was Mr. Hobart and he lived off-premises with his wife. The rest of the staff lived in a nearby residence hall. While the night porter and a skeleton staff remained on duty overnight, including in the kitchen, most would start before dawn.

The gentlemen headed to the smoking and billiards rooms in a raucous humor, while Aunt Lilian led the women to the small sitting room, flapping her program to usher us along.

"My program!" I said, stopping. "I left it in my coat pocket."

"It'll be there in the morning, Cleo," Flossy said.

"I want to read through it again."

She smiled. "You are so provincial."

I refrained from reminding her that I was from Cambridge, not the country. It wouldn't matter to Flossy. Anything outside of London was "provincial" to her and therefore dreadfully dull. Only London and its endless amusements could satisfy her zest for life.

Aunt Lilian joined us and asked Flossy to fetch her bottle of tonic from her dressing table. Flossy hesitated.

"Now," Aunt Lilian snapped.

Flossy bowed her head and hurried off.

I returned to the luggage room, which also acted as a cloakroom, and rifled through the pockets of my coat until I found the program. I was crossing the foyer again when the beak-nosed man who'd been talking to Mr. Hirst emerged from the stairwell beside the lift.

He scanned the area, spotted me, and hesitated. I smiled and he touched the brim of his bowler hat in greeting before heading for the front door.

On a whim, I said, "Mr. Clitheroe."

He kept walking.

He exchanged glances with the night porter. The night porter did not open the door for Mr. Clitheroe as he ought to do for a departing guest.

I joined my aunt, cousin and their guests in the small

sitting room, but didn't feel like joining in the conversation. Mr. Clitheroe had got me thinking. It wasn't just that he didn't respond when I said his name, or his furtive demeanor, it was also his clothes. He wore a well-made suit that wasn't out of place during the day, but didn't belong in a luxury hotel in the evening. All the gentlemen guests were dressed in tailcoats, bow ties, stiff white shirts with winged collars, and low-cut waistcoats with silk top hats, but Mr. Clitheroe wore a single-breasted coat and high-cut waistcoat with a simple necktie. A guest of the sort the Mayfair attracted wouldn't leave the hotel in the evening wearing his daytime suit.

Which meant the beak-nosed man was not a guest at all.

* * *

"HAVE you seen the papers this morning?" Harmony stood in the doorway connecting my bedroom to the sitting room, a folded newspaper in hand.

I sat up, blinking away sleep. "What time is it?"

"Eight."

"I asked you to wake me at nine today."

"Did you? I don't remember."

I lay down again and pulled the bed covers up to my chin. "Come back later. It was a late night, and I'm tired."

"Your breakfast will get cold."

My stomach rumbled. I pushed off the covers and picked up the dressing gown folded over the back of the chair. "I suppose you want to know all about the show."

"Oh yes, how was it?" Harmony led the way into the sitting room and deposited the newspaper on top of the tray's flat lid where I couldn't fail to see it. She proceeded to plump the sofa cushions until I invited her to join me for a cup of coffee.

She gave up the pretense of tidying and sat on the other chair at the small breakfast table. It was a little charade we went through every morning. She came to wake me, usually at eight, and sat with me while I ate breakfast, enjoying a cup of coffee. She should have been tidying my suite, and as far as the housekeeper was aware, that's precisely what she was doing, but I kept the rooms tidy myself. After breakfast,

Harmony often stayed to do my hair. The morning routine had given us time to become friends, as much as a woman and her maid could be friends. More often than not, we spoke to one another as equals. Harmony had quickly learned that I didn't put on airs and wasn't used to an idle, luxurious life like my aunt and cousin, and I'd realized she was clever and had a thirst for knowledge. I'd taken to borrowing books from the hotel library and giving them to her to read on her time off. Not that she had much spare time.

I handed her the program for the Hippodrome's opening show and described some of the spectacular acts. While she made all the right sounds, I knew she wasn't particularly interested. I cut my account short and turned to my breakfast tray and the newspaper she wanted me to read.

I didn't even have to turn the page to know what had piqued her interest. It was right there on the front in bold type: ACTRESS FALLS TO DEATH AT THE PICCADILLY PLAYHOUSE.

"How terribly sad," I said as I read the article. "That must be why the theater was in darkness last night. It says here the show was canceled following her death in the afternoon."

Harmony moved up alongside me. "It says it was suicide."

According to the article, Miss Pearl Westwood had thrown herself from the second tier dress circle. Her body had been found by the theater staff preparing for the evening's performance.

"The poor woman." I folded up the newspaper and set it beside the coffee pot and cups.

"Poor Lord Rumford."

"Why?"

She gave me an odd look. "She was his mistress. Didn't you know?"

I stared at her, aware that my mouth had dropped open. "Lord Rumford, the guest currently staying here at the hotel? *That* Lord Rumford?"

"The very one." Harmony sat on the other chair and poured coffee into the two cups. She handed one to me, a mischievous twinkle in her eye. "If only Miss Bainbridge could see you now. She'd call you provincial for not realizing gentlemen keep mistresses."

I closed my mouth and tucked into my breakfast of a boiled egg and toast. "I'm merely a little surprised. I met Lord Rumford. He seems nice. He even told me how his wife was currently in the country as she no longer liked London's fast pace." Lord Rumford must have been in his sixties, while the newspaper article claimed Miss Westwood was only twenty-six.

"How convenient that Lady Rumford prefers the country manor," Harmony said with a wry twist of her mouth. "Gives his lordship freedom to see his mistress while he's in London. Which he is a lot."

"She didn't come here to the hotel, surely?"

"She did sometimes."

I didn't know why it shocked me. I knew gentlemen guests kept mistresses, and I knew they sometimes brought them here. A foreign count even had his mistress stay with him in his suite as if she were his wife, while his actual wife was at home in Russia. But he'd been from the continent, and they did things differently there. I hadn't expected an English lord to parade his mistress openly at the hotel where he stayed while in the city.

Harmony scanned the newspaper article again. "I wonder why she ended it like that? She seemed to have everything she could want. Fame, money, adoring fans and an equally adoring lover."

"Those are hardly things that make one fulfilled and happy," I said. "And how do you know Lord Rumford adored her? Perhaps he was about to end their relationship and she threw herself over the balcony in despair."

Harmony shook her head, loosening one of the dark coils of hair she'd tucked behind her ear. It fell in front of her face and she tucked it away again, although I knew it wouldn't stay. The errant spring never obeyed for long. "I heard from Peter that he's very upset."

"How does Peter know?"

"He saw Mr. Hobart hurrying back and forth with a very serious face this morning. He was organizing flowers, notices for the paper, and sending little things up to Lord Rumford's room to show him the hotel cares."

"That's very kind of him." It was typical of Mr. Hobart to be so considerate of one of his guests. The manager always put them first, and always seemed to know what they needed, even before they asked. It was the sign of an excellent hotel manager, so Floyd told me.

"I think you should investigate," Harmony suddenly announced.

I choked on my final bite of toast. I coughed into my napkin, my eyes watering. When I finally recovered, I lifted my gaze to Harmony's. She was serious. "What are you talking about? What is there to investigate?"

"Perhaps it's not suicide." She shrugged. "The newspaper doesn't say why Miss Westwood threw herself from the dress circle."

"Probably because they either don't know what drove her to such a desperate act, or they chose to protect her privacy."

Harmony snorted. "No journalist is going to worry about her privacy. She's a star. The public want to know everything they can about her life, and particularly about her death. The first newspaper to find out and report it will sell thousands more copies than their rivals."

"So you think she was murdered?" At Harmony's nod, I shook my head. "If it is, the police will find the killer."

"Perhaps." She sipped her coffee with such an air of expectation that I knew she was going to say more on the subject. I was proved correct when she said, "But they didn't prove themselves to be very competent in the investigation into Mrs. Warrick's murder, right here at the hotel."

I opened my mouth to defend Detective Inspector Hobart but shut it again. She was right; the inspector had been rather slow at finding the killer. His determination to be thorough had been something of a hindrance, but on the other hand, it meant he hadn't accused the wrong man—like I had.

"Harmony, I'm not investigating Miss Westwood's death."

"But don't you want to be an investigator?"

I chewed the inside of my lower lip, regretting that I'd told her I was thinking about entering the private detective business. "I do," I said carefully. "But this is not the right case to take on. For starters, there is no client, and no client means no payment. And secondly, if it is murder, the police will investigate. I'll just get in their way, and Detective Inspector Hobart won't like it. He's only just forgiven me for getting involved in Mrs. Warrick's murder investigation."

Her eyes gleamed like polished jet as she watched me over the rim of her cup. "Or are you just worried about offending the father of the man you're sweet on?"

"I am not sweet on Mr. Armitage! What gave you that idea?"

"The way you look at him."

I sliced the top off my egg with such vehemence it missed the plate altogether and landed on the table. "Every woman looks at him like that. He's very pleasing to look at. Unfortunately, he has the personality of a man who knows he's pleasing to look at. He's arrogant and somewhat rude."

"I always found him charming."

"He can be."

Mr. Armitage certainly turned on the charm when he worked at the hotel. But as soon as he left, the charm slipped and his true nature revealed itself. Of course, that could just be for my benefit. I had cost him his job, after all.

Harmony glanced at the clock and sprang to her feet. "We better do your hair so I can get on with my work." She gathered up the dirty dishes and placed them on the tray then ushered me into the bedroom even though I hadn't finished my egg.

I sat at the dressing table and succumbed to her ministrations. Afterwards, I dressed while she tidied up the sitting room. When I emerged from the bedroom, she had the tray balanced on one hand and was heading for the door.

"We'll talk about Miss Westwood again later," she said. "Perhaps you'll change your mind."

I was hardly listening, however. A thought had occurred to me. "Do you know what Mr. Clitheroe looks like?"

"Who?"

"He's a guest here."

"What room number?"

"I don't know."

She shrugged. "Sorry. I only know guests by their room numbers not their names. Why?"

"No reason."

Her dark eyes narrowed. She didn't believe me, but she didn't pressure me for an answer either.

I headed downstairs and smiled at Goliath, waiting stony-faced beside a trolley stacked with a large trunk, two cases and three hat boxes. He gave me a fleeting smile, but it withered upon Mr. Hirst's glare. According to the new assistant manager, porters should be as invisible as possible. I wasn't sure how he expected someone as tall and well-built as Goliath to be invisible and had once joked to him about it. Mr. Hirst had laughed too, but it had rung false.

Frank the doorman signaled to Goliath to bring the luggage to the waiting carriage. The guests were still completing their check-out procedure with Peter at the desk as I passed them on the way to the senior staff offices.

Mr. Hobart's office door was open and he looked as though he was just about to leave. Unlike Mr. Hirst, the smile he gave me was genuine. We'd not started on a very good footing, after I'd been the cause of his nephew's dismissal, but he was quick to forgive me, thankfully. No matter how busy he was, he always had time to speak to me and never rushed me.

Today, however, I sensed his eagerness to get away. "Good morning, Miss Fox. Is there something I can do for you?"

"I wanted to ask you about a particular guest, a Mr. Clitheroe."

His clear blue eyes narrowed ever so slightly and the sense of eagerness vanished. He was very curious about my interest in Mr. Clitheroe but wasn't sure whether he should ask me why. No matter how much he'd decided to like me, I was still his employer's niece and not someone he should be demanding answers from. "What did you want to know about him?"

"What does he look like?"

The question seemed to catch him off guard. Whatever he thought I was going to ask, that was not it. "Medium height and build, brown hair. Rather typical for a man in his mid to late thirties."

"Does he have any distinguishing features?"

"Such as?"

"Such as his nose? Is it somewhat beaky?"

The corners of his mouth lifted slightly before he schooled his features. "Some would call it a little prominent."

"But you're too diplomatic to say it?"

That got his smile to break free. "Is there anything else, Miss Fox?"

"That's all, thank you."

We walked out of his office together, and he closed the door behind him. "May I have one of the hotel carriages brought around for you?" At my arched look, he indicated the coat and gloves in my hand. "You appear to be going out."

"I'll catch a cab to the station. I'm heading to Ealing to see your nephew, as it happens."

He stopped short. "Well, isn't that a lovely surprise. I'm sure he'll be very happy to see you."

I doubted that but smiled anyway.

"You're unlikely to find him there, I'm afraid. He moved out, much to my sister-in-law's disappointment. She enjoyed having him home these last couple of weeks. But it was time for him to go. A man his age can't live with his parents for long, especially when he's been away from home as many years as he has. If I give you his new address, can you remember it or do you want me to write it down?"

I hadn't expected him to give it to me so easily. I hadn't even told him why I wanted to speak to Mr. Armitage. "I'll remember it."

He gave me the address in Soho, a mere fifteen minute walk from the hotel. "Now," he said on a heavy sigh, "I have to see a bereaved man about funeral arrangements."

"Lord Rumford?"

He nodded. "Sometimes this job is disheartening. But you enjoy your day, Miss Fox. No need for such a sorry business to upset you."

It was kind of Lord Rumford to organize his mistress's funeral. Then again, perhaps she had no one else. I hoped his wife didn't find out.

That thought had me shaking my head at the direction my own moral compass was pointing. Three weeks ago, it had been straight as an arrow. Now it seemed not to know which way was the right way.

I accepted an umbrella from Frank at the door and headed off. My thoughts began with the "sorry business," as Mr. Hobart called it, but moved to the prospect of seeing Harry Armitage again. No doubt he'd be surprised by my visit.

He'd be even more surprised at my suggestion we should become partners in his new private investigation venture. After he recovered from his surprise, he'd give me an emphatic no.

But I knew how to convince him it was a good idea.

CHAPTER 2

My hopes of convincing Mr. Armitage that I should become his partner in his new enterprise were dashed upon arriving at the address his uncle had given me. It was not Mr. Armitage's home, but his place of business, and ARMITAGE AND ASSOCIATES: PRIVATE DETECTIVES had already been painted on the door. I wondered how difficult it would be to change it to ARMITAGE AND FOX. Probably as difficult as it would be convincing him he needed a partner.

Wedged between a barber shop and a café, the door was easily missed. While both shops sported clean windows and seemed respectable, there was a hint of the foreign origins of their owners in the translations below the English. I recognized the Italian words on the café window but not those painted on the barber's.

Soho was the poor relation of neighboring Mayfair, and up until a decade ago it had been a slum. Its Bohemian heart and close proximity to the wealthy meant it was the ideal location for the theaters and assorted restaurants and cafés that sprang up on the main streets. There was an energy about Soho that was not present in Mayfair. It was as if the area looked forward to the possibilities of the new century, while Mayfair was too busy looking back at past glories to notice that the world had moved on.

Mr. Armitage's office was not located on one of the busy Soho thoroughfares. The narrow street looked as though it was still struggling to leave its slum roots behind. The buildings' paintwork was either fading or peeling away, and rubbish blew down the street whenever the wind picked up. Yet despite the muck-filled gutters and lack of street lamps, the stoops were swept clean.

I pushed open the door to Armitage and Associates and climbed the stairs to the first floor landing where another door was painted with the sign for Mr. Armitage's business. The paint smelled fresh.

I hesitated a moment before knocking. The door was immediately opened by a smiling Mr. Armitage. The smile vanished upon seeing me.

"It's you," he said flatly.

"I'm sorry to disappoint."

"I hoped it was a potential client."

"Perhaps I am."

Mr. Armitage's gaze narrowed, clearly not believing me. He stepped aside, however, and invited me in. I brushed past him, very aware of his closeness. Harmony had been right when she said I found him handsome. I did. With dark hair and chiseled features, coupled with his height and broad shoulders, he was an impressive man.

A physical attraction was as far as my interest went, however.

The small office was as masculine as the man himself with its half-wall paneling and bulky furniture. He must have bought the desk and armchair secondhand. Both bore scratches and the leather of the armchair had faded to a mid-brown. Except for a clock, the walls were completely bare. There wasn't even a bookshelf, although a filing cabinet stood behind the desk.

"You ought to put up a picture of your parents," I said. "It'll make the place a little more friendly. And get a bookshelf and stock it with books. A few knick-knacks wouldn't go astray too, but don't clutter the place."

He slammed the door, making my nerves jangle. "Did you come here to give me decorating advice?"

"I'm simply trying to help. If you want clients to feel comfortable, you should add some small touches. You don't want to intimidate the clients, but you do want to create an air of competence. Your choice of furniture makes it seem as though you've been in business a while, which will be good for establishing your authenticity." I ran my hand over the back of the armchair. "This is nice. It's very homely."

His gaze narrowed further. "Are you angling for a commission?"

"Pardon?"

"I've heard of ladies offering their services as decorators."

"Good lord, no. That would involve shopping, and I'm not terribly good at that. Flossy would enjoy it, but she'd ignore your budget and shop at the high-end stores. Not that she'd be allowed to start such a business venture."

"Of course. Bainbridge women don't work."

The way he said it, I suspected he was lumping me in with Flossy. I'd long suspected he and everyone else thought I was wealthy. It was an easy mistake to make, considering my mother and Aunt Lilian were the only children of a wealthy businessman. Few people knew that Aunt Lilian inherited everything after my grandfather cut my mother out of his will when she married my father. My father, an academic at Cambridge University, had not been the sort of man my grandparents wanted their daughter to marry. At first, I wondered why everyone here in London didn't realize I was quite poor, when I had to move in with my uncle and aunt, but in time I learned they simply assumed I wanted companionship. They weren't to know that my only income came from the allowance Uncle Ronald paid every month.

Part of me wanted to set Mr. Armitage straight, but only a small part. My financial situation was my business, not his or anyone else's.

Mr. Armitage offered me the guest chair then sat behind the desk. "You said you have a case for me."

"No, I said *perhaps* I'm a potential client."

He tilted his head to the side. "So…you're not?"

"No."

He heaved a sigh. "Then why are you here, Miss Fox? Please be brief. I'm a busy man."

"Oh? You have a case already?" Perhaps it was a little cruel, considering he'd clearly just opened for business, but his brusque manner grated me the wrong way. I never thought I'd miss the charming assistant manager I'd first met on my arrival at the Mayfair Hotel, but today I did. As false as that charm might have been, it calmed my fractious nerves.

"I do, as it happens." He smiled one of his winning smiles when my face fell.

I quickly rallied, however. This could work in my favor. "That's marvelous. You'll need a partner to help with the case load."

"It's hardly a load yet, but hopefully it will lead to more clients."

"I'm sure it will. You ought to prepare for that eventuality now."

"By having a partner?" He shook his head. "I'll learn to walk before I run. Besides, I don't want a partner."

"You will when the right partner comes along."

He leaned back in the chair and regarded me. "Miss Fox, do you have someone in mind?"

"I do, as it happens."

"Please inform him I'm not looking for a partner. If I find I need help as I get more cases, I'll contact you for his details and I'll interview him. I can't promise anything, however, since I don't know his qualifications."

"She's very qualified. She solved a murder."

"She?" He laughed, but it quickly faded. "Are you putting yourself forward as an employee?"

"No. As a partner."

He laughed again, then stopped, then barked another laugh for good measure. I shifted in my chair, willing my face not to flame. Unfortunately it betrayed me.

I gathered my wits about me and forged ahead. I was here now, and it was too late to turn back. "Why do you find it so amusing? You can't possibly know anyone more qualified than me who is willing to work with you for no pay until the client settles the account."

He tilted his head to the side and studied me. "You're serious, aren't you?"

"Would I subject myself to your humiliating reaction if I weren't?"

He gave the smallest wince and put up his hands. "I'm sorry. My reaction was uncalled for." It was nice to see that he could still act the gentleman in my presence. He did spoil it somewhat when his lips twitched as he tried not to smile. "Please allow me to explain why I can't accept you as a partner, even if I were looking for one. First of all, we don't get along."

"We could if you forgave me for getting you dismissed from the hotel."

"I have forgiven you for that. I have not forgiven you for putting my uncle through the distress of losing a job that's very dear to his heart."

It was my turn to wince. I regretted every moment of the meeting in my uncle's office when he'd dismissed both Mr. Hobart and Mr. Armitage for keeping the secret of Mr. Armitage's arrest. "I helped get him re-employed by putting in a good word with my uncle." It sounded pathetic. I swallowed and looked down at my lap.

Mr. Armitage sighed. "And for another thing, your family would not approve."

I lifted my gaze to his. "That's for me to worry about."

"I don't want my fledgling business blacklisted by a man as powerful as Sir Ronald Bainbridge. Not when I plan to use his hotel as a source for my clients, at least initially. And finally, I will never have a partner."

"Then let me be an associate."

"No."

"But you already have 'Associates' painted on the door. Why put it there if you don't plan to hire staff?"

"I do plan on it, just not yet. There isn't enough work. And may I point out *again*, that I wouldn't hire *you*."

I chose to ignore the latter part of that statement and latch onto the former. "There will be enough work when I tell you about a potential case for a paying client. That will mean two cases. You can't possibly work them both at the same time."

He simply smiled, but there was a brightness to his warm eyes now that hadn't been there before. I'd piqued his interest. "What's the case?" he asked.

"I'm not telling you unless you hire me."

"Blackmail, Miss Fox?" He clicked his tongue. "What would your family say?"

"My uncle would congratulate me on sticking to the course I've mapped out. He is a businessman, after all."

He watched me from beneath those long dark lashes of his, the warmth in his eyes having vanished. It was difficult to know what he was thinking. The steady gaze unnerved me, and I lowered mine to the desk. It was a very clean surface. There were no notes, no files, just a blank notepad, pencils, pens and ink.

I lifted my gaze to see him still studying me. I tried not to show how much it disarmed me. "There isn't a case, is there?"

He blinked, breaking the spell. "Pardon?"

"If I open the drawers of that filing cabinet, I'll find it empty except for the lease agreement to this office. Is that correct?"

It was his turn to look away.

"You don't have a case yet, do you?" I pressed.

He drew in a deep breath and let it out slowly. I'd dented his masculine pride by calling out his white lie, but to his credit, he wasn't going to let that defeat him. "Two can play that game, Miss Fox."

"What game?"

"The guessing game."

So I was right. He had lied about having a case. "And what are you going to guess about me?" Perhaps he'd used his powers of deduction and realized I couldn't possibly be as wealthy as my Bainbridge family, considering I'd arrived at the hotel dressed in the out-of-date clothes of an ordinary woman.

He crossed his arms and sat back with a satisfied look on his face. "Your client resides at the hotel. Or perhaps the hotel itself is the client."

"How do—" I cut myself off, but his smile widened. "What makes you think that?"

"You're new to London and have no friends here outside your family and their circle. Your entire life revolves around the hotel. Where else would you have learned of a case requiring an investigation?"

I remained still so as not to give anything away.

That only made him smile more. "Since I'm right, I don't need you to bring me the case, Miss Fox. I simply need to ask my uncle. He knows everything that's going on at the Mayfair."

I gasped. "You'd steal my case from me?"

"It's not stealing. You can't investigate it. You're not a private detective. I am."

"Anyone can be a private detective, including women. One doesn't need a license or even an office." I stood. "And your uncle doesn't know about this situation. If he did, he would have done something before now."

I strode to the door, opened it and left without so much as a goodbye. The man didn't deserve it. The fleeting glimpse I'd caught of the disappointment on his face before closing the door was satisfying, and probably explained why my anger quickly dissolved. By the time I'd reached the street, it had gone altogether and reason returned.

Mr. Armitage was right. I wasn't a private detective. I couldn't ask for money from Mr. Hobart to investigate the beak-nosed man's presence in the hotel. Indeed, I wasn't even sure if there was something illicit going on at all.

I glanced along the street just as a gust of wind blew a newspaper sheet into my skirts. I kicked it away and watched it turn end over end before running out of steam outside a leather shop. This really wasn't the best address for a detective agency hoping to attract a well-to-do clientele.

I sighed. Mr. Armitage needed the money more than me. He needed this career to work more than I did. I had a lovely roof over my head and an income from my allowance. He had nothing, and that was thanks to me. I owed him this first case.

I turned back to the door just as it burst open and Mr. Armitage rushed out. He barreled into me, and I was only saved from being knocked off my feet by his two strong hands gripping my arms.

"Miss Fox!" He was as surprised to bump into me as I was at being bumped into. "You're still here."

"Yes," I said, somewhat breathless. "Yes," I said again, louder.

His thumbs skimmed over my arms before he released me. "I'm sorry. Are you all right? Did I hurt you?"

"I'm fine, thank you. I can see you're in a hurry, so I'll be quick. I have something to say, which is why I haven't left."

He adjusted his tie and stretched his neck out of his collar. "Let me speak first, please. I'm not on my way out." He cleared his throat. "I wanted to catch you, as it happens."

"Oh?"

He glanced up at the gray sky. "I, uh—I wanted to apologize for my behavior in there. I don't know why, but you bring out the worst in me. I'm not usually so…"

"Unkind? Arrogant? Condescending?"

He laughed softly. "I was going to say ungentlemanly."

"There's no need to apologize. I'm just as much to blame. It seems you bring out the worst in me too."

He indicated the door behind him. "That's your worst?"

"I don't usually storm out of offices when I don't get my way. I like to think I've grown out of such childish petulance."

He gave me a tight smile. "Well then. I'm glad we cleared the air. Good day, Miss Fox." He turned to go inside.

"Wait a moment. I want to tell you about the case."

"You mean *your* case."

I shook my head. "It's yours now. That's if it is a case at all. I'm not yet sure if there is something requiring investigation, but you can talk to your uncle to see what he thinks. I promise not to interfere. The investigation is entirely yours."

"Why the change of heart?"

He might get offended if I told him I felt sorry for him. Since I couldn't come up with a different reason quickly, I ignored his question altogether. "Let's talk about it in your office."

"I have a better idea. Luigi brews great coffee."

He opened the door to the Roma Café and the delicious smell of roasting beans enveloped me. The two men sitting on stools at the counter looked up. Both had the craggy faces of men well past middle-age with the swarthy complexion of Italians. They nodded at Mr. Armitage, who nodded back.

The man behind the counter threw his hands in the air and smiled broadly. "Harry! Come in, come in." His Cockney accent was at odds with an appearance that was as tanned as the two customers. He was much younger, however. I guessed him to be no more than thirty-five.

Mr. Armitage introduced him as Luigi, the café owner. Luigi reached across the counter and clasped my hand between both of his. *"Bella signora. Benvenuti nel mio caffè."*

"Grazie, signore. Il caffè ha un profumo delizioso."

Luigi and his two companions stared at me. "You speak Italian?"

"Just enough to get by as a tourist in Italy."

"Have you been?"

The notion that I could ever afford to go to Italy seemed so absurd that I laughed. "No."

He sighed. "I ain't been either, but I will one day." He indicated the table in the window laid out with a red and white checked tablecloth. "Take a seat and I'll bring you the best coffee you've ever tasted."

Mr. Armitage pulled out the chair for me. "Did your mother teach you Italian?"

"My father."

"I thought he was a professor of mathematics."

I was surprised he knew that much. We'd not talked in great depth about our parents. "He was, but he had a lot of other interests. He taught me a little Italian, among other things." It was fortunate I'd remembered as much as I did. My education in foreign languages had mostly ended with my parents' deaths. I'd tried to continue alone but found it too difficult when there was no one to converse with.

"You had an unusual upbringing."

I blinked at his comment. My upbringing had been ordinary compared to his. "Only if by unusual you mean cerebral. If there's one thing my parents had in common it was their love of learning about anything and everything. They instilled that love in me, and my grandparents continued my education after my parents' deaths. I'm afraid I've spent much of my life with my nose in a book or attending lectures."

"At the university?"

"Occasionally, and only those women were allowed to attend. I also belonged to several societies and women's institutes that had guest lecturers presenting on all manner of subjects."

"I would have liked to attend university," he said. "But I needed to work and the hotel was as good a place as any." There was no bitterness in his tone, no regret, merely a statement of fact.

"What would you have studied?"

He thought about it a moment. "Engineering. Ever since watching Tower Bridge being built I've been fascinated by construction."

Luigi deposited two cups of coffee in the smallest cups I'd ever seen outside of a doll's house. I closed my eyes and breathed in the aroma. When I opened them again, Mr. Armitage was watching me, a curious expression on his face.

"I wonder if this is what Italy smells like," I said.

Mr. Armitage picked up his cup. "You should travel there one day and find out."

"If only it were that easy. Now, about the case." I sipped. "I do hope it comes to fruition, for your sake. But I also hope it doesn't. You see, it involves your replacement, Mr. Hirst."

Mr. Armitage lowered his cup with a frown. "What about him?"

I told him how I'd seen Mr. Hirst talking with a fellow who didn't seem to belong in the hotel. "He told Uncle Ronald it was Mr. Clitheroe, a guest, but my uncle seemed unconvinced, although he didn't press the point. Later, I got a better look at the fellow and it struck me that he was not dressed the way a gentleman guest would usually be in the evening. Even more strangely, after having a word with the night porter, the night porter didn't open the door for him."

"Was James or Phillip on duty?"

"James. This morning I asked your uncle for a description of Mr. Clitheroe. The man I'd seen the night before had a very prominent nose, you see. Your uncle said Mr. Clitheroe's was merely somewhat prominent." At Mr. Armitage's shrug, I added, "You're right, I could be seeing suspicious behavior where there is none. I'm sure Mr. Hirst wouldn't lie. He has an excellent reputation, after all."

"And yet he was eager to join the Mayfair even though it wasn't a promotion."

"Perhaps he simply wanted to gain experience under a different owner and manager."

Mr. Armitage tapped the side of the cup with his finger then suddenly picked it up. "Finish your coffee, and I'll accompany you back to the hotel. I'll question my uncle first and see if there is a potential case here."

"Have him point out the guest named Clitheroe to me. I'll know immediately if he was the same man or not." I opened my purse to pay for coffee, but Mr. Armitage refused.

"You gave me the case, Miss Fox. The least I can do is pay for your coffee."

The walk to the hotel was brisk, and I was a little out of breath by the time we reached it. But instead of going through the front door, Mr. Armitage merely greeted Frank and kept on walking.

I raced after him. "Where are you going?"

"Down here." He pointed to the side street. "I prefer to use the staff entrance."

"Why?"

"Because I'm not a hotel guest."

I followed him when he turned into the side street.

He stopped. "You can't come this way."

"Why not?"

"Because you're not staff."

"That's ridiculous. You once said family can go wherever they wish in the hotel."

He crossed his arms and arched his brows at me. "The staff will feel uncomfortable if you use their entrance."

"But the staff like me." I winced at the whine in my voice.

He gave me a benign smile, as if to say the staff were being polite as their employment depended upon it. I sighed. He was probably right.

"Thank you for your help so far, but this is my investigation now." He lowered his arms and continued on. "Goodbye, Miss Fox," he tossed over his shoulder.

I trudged back the way I'd come, entering the hotel through the front door, which Frank held open for me. "You like me, don't you, Frank?" I asked.

"Of course I do, Miss Fox," he said smoothly.

"You're not just saying that because I'm Sir Ronald's niece."

"Not at all. You're one of my favorite people."

I sighed and headed inside. If Frank had instilled a little more sincerity into his response, I might have believed him.

I paused in the foyer, but decided not to go in search of Mr. Hobart. Mr. Armitage was right and it was his investigation now. I'd done my part.

I went in search of Flossy instead and found her coming out of her parents' suite. She looked troubled.

"Is something the matter?" I asked.

"My mother's headache is dreadful today. I knew last night would be too much for her. She shouldn't have had that second dose of tonic."

"I don't understand. Doesn't the tonic make her feel better, not worse?"

"It does, temporarily, and then the headaches return, crueler than ever."

She looked so sad. Flossy was such a bright, happy spirit that I hated seeing her like this. I clasped her hand and squeezed. "Is there anything I can do?"

She gave me a weak smile. "No, thank you, Cleo."

"Perhaps I can sit with her later. We can have a quiet talk while you go out for some air, with a maid as chaperone, of course."

She nibbled her lower lip and glanced at her mother's door. "I suppose I could go to the dressmaker's and milliner's on Bond Street."

"I'm sure the air on Bond Street will do you some good."

"It will, won't it?" She kissed my cheek. "Thank you, Cleo."

Harmony emerged from the stairwell and jerked her head towards the door to my suite. I excused myself and joined her there. She slipped into my suite behind me.

"We're in luck," she announced with a level of excitement I'd usually associate with Flossy, not Harmony. "Miss Westwood *was* murdered."

"That doesn't sound very lucky for her."

She gave me an arched look. "This is no time for jokes." She reached up to unpin my hat. "You ought to see Lord

Rumford while he's in his suite. Room four-fifteen, just down the hall."

I relinquished my hat and gloves when she asked for them too. "Why do you think Miss Westwood was murdered? And are you suggesting Lord Rumford is her murderer?"

"He's the one who thinks she was murdered. He doesn't believe she killed herself. He says she had far too much to live for and was a very happy person. But the police don't believe him and are refusing to investigate further. They're too lazy, if you ask me. Suicide is the easy verdict and saves them the trouble of finding out what really happened."

"Detective Inspector Hobart isn't lazy."

"He might not be the investigator on this case. There must be many other detectives in Scotland Yard." She shooed me towards the door.

I planted my feet on the floor, refusing to budge. "I don't know."

She thrust a hand on her hip. "If it is murder, he or she should be uncovered for poor Miss Westwood's sake."

"I suppose."

"And if the police won't do it, who else is there?"

"Harry Armitage is a private detective now."

"Mr. Armitage can find his own clients. Besides, I don't know if Lord Rumford will pay. He made no *specific* mention of hiring anyone."

"How do you know all this?"

"I have eyes and ears."

"You've been eavesdropping?"

She remained silent, which was probably wise. That way she couldn't be accused of anything.

I sighed. "Very well, but only because I have nothing better to do."

"Very true."

I eyed her sideways. "And if Miss Westwood was murdered, her family should have justice."

She beamed. "Excellent. I'm so glad you agree." She gave my shoulder a little shove. "Let's do it now before he heads out again."

"You're coming with me?" I asked as she followed me along the corridor.

"Of course. You need a chaperone. We can't have your reputation ruined."

I swallowed my laugh when she gave me a sharp glare. Sometimes Harmony could be more censorial than a parent.

Perhaps she was right to be protective. Although I was used to going where I wanted without being accompanied, I was now part of the Bainbridge household, and they lived by different rules than my middle class grandparents.

Lord Rumford looked like a man in need of sleep. Dark shadows circled his eyes, the whites of which were webbed with tiny veins, and his gray beard and hair were in need of a comb. While he didn't smile in greeting when he opened the door on my knock, he didn't bark at us either. He simply sighed and said, "Yes?"

"My name is Cleopatra Fox and this is Harmony Cotton." At his blank expression, I added, "I'm Sir Ronald Bainbridge's niece."

He shook my offered hand. "Very pleased to meet you."

I wasn't sure what to say next. "I'm going to uncover your mistress's killer" sounded presumptuous.

Harmony came to my rescue. "Miss Fox is going to investigate Miss Westwood's death and wishes to ask you some questions. May we come in?"

A spark lit Lord Rumford's eyes. "You are not what I was expecting."

"You were expecting someone else?"

"Someone a little older and…"

"Male?"

His smile was kind. "Admittedly, yes."

"Miss Fox is very experienced," Harmony said. "She solved the case of the hotel's murdered guest a couple of weeks ago."

"The Christmas Eve Killer?" he asked, citing the name the journalists had dubbed Mrs. Warrick's murderer. "You weren't mentioned in the papers."

"Miss Fox is Sir Ronald's niece." Harmony didn't need to say more. Lord Rumford understood that it was unseemly to associate the Bainbridge name with the solving of a murder, particularly when the sleuth was a female member of the family.

"You won't want to attract attention to yourself then," he said to me.

"I don't."

"Good. Because I don't want to attract attention to myself either. Not in relation to Pearl's death."

"Or her life?"

"Precisely." He glanced up and down the corridor then, seeing it empty, stepped aside. "Do come in. I'd be very happy to hire you as long as my name is kept out of it."

CHAPTER 3

The fourth floor of the hotel had the largest suites and was used by the Bainbridge family and important guests. Lord Rumford's suite resembled mine, with a sitting room and adjoining bedroom. The only difference was the view over Green Park. His was from a more easterly perspective.

He indicated we should sit on the sofa. I sat but Harmony hung back, keeping her distance while being close enough to overhear us.

"I'm sorry for your loss, my lord," I began.

"Thank you. It's come as a shock. I only saw her early yesterday afternoon. It must have been shortly before…" He passed a hand over his jaw and drew in a shuddery breath.

I hesitated. I hadn't expected such grief. I'd assumed Pearl Westwood was the latest mistress in a long line that stretched back decades and would soon be replaced. It seemed as though he truly cared for her. It was no wonder he wanted to find her killer. "Why do you think she was murdered?"

"When I saw her before Christmas, she was happy. She was typical Pearl—lively, fun, not a care in the world. Then, when I returned to London two days ago, she'd changed. She was troubled."

"Forgive me for saying this, but whatever caused the change could be the reason she committed suicide."

"She was troubled but not sad. Not desperately so that she would end it all. She asked for money, you see. She didn't say why, just that it was important. She was dreadfully apologetic about it."

I hesitated, not sure if I ought to ask the question that was on my mind. It was terribly impolite. Thankfully Lord Rumford guessed anyway.

"You want to know the details of our arrangement," he said.

I nodded.

"I paid for her flat and gave her gifts from time to time. No money passed between us. It was all quite dignified."

Sometimes it amazed me how people justified their actions to themselves. If he thought not giving Pearl money meant she was not a prostitute, and he wasn't her customer, he was wrong. It was precisely that. Neither his intentions nor his feelings towards her mattered. I would have liked to know what she'd felt about him. Had she cared for him? Or was he a means to an end?

"Did you give her the money when she asked?"

He looked down at his hand, resting on the chair arm. "I hadn't got around to it."

"Did she know that you planned to give it to her?"

"I hadn't got around to telling her." The hand on the chair arm fisted. "The point is, she needed money and she wouldn't say why. I believe someone was blackmailing her."

"About her arrangement with you?"

"Yes."

"Then wouldn't she tell you?"

"She's very proud. *Was* very proud." He swallowed heavily. "Knowing her, she would try to deal with it on her own. Pearl was like that. Very independent. She didn't like relying on me to rescue her, you see."

"Are you aware of anyone in her life who might blackmail her about your relationship?"

"No."

"Who else knew about you two?"

He shrugged. "I'm not sure. We were very discreet, but those close to us knew. There is a sister, but I can't recall her name. The other actors and theater staff knew too. Ask the manager. She was close to him. Culpepper, his name is. Good fellow. He introduced us."

I rose to leave. "Thank you, my lord. Can you give me the address of Miss Westwood's flat?"

He wrote down an address on a piece of paper at the desk and handed it to me along with two keys. "Thank you, Miss Fox. I appreciate you doing this."

I bit my tongue. I ought to ask if he was going to pay me but refrained. I would investigate regardless. Harmony was right; I had nothing better to do with my time.

Harmony and I emerged into the corridor. Just as the door closed behind us, Harry Armitage stepped out of the stairwell.

"Good morning, Harmony. Miss Fox, we meet again." He looked past me at the door labeled four-fifteen. Time seemed to slow. His lips parted in surprise then pressed together. Hard. His face darkened. "You stole my client."

I stiffened. "I did no such thing!"

He grabbed my elbow and marched me away from the door. "Are you investigating Pearl Westwood's murder?"

I shook my arm free. "Yes."

"Then I repeat: you stole my client. I can't believe this. I trusted you!" He dragged his hand through his hair and shook his head.

I was about to protest again when Harmony mumbled something about work and hurried off. It would seem I'd get no help from her.

"You sent me on a wild goose chase about some mysterious beak-nosed fellow just so you could distract me from your real quarry."

"What?" I blurted out.

He jutted his chin at room four-fifteen. "Don't deny it. I saw you leaving."

"I'm not denying I was inside speaking to Lord Rumford. But I will deny that I sent you on a wild goose chase to deliberately distract you. First of all, it isn't a wild goose chase. I think there is something going on with Mr. Hirst and that fellow, whoever he is. Probably."

He crossed his arms and gave me a look as if he didn't believe me.

"And secondly, I wasn't going to investigate Miss Westwood's death until Harmony suggested it to me *after* I returned from having coffee with you. It was she who said I should have a word with Lord Rumford after she overheard him say he suspected his mistress had been murdered."

"And how did she hear that?" He arched his brows. "Let me guess. She was eavesdropping on Lord Rumford's conversation with my uncle."

"She didn't say."

He rolled his eyes to the ceiling. "Lord Rumford approached my uncle earlier asking for the name of someone discreet to look into Miss Westwood's death. My uncle didn't give Lord Rumford my name, as he didn't know if I had the time to dedicate to the case. He told Rumford he'd send someone to his room if available, or a note if not. When I showed up in his office a few minutes later, he told me all about it, and here I am." He watched me with a glare so icy I shivered.

"Why did it take you so long to come up here to speak to Lord Rumford?" I asked.

"Because I was talking to Uncle Alfred about Hirst and the guest named Clitheroe."

"And?"

"And he doesn't think there's anything to worry about, hence the wild goose chase."

"Oh."

"My delay gave you just enough time to swoop in and take my client from under my nose."

I was growing a little tired of his accusation. He mustn't hold me in very high esteem if he thought that of me. Considering prior events, perhaps that was understandable, but it still hurt. "I can see how it looks, but I assure you, my intentions are innocent. Harmony must have been eavesdropping on your uncle and Lord Rumford and decided to put me forward as an investigator. She wouldn't have suggested it to me if she knew Mr. Hobart was going to ask you."

I wasn't entirely sure of Harmony's complete innocence in

the matter, but I would try to defend her as best as I could. She was going to get a talking to from me later, however.

"Anyway, Lord Rumford is not my client," I went on. "I don't think he's paying me."

"Because you insisted you didn't want to be paid."

"No, because he didn't offer."

"He didn't offer because discussing something as *vulgar* as money with Sir Ronald's niece isn't the gentlemanly thing to do to." He put an ugly twist on the word vulgar which summed up perfectly what Lord Rumford and his ilk thought of any kind of financial discussion, particularly around ladies.

I sighed. I really hadn't wanted to step on Mr. Armitage's toes. "We'll talk to him now and tell him you're the official investigator and I'm just…" I sighed again. "Sir Ronald's nosy, bored niece."

I crossed the corridor to the door and raised my hand to knock.

Mr. Armitage closed his hand around my fist and drew it away. We stood so close my shoulder brushed his chest. When I looked up, his face filled my vision.

"Don't," he said softly.

"Why not?" I whispered.

He simply shook his head and let me go. He walked off, his long strides quickly taking him away from me.

I picked up my skirts and ran after him. "Mr. Armitage."

He did not slow down.

I quickened my pace. "Mr. Armitage."

He didn't respond.

"Harry, stop!"

Finally he halted and turned to me. "You won the case. I won't say fair and square, but I can't say I would have been any less devious."

"Harmony was the devious one, not me," I pointed out.

"Keep the case. I don't want your charity."

"It's not charity, it's…sharing. We'll share the case."

He firmed his jaw and set off again.

I got the feeling I'd insulted him. Idiot men and their idiotic pride. It served him right if he had to wait a while longer for his first case. It wasn't my fault. He wasn't going to starve in the meantime anyway. His mother would feed him every chance she got, and his father would lend him money if he needed it. Harry Armitage would be just fine.

And I had a murder to investigate.

* * *

PEARL WESTWOOD'S flat was on the ground floor of a modern complex a mere ten minute walk from the Piccadilly Playhouse, which meant it was also within walking distance of the hotel. Not that I could imagine Lord Rumford ever walking to his mistress's place. He was quite portly and very rich. He would be driven.

One of the keys Lord Rumford had given me fitted into the iron gate positioned within the archway that led from the street into the building's hallway. The gate creaked as it swung closed then relocked itself.

I headed along the hallway to the twin doors at the end and was about to insert the other key into the lock of the one marked 1B when the door suddenly opened. The woman standing there emitted a small squeal then let out a breath.

"Goodness," she said. "You surprised me. I wasn't expecting anyone."

The woman was in her early thirties with light brown hair and a heart-shaped face. She was otherwise unremarkable, as was the plain woolen coat she wore over a black dress. The little girl holding her hand had the same shaped face as her mother. A red bow in her blonde hair provided a pretty dash of color to an otherwise bland outfit of ill-fitting gray coat. She must have been about four years old. In her other hand, the woman held a carpet bag.

"I'm sorry, I thought this was the home of the late Pearl Westwood," I said.

The woman drew in a shuddery breath. "It is. I'm her sister, Mrs. Larsen."

"Oh, I am so sorry. I didn't mean to intrude. I'll leave you in peace and come back later." I turned to go.

"Why do you have a key to my sister's home?"

"It was given to me by her…" I glanced down at the girl. She didn't seem to notice me. She stared straight through me, humming quietly to herself. "By a gentleman by the name of Lord Rumford."

Mrs. Larsen's lips pressed together in disapproval.

"My name is Cleopatra Fox. I'm investigating the death of Miss Westwood on his lordship's behalf."

She glanced down at the little girl then back up at me. "Why?"

"He doesn't believe she ended it herself." I didn't want to use the words kill or murder in front of the girl. Such talk was too grim for tender ears. "He thinks someone else…" There was no need to finish the sentence. I could see from Mrs. Larsen's shocked face that she understood my meaning.

"He thinks that, does he? Good lord." She swallowed heavily. "And he hired you to…" She looked down at the little girl and led her back inside. "Will you stay for tea, Miss Fox?"

"Thank you, that's most kind, but only if you can spare the time. I know how much there is to do when you lose a loved one."

I followed her into a parlor decorated with dusky rose pink wallpaper and a darker pink, blue and cream Oriental carpet. Although not large, the parlor managed to fit an upright piano, sofa, two pink velvet armchairs with matching footstools, and three tables. Ash swirled in the grate as a gust of wind blew down the chimney, chilling the cold room even further.

Mrs. Larsen stood the girl in front of an armchair and set down the bag. "Now sit here and be good. Don't make a fuss. I have to talk to this lady."

The girl continued humming.

"Do you hear me?"

The girl nodded and put her arms up to be lifted onto the chair.

Mrs. Larsen deposited her on the armchair and indicated I should sit on the sofa. She disappeared into the adjoining kitchen.

It gave me a few moments to study the framed photographs on the table nearest me. The same woman appeared in all of them, accompanied by different people in each. In many, they wore costumes—Egyptian pharaohs, medieval peasants, bathing and dancing outfits which showed off Pearl's shapely legs. The only photograph where she was not in costume was one of her standing beside Lord Rumford, seated on an armchair, her hand on his shoulder. They wore formal evening clothes, as if they were just about to head off to the opera. The woman sported a tiara in her hair and a pearl choker at her throat.

She must be Pearl Westwood, although I did think it a little odd she was in all of the photographs and there wasn't a single one of her sister or niece.

Pearl was also the subject of a large painted portrait in a gilded frame hanging above the fireplace. She wore a pink chiffon dress that left her shoulders bare and a diamond pendant nestled in the deep V of her bosom. Her dreamy expression was so different to the smiling photographs on the table, yet she was no less beautiful. While I could see the family resemblance to her sister, Pearl's features were arranged in a way that captured the onlooker's attention and held it. It was as if two sculptors had taken two identically shaped molds, yet the amateur had sculpted Mrs. Larsen's features and the experienced artist had used his superior skill to sculpt Pearl.

"That's her," Mrs. Larsen said as she returned carrying a tray of tea things. "She was so beautiful, but as I always told her, beauty doesn't last and she shouldn't rely on it. Not that it matters now," she added quietly. She poured the tea and handed me a cup and saucer. "I'm afraid there isn't any cake. My sister wasn't one for keeping sweet things in the kitchen. Too tempting, she used to say. She had a tiny waist but was terrified of getting fat. Silly, silly girl." Her face crumpled and she had to put her cup and saucer down when her shaking hand made them rattle. She reached into her sleeve and pulled out a handkerchief. "I can't believe she's gone."

"I'm so sorry for your loss," I said. "It must have been a shock."

"It was. We didn't see eye to eye on many things, but she was still my little sister. To think I'll never see her again... It hasn't really sunk in."

I gave her a moment to compose herself and watched the

girl swinging her legs back and forth on the chair. She seemed quite content to sit there and wait for us to finish.

"You must want some things to remember her by," I said to Mrs. Larsen.

She followed my gaze to the carpet bag. "I took a dress and pair of shoes as well as some personal items as keepsakes. The funeral director asked me to find her something to wear and my sister had a pretty blue dress that will look lovely."

"When is the funeral?"

"Tomorrow morning at ten. That man is doing something, at least, and paying for the service and burial at Kensal Green cemetery."

"That man?" I asked.

Her lips pursed. "Rumford. He wrote to me and said he'll arrange it."

"That's very generous of him. He must have loved her very much."

She picked up her teacup and took a long sip.

"As I said when I arrived, Lord Rumford asked me to look into your sister's death as he doesn't believe it was suicide." I whispered the word so that the girl couldn't hear. "But I'd like your opinion."

Mrs. Larsen sipped again then, frowning, placed the teacup back in the saucer. "To be honest, I didn't know Nellie very well."

"Her real name is Nellie?"

She nodded. "There was already a famous Nellie on stage —Melba—so she was advised to change it. Westwood is also made up. It's been six years since she began calling herself Pearl Westwood. The change of name also coincided with a change of character."

"Oh?"

"She was always an outgoing girl, and very confident. Excessive beauty can do that to a woman. People told her she was beautiful her entire life and some put her on a pedestal because of it. Not just men, either, although they were the worst. It was only natural she became too confident. I don't blame her for it." She stared down at her cup. "As her star rose, her life changed. She went to parties, drank to excess and became one of those women you read about in the papers in the company of scoundrels." Her mouth turned down in distaste. "We grew apart. Her world was very different to mine, and neither of us wanted much to do with the other. She saw me as dull, and I saw her as someone of loose moral character. Being apart was better for us both—fewer arguments, you see." She nodded at the girl. "I also didn't want her to be a bad influence on Millie. Do you understand why I can't really answer your question, Miss Fox?"

"I do. What about Christmas? Did you see her then?"

"Christmas Day was the only time we really saw each other in the last few years. She dined with us at our home."

"How did she seem?"

She shrugged. "The same as always. She talked about her shows, the parties, and the latest gift that man had given her. She mentioned that he wanted to take her on a holiday to Switzerland next autumn. She was very excited about it."

That didn't sound like someone who would commit suicide. "Did she seem troubled?"

"No."

"Did she mention she needed money?"

Mrs. Larsen seemed surprised. "Money? No, she didn't." She indicated the room with its gilded frames, the marble statue of a Greek goddess reclining on a rock, and ostrich feathers shooting from a black marble vase. "My sister wasn't poor."

"All of this would have been paid for by Lord Rumford. If she lived a fast life, she could have spent quite a sum of her own to keep up. Perhaps she had debts."

"If she needed money, she could have sold some of the jewels he gave her. Or she could have just asked him for it."

"She did. He never got around to giving it to her before she died."

"Oh," she murmured. "I see. Do you think the reason she needed money is linked to her murder?"

"I don't know yet."

She sipped her coffee thoughtfully. "The last time I saw her was Christmas Day, but I can tell you she seemed quite her usual self. If she had financial problems, she didn't confide in me or my husband."

"Do you know anyone she might have confided in? A close friend, perhaps?"

She shook her head. "Nellie didn't keep her childhood friends. She shed them along with her real name. And I'm afraid I didn't see her enough lately to know her new friends."

"You never met any when you visited her at the theater?"

"I never went to the theater. Not the Playhouse, anyway. I did see her after a show once, early in her career at a different theater. After seeing the constant stream of admirers coming into her dressing room that evening, I learned I didn't want to repeat the experience. She didn't care that they saw her half-dressed and they didn't care that her older sister was present. If you want to know who her friends are now, you'll have to ask around at the Playhouse. She performed there for most of her career."

"I will, thank you."

She glanced at the clock on the mantel and apologized. "I'm afraid I must leave. Do you have any more questions?"

"No, but I was hoping to look around the flat. I might find some letters from her friends, or a reason why she needed money."

She glanced at the clock again.

"You don't have to stay," I said quickly. "I have a key to lock up. Leave the teacups; I'll wash and dry them before I go."

She gave me a wan smile. "I don't see why not." She crossed to a mahogany escritoire and flipped the lid on an inkwell. She wrote an address on a piece of paper and handed it to me. "Please keep me informed if you learn something. You can find me here."

She and Millie saw themselves out, and I headed into the kitchen to wash and dry the dishes. A quick look in the cupboards proved Pearl kept very little food. There were no baking utensils and the oven and stove were spotless.

I searched the parlor next, starting with the escritoire. Pearl wasn't much of a letter writer. There was no personal correspondence, just some legal and banking documents. One was a contract to work exclusively for the Piccadilly Playhouse which ended at the end of 1901 with the option to extend if both parties wished it. It was signed by the theater manager, Mr. Culpepper. The bank statements showed she had some money in her own name, but not much. There were some doctors' bills and several shop bills, most of which had been paid with the only outstanding ones being for recent purchases. They were not yet due. If Pearl needed money, it wasn't to pay off creditors.

Aside from a very well stocked drinks trolley, there was nothing else of note in the parlor, so I moved on to the bedroom. I finally found the personal correspondence I'd hoped to find in one of her dressing table drawers. I undid the pink ribbon tying them together and went through them, one by one. There were thirty-eight, all written by Lord Rumford and dated over the previous two years. After reading the first two, I decided not to read further. Their contents made my cheeks burn, and he wasn't a suspect anyway.

I searched the rest of her dressing table and moved on to her wardrobe, only to come up empty handed. I sat on the bed and looked around the room, trying to put myself in Pearl's shoes. If I had jewels, where would I hide them?

After another search for loose floorboards, false bottoms and cavities in the walls, I decided that the jewelry couldn't be in the flat at all. Mrs. Larsen must have taken them with her in the carpet bag as part of the personal effects she'd mentioned. As next of kin, they were hers to take, unless Pearl had left a will that excluded her sister. Lord Rumford clearly wasn't expecting them back or he would have asked me to retrieve them while I was here.

I locked up the flat and returned to the hotel. It was late afternoon and many of the daytime staff should have left, while the number of kitchen staff would increase before the wait staff arrived. Frank was still on the door and he welcomed me back by telling me Harmony had been looking for me.

Goliath greeted me in the foyer. "Harmony wants to see you," he said as he passed.

Peter looked up from the reservations book and beckoned me over. "Harmony is waiting for you in the staff parlor."

"So I heard," I said wryly.

"How is the investigation coming along?"

"You know about that?" I asked.

He looked offended. "Of course. Harmony told us."

"Us?"

"Me, Goliath, Frank and Victor." He gave me a blank look. "Why wouldn't she tell us? We proved to be a great team last time."

"Very true. Your help was invaluable in solving Mrs. Warrick's murder. But this time the murder has taken place outside of the hotel. I don't know how much help you can provide."

"True enough, but if there's anything we can do, you know where to find us." He flashed me one of his characteristic smiles.

Of all the staff, Peter was the sweetest, with a genuinely pleasant nature. I was told that was why he was on the front desk. He made guests feel welcome, and since he was often the first person they spoke to upon arrival, and the last before they left, it was important for the hotel to put its best foot forward. Frank was the most cantankerous, although he usually managed to hide it as he opened the door for guests. He had not hidden it for me when I first arrived at the hotel, however. Seeing me dressed in clothing not suited to a luxury hotel, he assumed I was in the wrong place and treated me as though I couldn't afford to set one toe across the threshold. He'd tripped over himself to be nice to me after finding out I was Sir Ronald's niece, but my initial opinion of him hadn't changed much.

Goliath, the extraordinarily tall porter, had a nature that was at odds with his physical appearance. He was rather boyishly innocent, preferring jokes to serious conversation. He liked rubbing Frank the wrong way, like a younger brother likes to irritate his older sibling. Frank always reacted badly, which was just what Goliath wanted.

Then there was Victor, one of the junior cooks. He was the most mysterious, and I hadn't quite made up my mind if he was dangerous or not. He had an affinity for knives, but had thankfully channeled that aptitude to honest work rather than being a menace on the streets. From the hints Harmony had given, and the way he helped me break into the Dean Street school for orphaned boys, clearly his past had been somewhat murky, but I was yet to uncover the details.

I smiled as I headed to the staff parlor behind the lift well. Mr. Armitage had been wrong. The staff did like me, enough to want to help me, at least. It would seem the only person who didn't like me was Mr. Armitage himself. I didn't know how to change that. I dearly wished I did.

CHAPTER 4

I found Harmony in the staff parlor reading one of the books I'd loaned her. When I entered, she slammed the book closed and hugged it to her chest, covering the cover. When she realized it was me, she let out a breath and lowered the book. Since staff were not allowed to borrow books from the hotel library, she was right to be cautious. If one of the senior staff caught her with it, she'd be in trouble. Mr. Hobart might merely chastise her, but Mrs. Short, the new housekeeper, could dock her pay. Mrs. Short had proved to be just as mean as her predecessor. Harmony had once quipped that it seemed to be a requirement of employment for housekeepers to be mean to their maids.

"Why didn't you return home?" I asked her. "You've been up since before dawn. You must be exhausted."

"I couldn't leave without finding out how you went at Miss Westwood's place." She offered me a cup of tea. There was always a warm teapot in the staff parlor with spare cups to use. The maids or kitchen staff must replenish the pot and cups as needed.

"No, thank you, I just had a cup."

She gasped. "You helped yourself to a dead woman's tea?"

"Her sister was there retrieving some clothes to dress Miss Westwood's body."

Harmony pulled a face. "What an awful thing to have to do."

It was. While I'd been too young to take on such a task when my parents died, I'd helped my grandmother press my grandfather's best suit after his death, and gone through her wardrobe to decide what to dress her in for her funeral. It had been among the hardest things I'd ever had to do.

I sat and was about to tell Harmony all about my afternoon when the door opened and Victor sauntered in. Dressed in clean chef whites, he must not yet have started his shift. The knife belt strapped around his hips was fully stocked until he perched on the edge of the table and removed the small paring knife. He twiddled it as if it were a pencil, not a sharp blade that could slice off a fingertip. It was no wonder he had scars on his hands and another on his face.

"What are you doing here?" Harmony asked him, her tone brisk.

"I heard Miss Fox was back." He nodded a greeting at me. "Afternoon."

I nodded back. "Good afternoon, Victor. When do you start?"

He glanced at the clock. "In fifteen minutes, so you best be quick."

I arched my brows. "With what?"

He caught the knife and for a moment, his hands were still. "Telling us about your visit to the actress's home."

Harmony bristled. "Who told you?"

"Goliath."

She rolled her eyes. "I need to have a word with him about loose lips sinking ships."

I smiled. "It's quite all right. One more knowing that I'm investigating won't matter. Just don't tell anyone that Lord Rumford has asked me to look into it. He doesn't want a scandal."

He nodded just as Goliath entered, followed by Frank. They removed their brimless hats, threw them on the table, and poured themselves cups of tea.

"Have we missed anything?" Goliath asked, turning to face us.

"Miss Fox was just about to tell us what she discovered at the actress's flat," Victor told him.

Harmony glared at him. "She was just about to tell *me*. The three of you weren't invited to this meeting."

Goliath pouted, his shoulders slumping forward, and Frank stared into his teacup.

Victor merely shrugged. "Just pretend we're not here." He twirled the knife again.

Harmony's jaw set so hard I could hear her back teeth grinding.

"Apparently we're a team," I told her before she could scold him again. "Along with Peter, of course." I glanced at the door, expecting him to walk in at any moment. But it remained closed.

She lifted her chin. "You and I are a team." She sniffed. "Although I'll concede that we may require their help on occasion."

"Good of you to see it that way," Victor said evenly. It was difficult to tell when he was trying to rile her. Sometimes I was quite sure of it, but at others, his face was so straight that he couldn't possibly be anything other than serious.

"But this is not one of those occasions," she finished.

Frank eased himself onto a chair with a groan. "That's better."

Goliath slapped him on the shoulder. "Quiet, old man. Miss Fox doesn't want to shout over your creaking bones."

"I'm only a few years older than you."

Goliath snorted. "If a few is fifteen, then sure."

"Fifteen! How old do you think I am?"

"Stop it," Harmony hissed. "Let Miss Fox speak."

With the group quiet, I told them about meeting Mrs. Larsen and what she'd told me of her sister's nature and their fractured relationship. I described the flat with its many photographs of Miss Westwood and the lack of jewelry and personal letters, except for those written by Lord Rumford.

"Where did you look?" Victor asked.

"Everywhere," I said.

"Where *exactly*?"

"The dressing table, writing desk, wardrobes, and cupboards."

"Did you look in the jars in the cupboards?"

"Yes," I said, feeling pleased that I was a step ahead of him.

"What about under the carpet?"

"I pulled back the rugs and felt for loose floorboards. I tapped the walls looking for hollowed spaces, and checked for hidden triggers to open false bottoms in the desk and dressing table."

"What about inside the mattress and cushions?"

My bubble of satisfaction deflated. "No. But I don't think I would have found any jewelry. I think her sister took them with her when she left."

He tucked the paring knife in his belt and crossed his arms. "If you want to go back, I can pick the lock and get you in."

"Victor!" Harmony cried. "What's wrong with you?"

"Yes, Victor, what's wrong with you?" I mocked. Harmony didn't know that Victor had helped me break into the boy's orphanage, but she must have suspected since she'd pointed me in his direction when I'd asked for someone who could help. "There's no need to break in." I held up my purse. "I have the key."

Victor almost smiled. Despite his seriousness, I was quite sure he had a sense of humor, particularly when it came to teasing Harmony.

"She was a beauty, all right," Frank said, as if we'd just been talking about Pearl's looks. "I went to see her perform once, but I couldn't afford the good seats. But her presence on the stage carried all the way back to me." His gaze took on a dreamlike quality as he remembered the show. "Rumford was a lucky man."

Goliath smacked him in the shoulder. When Frank frowned at him, Goliath tried to surreptitiously indicate me with a sideways glance.

Frank shrugged and said, "What?" with oblivious innocence.

"It wasn't luck," Harmony said. "Rumford paid her to be with him. Not that I blame her for being his mistress." When the men all blinked at her, she added, "At least she got something out of the arrangement. Unlike a wife."

The men continued to stare.

"I don't blame Pearl either," I said. "Her beauty was a gift, and must we not use our natural gifts in whatever way we can?"

"It's a gift that wouldn't last," Harmony pointed out.

Mrs. Larsen had said the same thing, that she'd tried to tell her sister her beauty would fade and that she shouldn't rely on it. I didn't think Mrs. Larsen was jealous of Pearl, simply a more practical person.

"From looking around her flat, I do think Pearl was rather vain," I said. "From the photographs, I'd say she knew how to pose, how to look her best, and how to appeal to men. Almost all of the photographs had her standing with one or more men."

"Maybe a jealous lover killed her," Victor said. "Someone who hated that she was Rumford's mistress."

"Someone who didn't have enough money to compete against Rumford," Harmony added. She turned to me. "You should find out if a man came to the theater asking after her."

"I'm planning to," I said. "Considering she died at the theater, the murderer is probably someone she knows from there. An actor who was in love with her, perhaps, or a jealous actress, or a besotted audience member. I'll go tomorrow afternoon, after the funeral."

"Why go to her funeral?" Goliath asked.

"To see who cared enough about her to show up."

Our meeting over, we exited the parlor. Goliath and Frank disappeared into the service rooms behind the parlor, while Victor peeled away from them to head down the stairs to the basement kitchen.

I held Harmony back. "Did you overhear Lord Rumford talking to Mr. Hobart about his suspicions that Pearl was murdered?"

"Yes."

"Were you listening in from the other side of Mr. Hobart's office door?"

She looked somewhat sheepish and yet defiant at the same time. "I was dusting in the corridor and saw him go in. I didn't plan to listen in, it just happened."

I narrowed my gaze. "Mr. Hobart was going to tell Mr.

Armitage about the investigation. Mr. Armitage accused me of stealing the case from him."

She cringed. "In my defense, Lord Rumford didn't once specifically say he needed the services of a private detective."

"It was implied, and you know it."

She chewed on her lip. "Was Mr. Armitage very mad?"

"Yes, but he calmed down eventually. And thank you for leaving me to face him alone, by the way. I hadn't pegged you as a coward."

"He used to be my superior. It's hard to think of him as an equal now. Anyway, you were better off being alone with him, without me interfering."

"Why?"

Mr. Chapman, the restaurant steward, came around the corner and stopped short upon seeing us. Dressed in the tail-coat all the senior male staff wore, the rosebud he always added to one of the buttonholes each evening was already in place. He was tall, but unlike Mr. Armitage and Goliath who were also tall, Mr. Chapman took advantage of his superior height to look down his nose at us.

"Harmony, stop bothering Miss Fox," he said snippily.

"She wasn't," I said.

I might as well not have said anything. He ignored me and glared at Harmony until she bobbed a curtsy and hurried off, the book hugged to her chest again.

"That wasn't necessary," I said. "Harmony is finished for the day so she isn't taking time off from her duties, and we were just having a conversation. She certainly wasn't bothering me."

He tugged on his shirt cuffs until they appeared just beneath his jacket sleeves. "Friendships between staff and family or guests shouldn't be encouraged. It leads to liberties being taken."

I rolled my eyes and marched off. There was no point in arguing with him. He wasn't going to change his opinion because of something I said. I hoped Harmony would suffer no repercussions.

* * *

I SAT with Aunt Lilian until it was time to dress for dinner. She would not be joining us in the dining room, as her headache was too intense, but she wanted me to stay to keep her company for awhile.

"I can only rest so much," she said with a twitch of her lips which I took as an attempt at a smile.

We sat in the sitting room in her suite, me on an armchair, Aunt Lilian reclining on the sofa. A blanket covered her legs and feet, and her slender fingers fidgeted with the edge, teasing and twisting the fringe. She looked so delicate lying there, like a flower past its spring bloom. According to all of the photographs I'd seen, Aunt Lilian had been a beauty in her youth.

"Last night's party after the show took it out of you," I said gently.

"Oh, but what a wonderful evening it was. Did you enjoy yourself, Cleo?"

"I did, thank you." I'd retired before my aunt, uncle and cousins. While I had liked the evening, my family appeared to enjoy it more than me. They were *their* friends, after all, not mine.

She reached out a hand to me. It shook violently. I took it gently, afraid of snapping off her boney fingers. "I'm so glad. Your mother would be proud of you, carrying on with such courage after your grandparents' deaths. I don't know if I could have been as brave as you at your age. To think you've journeyed to a new city and left your life behind!"

It hadn't been a difficult decision. If I'd stayed in Cambridge I'd have lived in poverty. But I didn't say that.

"We're very glad you wanted to live with us," she said. "Very glad indeed. Already I can see what a steadying influence you're having on Flossy. She looks up to you."

"She's been very good to me," I said. "You all have. It made settling in so much easier. The hotel already feels like home." I hadn't expected it to be this easy. Before coming to London, I'd been rather terrified of meeting my mother's sister and her family. I'd been expecting a tyrant in my uncle and a snob in my aunt. While he'd proved to have a temper, and they'd all displayed some snobbery at times, they were far from intolerable.

My comment about home brought a smile to my aunt's face. "I am so glad to hear you say that, Cleo. So very glad." She smothered a yawn with her hand. "How can I possibly be tired after resting all day?"

She might be tired, but she was also restless. Her fingers resumed their fidgeting of the blanket fringe and her legs and feet shifted constantly. Her gaze darted too, sometimes flicking over me before scanning the room, then once again settling on me.

"Forgive me for asking," I said carefully, "but what ails you? Do the doctors know?"

She hesitated before answering. "They say it's melancholia."

In my experience, melancholia was a general term used to describe a lowness of spirits, the cause of which was unknown. "Is there a cure?" I asked, although I was quite sure of the answer.

"No. The new tonic the doctor gave me helps revive my spirits for occasions such as last night, but I mustn't take it all the time. It makes the headaches so much worse when the tonic wears off. Unfortunately, it's not as effective as it used to be. It used to lift my spirits all night, but now it lasts only a few hours."

"What would happen if you stopped taking it altogether? Would the headaches disappear?"

"I don't know, but I must take it. I'd be terribly dull otherwise, and no one wants a dull hostess or party guest." She laughed, but it didn't ring true. She believed what she said.

"I'm sure no one would think you dull, Aunt. I don't."

"That's kind of you to say, but my conversation is limited. Your mother inherited all the wit and intelligence, not to mention beauty." Tears welled in her eyes, and my own eyes filled in response. "She wasn't too keen on large parties, but other than a reservation around strangers, she had every natural advantage. Everyone liked her when they got to know her. That's why it was so strange when she chose your father."

I emitted a small gasp of air and stared at her.

"Oh!" She covered her mouth with her hand then lowered it to her throat. "I am sorry, Cleo. I didn't mean to imply there was something wrong with him. There wasn't. He was handsome and witty too, and very intelligent, of course. But he came from nothing. That's all I meant. Your mother could have married a nobleman, either English or foreign, but she chose love."

"And your parents couldn't abide it." I didn't want my bitterness to come through in my tone, but it did.

"No, they couldn't." It was spoken so softly I could barely hear it.

This was new ground we were venturing into. So far, I'd avoided the sensitive topic of the estrangement. I'd not wanted to get into an argument with my aunt and uncle, who would naturally defend her parents. It had happened so long ago, and my parents and grandparents were gone, that it seemed unnecessary.

"This is what I mean when I say I need my tonic." Aunt Lilian's pained gaze fell on the closed doors to her bedroom. "If I don't take it, I say silly things like that. I'm a dreadful person, Cleo."

My annoyance dissolved. I reached forward and touched her hand. Her busy fingers stilled. "I know you had no choice in the estrangement."

She nodded, blinking tear-filled eyes.

"Your parents would have scolded you if you fought against their wishes, or worse, and Uncle Ronald wouldn't have liked it either." Perhaps I was overstepping, but I wanted her to know that I didn't blame her. I could see now that she didn't have the strength to stand up to a man with a temper as fierce as her husband's.

She blinked at me. "You have it a little muddled, Cleo. While my parents cut out your mother from their lives, Ronald and I tried to keep the line of communication open. But my sister—your mother—wanted nothing to do with any of us. We tried again, after my parents died, and still she refused to see us. Then, after your parents' accident, we asked your grandparents if we could take you in. They refused, saying your parents wouldn't wish it. Ronald offered them money for your education and upkeep, but they only allowed him to give you a small amount each month. We asked if we could at least visit, so you would know us, but if they answered our letters at all, it was just to reply with a brief no. When you came of age, we wrote to you, but you never answered."

I sat there, stunned. I couldn't even form a coherent thought let alone a response.

"I thought you knew," she murmured.

After a long while, I sucked in a shuddery breath. "I didn't."

"Ronald suggested as much, but… I wasn't sure until you came here. Once I realized how lovely you are, I knew it must have been your grandparents' doing."

My grandmother had always collected the mail before me. Always. And when I asked about my London family, neither she nor my grandfather wanted to talk about them. All they would tell me was that the Bainbridges were snobs and wouldn't like me because they felt my father was beneath them, and my maternal grandparents had been cruel in cutting us out of their lives. While the latter might be true, the former wasn't.

How could my beloved grandparents have lied to me?

"I have their letters somewhere." My aunt rubbed her forehead. "Where have I put them?"

"It doesn't matter," I said weakly. "I believe you."

She looked relieved.

"You're owed an apology for the way my grandparents responded to your letters," I said.

"Yes, but not by you, dear. No more than I need to apologize for the way my parents treated your mother and father." She patted my hand. "I admit to being angry when your mother chose him over me. I looked up to her so much, you see. I adored her. And by choosing your father, she knew she might never see me again. That was painful, at the time, and my last words to her were angry ones. I was foolish and jealous, still just a silly girl, in many ways. I regret parting with her like that."

She sank back into the sofa and her gaze took on a faraway look. She'd been hurt by her parents' cruelty just as much as my mother had, and had lost a sister too, yet her gaze seemed more wistful than sad.

"I'm glad we had this conversation," she suddenly said.

I kissed her cheek. "Me too."

* * *

I SAW Mr. Hobart in the foyer while I waited for Frank to hail a cab to take me to Kensal Green cemetery. He greeted me cordially, but there was a slight strain to his smile. Mr. Armitage must have informed him of my involvement in the murder investigation.

"Let me explain," I began.

"There's nothing to explain. Harry told me you weren't aware Lord Rumford had approached me about his suspicions and I was going to give the investigation to Harry."

"Did he also tell you I tried to offer it to him but he refused?"

He nodded.

"You're upset with me," I said.

"Of course not."

I gave him an arched look. "Your disappointment is written all over your face, Mr. Hobart. I can read it as clearly as a book."

He sighed. "I'm not disappointed in you, as such, just disappointed *for* Harry. If it does turn out to be murder, and he could prove it, his name would get into the papers. It would have led to more clients."

I sighed too. "I know. I really do want to share the case with him, at the very least."

"His pride won't allow it. He thinks you're offering out of charity."

"How can I get him to change his mind?"

Frank opened the front door and cleared his throat. "Your cab is waiting, Miss Fox."

"Just a moment." I turned back to Mr. Hobart. "What shall I do?"

"You'll think of something when the time comes." He frowned at Frank. "You ought to be riding in a hotel carriage, not a cab. Frank, next time, have a conveyance brought around for Miss Fox."

Frank stiffened. "Yes, sir."

"There's no need for a fuss," I told them both as I slipped

on my gloves. "Now if you'll excuse me, I have a funeral to get to."

* * *

IT HAD BEEN RAINING STEADILY since I awoke and it hadn't eased by the time the burial began. The small crowd huddled under umbrellas at the plot as cemetery staff lowered Pearl's coffin into the ground. Her sister wept. Beside Mrs. Larsen stood a man, most likely her husband. They hadn't brought Millie.

When Lord Rumford took up a position beside the plot, Mrs. Larsen had moved to the other end, her husband following. If he'd noticed, Lord Rumford gave no sign. He seemed lost in his own thoughts as he stared down at the coffin.

I took note of the other faces in the small gathering. Some wept, but most didn't. The majority of the thirty-five mourners were men. The funeral had not been announced in the newspapers, however this morning's editions reported there would be an informal public memorial held at the Piccadilly Playhouse this afternoon. The show would resume tomorrow night with Pearl's understudy in the lead role.

I'd already added her to my list of suspects.

A movement at the edge of my vision caught my eye. A man stood a little distance away, almost hidden by the trunk of a chestnut tree. He had no umbrella and hunched into his great coat, but I could just make out his face and the wart-like rash at the corners of his mouth.

The service came to an end and the crowd dispersed. I hurried off in the direction of the man, but he'd already disappeared. I followed the path to the cemetery's entrance just in time to see a brougham drive off. Instead of the ubiquitous black, its doors were painted dark green and the curtain fabric matched.

I waited as the other mourners left and nodded at Lord Rumford. I had assumed he wouldn't want to acknowledge me, but he approached.

"May I offer you a lift back to the hotel, Miss Fox?"

"No, thank you. My lord, do you know a man with warts on the sides of his mouth?"

"No."

He did not ask me why I asked. He touched the brim of his hat and headed for the waiting carriage emblazoned with the Mayfair's insignia on the door. The exchange had been all rather mechanical, as if he were an automaton going through the motions after someone wound him up.

Mrs. Larsen and her husband arrived next. She introduced me to him and after exchanging the obligatory niceties about the service, I asked, "Did you see the man standing behind the tree watching the burial? He had some warts or lesions on his face."

"I'm afraid not." Mrs. Larsen looked to her husband but he also shook his head.

"Did you recognize any of the other people attending the funeral?"

They both shook their heads. "As I said, I didn't know any of Nellie's new friends or people she worked with," Mrs. Larsen said. "No one from her old life showed up, but that's understandable given she never tried to keep up the connections."

"Are you going to the memorial at the theater?"

Her lips pinched. "No."

"It's not really our sort of thing," Mr. Larsen added. "We'll go home and mourn Nellie in our own way."

"Quietly," his wife added with a pointed glance at the last of the cabs driving off with the theater set.

I caught my own cab back to the hotel for a light luncheon and a change of clothes, since my dress was wet from the knees down. By the time I set off again, the rain had stopped, and I was able to walk to the Piccadilly Playhouse without putting up my umbrella.

All of the Playhouse's lights were blazing, despite it being mid-afternoon. Several bouquets of pink flowers had been placed on the pavement beside the theater's doors, as well as cards and messages that had run in the earlier rain. A burly doorman stood beside a portable blackboard. MEMORIAL FOR MISS PEARL WESTWOOD: ENTRY 1/- it read.

A shilling was a lot to ask for the public to pay their respects, and it explained why many turned away without going in. I paid the doorman and entered just as two people left.

Inside, those who'd paid the entry fee wandered up and down the foyer, admiring the many posters, costumes and props from various shows that had starred Pearl. Interspersed between the items were photographs of Pearl with her co-stars or other theater staff. They looked similar to the ones I'd seen in her flat. The refreshment counter was open, and drinks could be purchased, although few did. A string quartet at one end of the foyer played somber music. Some patrons cried while others caressed or kissed the framed photographs of Pearl. I wondered how many of these people actually knew her or were merely theater-goers who'd adored the star but never known the real person wearing the costumes.

It didn't take long before I recognized a man from the funeral. He stood in the middle of the foyer and accepted the sympathies of passersby with a grave air. I stopped a busboy collecting empty glasses and asked him the man's name.

"That's Mr. Culpepper," the busboy said. "The Playhouse's manager."

He was younger than I expected, about mid-thirties, with a thin mustache and slicked-back hair. I waited for him to finish speaking to a couple who appeared to be giving their condolences and approached before anyone else could.

"Mr. Culpepper? I'm Cleo Fox."

His smile was polite but sad. "Welcome to the Playhouse, Miss Fox. Thank you for coming. Have you had a chance to look around at all the things our precious Pearl touched?"

"I'm an acquaintance of a friend of hers. I've been tasked with making discreet inquiries into her death."

The muscles in his cheek twitched. "I don't understand."

"Is there somewhere we can talk in private?"

"I must be out here." He looked over my head, perhaps searching for someone to rescue him, but the mourners were occupied with quiet chatter amongst themselves, or admiring the photographs and props as if they were items in a museum.

"Do you think Miss Westwood killed herself?"

His gaze snapped to mine. "Pardon?"

"Is she the type to kill herself?"

He stroked his mustache with his thumb and forefinger. "Ordinarily I'd say no, but…"

"Go on."

"But she seemed troubled these last few weeks. Ever since we resumed performances after our mid-winter break, she was different."

"Different how?"

He gave a small shrug. "Worried."

"Enough to kill herself?"

He gave a small wince. "I…I can't say for certain." He looked away and swallowed heavily.

"The person I'm working for doesn't think she killed herself, so I'm asking some questions of those who knew her. I'm afraid some of my questions might be painful to answer, and I am deeply sorry about that. But it's important we get to the truth."

"I understand. And if she didn't kill herself, then I'd like answers too, of course. Pearl deserves that." He finally met my gaze. There was genuine sorrow in his eyes. "Do you work for Rumford?"

"I'm not at liberty to say. Mr. Culpepper, do you know someone who'd want to kill her?"

"Kill her? Miss Fox, I thought you were implying she met with an accident and merely fell over the balcony."

"Is that easy to do? Fall over the balcony?"

He swallowed again. "I suppose not. Good lord," he murmured. "Someone murdered her. We must notify the police."

"The police aren't interested in classifying this as anything other than suicide, unless I present them with firm evidence. So if you could answer my questions, Mr. Culpepper."

"Very well. No, I don't know anyone who'd want to kill her. Everyone adored her." He indicated the mourners. "Pearl was the life of the party. She lit up the room with her presence. On stage, she was the brightest star in the sky." His smile was wistful. "She was a little forgetful of her lines, but it didn't matter. The audience adored her."

"Such adoration can invoke jealousy in others. Do you know anyone who might have been jealous of her?"

He hesitated before saying, "No."

"Other actresses, perhaps?"

He shook his head.

"What about the understudy who will be taking over Pearl's role in *Cat and Mouse*?"

"No! Absolutely not. Dorothea Clare was a friend of Pearl's." He nodded at a young blonde woman chatting to two men. I'd seen her and both men at the funeral earlier. Miss Clare had not cried, but I'd noticed one of the gentlemen wiping away tears.

"What about former lovers?" I asked.

His gaze sharpened. The lips beneath the mustache thinned. "I beg your pardon?"

I steeled myself for his anger and forged on. No matter how awkward the subject was for her friends to hear, it had to be discussed. "Did she have other lovers?"

"I believe there was only Rumford."

"And before him?"

"That was two years ago. I can't remember."

"Please try. Could there have been a gentleman who had warts on his face?" I indicated the area near my mouth.

Mr. Culpepper looked appalled. "No! Pearl would never be with anyone with a disfigurement."

"They could be sores or lesions, not permanent."

The disgusted face he'd pulled did not change. "I don't remember who she was with before Rumford."

"But there was someone?"

He merely lifted a shoulder and looked over my head again.

"You introduced her to Lord Rumford, didn't you?"

He snorted. "Introduced? He demanded to see her after a show. I couldn't refuse him, could I? Not a bloody lord." He suddenly straightened. "Do you know, Miss Fox, I think she might have killed herself, after all."

"Why do you say that?"

"I think she killed herself and *he* was the reason. Rumford. I'm sure he was giving her up, or had at least threatened to. That's probably what was troubling her these last few weeks. He was threatening to give her up because he knew she didn't love him."

"I don't understand. If she didn't love him, why would

she kill herself if he was going to give her up? Wouldn't she be pleased, or at the very least, relieved?"

"Relieved to give up the trinkets and flat? Not Pearl. She might not have loved him, but she loved his gifts." His jaw hardened and his eyes turned cold. "I'm sure it was suicide, and *he* drove her to it by threatening to withdraw his generosity. You ought to confront Rumford about it. He deserves to feel guilt. He deserves to rot in self-loathing and pity for sending her to her death."

It hardly seemed like a reason to throw oneself off a balcony. Pearl was still young and beautiful; she could find another benefactor. Not only that, but Mrs. Larsen had mentioned her sister was excited about going on a holiday with Lord Rumford in the autumn. That didn't sound like he was going to give her up soon.

I was beginning to think Mr. Culpepper was jealous of Lord Rumford and was trying to place the blame onto him for Pearl's death. That was the action of a guilty man.

CHAPTER 5

I managed to speak to Dorothea Clare before she left the memorial, but not on her own. She was always surrounded by an admirer or colleague, sometimes several. I took my chance as the memorial drew to a close, when she was with just one other man, the fellow I'd seen crying at the burial.

He introduced himself as Perry Alcott and bowed over my hand. Like Mr. Culpepper, Mr. Alcott was slickly groomed with an impressive head of hair sculpted into a wave above his forehead. He was cleanly shaved and wore a fine pin-striped suit with a pink tie and matching pink rosebud in the lapel. The color must be chosen for Pearl.

"I am so sorry for your loss," I told them both. "It must be very difficult for you."

"It's been awful," Mr. Alcott said. "Just awful."

"A very distressing day," Miss Clare agreed. She couldn't have been more than twenty or twenty-one, with wide gray eyes fringed with dark lashes and full lips. She wore makeup, but it was subtle, and an evening gown of cream silk that seemed an odd choice for the occasion.

"I saw you at the funeral and wondered where you fitted into Pearl's life," Mr. Alcott said. It wasn't posed as a question, but he was certainly fishing for information.

I told them what I told Mr. Culpepper, without

mentioning that it was Lord Rumford who hired me. Like Mr. Culpepper, Mr. Alcott guessed anyway.

"I agree with his lordship," Mr. Alcott said. "Anyone who thinks Pearl killed herself didn't truly know her. She would not do that. Not in a million years. Pearl had everything to live for. Her career was like a dream, she had an attentive friend in Lord Rumford, and an adoring public. Don't you agree, Dotty?"

Miss Clare nibbled on her lower lip. When she let it go, a little lip color had come off on her teeth. "She *was* a little upset lately."

Mr. Alcott put his hand on an outthrust hip. "Upset? Darling, she was hardly upset enough to throw herself over the balcony." He turned to me. "Something certainly troubled her, but not enough to take her own life."

"Dearest Perry, you would defend her." The acerbic edge to Miss Clare's otherwise sweet tone was unmistakable. "How can you say that when she never told you what the problem was?"

Mr. Alcott sniffed. "She might not have confided in me, but I don't believe it was *that* bad, and you must stop suggesting it, Dotty. Pearl was a dear friend, and I won't hear a thing said against her now she's not here to defend herself."

Miss Clare turned her back on him to face me. "The truth of the matter is, the police think she killed herself and so do I. Nobody wanted to kill her. The suggestion is ridiculous."

"What about a jealous admirer?" I asked. "Someone she rejected, perhaps."

"I can't think of anyone."

Mr. Alcott barked a laugh. "Can't you? I can. Men wanted to see her after every performance. She would flirt with them, but that was all. She never accepted their offers. She was content with Lord Rumford and not looking to move on yet."

"Not until she'd milked him for everything she could get."

Mr. Alcott's jaw dropped, and he stared at Miss Clare.

Miss Clare tossed her head, making her blond curls dance jauntily. "Lord Rumford was good to her, and Pearl was indifferent, at best. I'm not suggesting she entertained other men, but she should never have allowed them into her dressing room after the show. Someone ought to tell Lord Rumford now that she's dead, just so he knows what she was truly like."

"Looking to step into her shoes in more ways than one, Dotty?" Mr. Alcott sneered.

"I simply feel sorry for him. Pearl had a fickle nature."

"They'd been together for two years!"

"Did either of you see another gentleman at the burial this morning with warts on his face?" I asked. "He was half-hidden behind a tree and left before the end."

They both shook their heads.

A gentleman entered and glanced around the foyer. When his gaze fell on Miss Clare, she smiled broadly and excused herself.

Mr. Alcott watched her as she accepted the gentleman's kiss on her cheek. "She's going to be a handful, that one, if she ever becomes a star of Pearl's stature. Pearl might have lived a fast life, but she was never mean to others, she never put anyone down. She was just too carefree and frivolous to be mean." He nodded at Miss Clare and the gentleman. "He hasn't come to pay his respects to Pearl, he's come to see Dotty. Little does he know, he'll be overthrown by mid-year."

"Why?"

"Because Dotty is taking over the lead female role in the play, and her star will rise just as quickly as Pearl's did. When that happens, Dotty will aim higher than that poor man. He's not rich enough or influential enough to satisfy her ambition."

"How ambitious is she?"

His gaze slid to mine, but he took a moment to answer. "Dotty was jealous of Pearl. Pearl had what Dotty wanted—fame, adoration, the best roles."

I arched my brow, hoping I didn't have to ask the question outright.

Fortunately he seemed to understand. "Dotty wouldn't have resorted to violence to satisfy her ambition. She is young; she simply had to bide her time before Pearl's star began to fall." He did not sound convincing, however. Pearl hadn't been very old, after all. Her career and stardom could have lasted several more years.

"You say you were Pearl's friend, but how well did you know her?" I asked.

"Probably as well as anyone here, except Culpepper." He nodded at the manager, seeing off some mourners at the door. "They go back quite a few years. She played minor roles in other theaters, until he cast her in her first leading role here at the Playhouse. She worked for him ever since."

"Were they ever intimate?"

"I don't know. I often wondered, but I never asked. They had a good working relationship, but they occasionally argued."

"What about?"

He shrugged. "I'd see her storming out of his office, or hear raised voices but not the words. I asked her about it once and she said Culpepper was being unreasonable and that was that. I assume he'd asked her to add an extra performance, or to sing a song that didn't suit her voice. She had trouble with the high notes," he said as an aside.

"Did Pearl ever mention her family?"

"Very rarely and it was usually in casual conversation. Most recently, I asked her what she was doing for Christmas, and she said dining with her sister's family. That's what I mean by casually. I got the feeling she hardly saw them, but I don't think there was any ill-feeling between them. Pearl never made a face when she spoke about her sister, for example. They probably just grew apart. It can happen in our business. Some family members don't like our choice of career."

"Or lifestyle?"

He gave me a humorless smile. "Quite. Do you know, today at the funeral was the first time I'd ever seen her sister. She looked a little like Pearl, although not nearly as beautiful."

"Did Pearl ever ask you for money?"

My question seemed to surprise him. "No, but she knew I couldn't give her any. I only ever get minor roles, you see, and I have expensive tastes in suits and lovers." His eyes flashed wickedly. "Does that shock you, Miss Fox?"

"Not at all," I said smoothly.

"Then you're a woman of the world." He removed a silver

cigarette case from his jacket pocket. "Care to join me in the smoking room?"

It was nice to be asked. When I'd attempted smoking in order to glean information from a suspect in the last murder, the men in the hotel's smoking room had judged me to be a certain type of woman. It seemed Mr. Alcott was not like other men.

"Thank you, but I must be getting home. If you think of anything relevant, would you please send word to me at The Mayfair Hotel."

His eyebrows rose. "Rumford's putting you up at the Mayfair while you investigate? You must be good."

I almost didn't tell him, but it seemed wrong not to be honest. "Actually I live there and just happened to overhear Lord Rumford saying he suspected Pearl's death wasn't suicide. I offered to investigate."

He wagged a finger at me. "I know who you are! You're the niece of Sir Ronald Bainbridge. I've heard about you."

I didn't know what to say. We'd kept my involvement in the previous murder out of the newspapers, and few people outside the hotel staff and the Bainbridge's friends even knew I existed.

"You look like a startled deer, Miss Fox. It's all right. Your secret is safe with me." He winked.

"What secret?" I asked weakly.

"How you solved the case of that guest's death. I've already been sworn to secrecy by a very good friend of mine."

"And who is your friend? My cousin, Floyd?"

He laughed. "Lord, no. Your cousin is the sort to be friends with women like Pearl and Dotty, not men like me. No, it was a young friend of mine who works there. Danny. He's a footman. You probably don't remember him, but he credits you with getting him off the hook with the police"

I certainly did remember Danny. He'd been the police's main suspect in the Christmas Eve murder, but all the staff knew he hadn't done it. He'd finally been freed after admitting where he'd been at the time of the murder—in another man's bed.

"Danny is very sweet," I said.

Mr. Alcott's eyes sparkled with his smile. "Yes," he said softly. "Yes, he is."

He headed off while I made my way to the door. It wasn't until that moment that I realized there was one very important question I'd failed to ask everyone. Pearl's funeral had not been announced in the newspapers. Lord Rumford had insisted it be a private affair for those closest to her. If no one knew the man with the disfiguring warts, how did he come to be at the funeral? How did he know when and where it would take place? If he hadn't made inquiries of the theater manager, two of her friends, or her sister, then who had told him?

I exited the theater and found the doorman standing exactly where he had been earlier, beside the blackboard sign. "Excuse me," I said. "Do you always work here on the door?"

"Only during performances, and at special events like today." He jerked his head towards the sign.

"Were you on the door last night even though there was no performance?"

"Aye. Mr. Culpepper needed me to keep everyone out. Miss Westwood's admirers wanted to get in and pay their respects, see."

"Did anyone ask about her funeral?"

"Several, but I didn't tell them. Mr. Culpepper said it was supposed to be a private service and I weren't to tell no one about it, so I didn't. I swear to you, miss, I told no one."

The man doth protest too much. A little nudge should procure a confession from him. "Come now, nobody expects you to withhold the details from her most intimate friends. That wouldn't be fair, would it? They deserve to attend her funeral too."

"That's not for me to decide."

"But you did tell one person, didn't you?" I pressed. "He gave you a very large incentive to tell him, didn't he?"

The doorman stared straight ahead. He was considerably taller than me and very well built. His collar struggled to contain his neck and he wore no gloves, probably because he couldn't find any to fit his broad hands. He could snap me like a twig if he wanted to. And yet he looked worried by my questioning.

"I won't tell a soul, and certainly not Mr. Culpepper," I said quietly. "Your secret is safe with me. But this is a murder investigation and I need to know about the man who paid you a considerable sum of money to tell you when and where Miss Westwood's funeral would be. If you don't, I'll have to inform the police that you wouldn't co-operate."

"The police!" He rubbed the back of his neck. "All right, but there's not much to tell. He came here last night when Mr. Culpepper was inside with the others, having a drink in Miss Westwood's honor. When I wouldn't let him in, he asked me about her funeral and I told him. He said he was a real good friend of Miss Westwood's and, like you said, a good friend has a right to farewell her."

I suspected the man had paid him too, but admitting as much went against the doorman's code of honor. "What did he look like?"

"I don't know."

"Did he have warts or sores on his face?"

"I didn't see his face. It was dark and he wore his coat collar up."

Damnation.

"There was one distinguishing thing about him, miss," the doorman said.

"Oh?"

"His carriage. The doors were green."

The doors of the carriage the warty gentleman had driven away in were green. It had to be the same man. I opened my bag and pulled out some coins. How much did one pay for this sort of information?

The doorman put up his hand to halt me. "Keep your money, miss. I really didn't see his face and that's the truth."

I thanked him and headed off into the busy early evening throng of Piccadilly Circus and wondered what path to follow next. While I'd learned quite a bit about Pearl from those who'd known her, I was little better off than I'd been at the start of the day.

* * *

I WAS in luck and caught Mr. Hobart just as he was about to leave the hotel for the day. "Did you think of something that I can do to involve Mr. Armitage in the investigation?" I asked.

He plucked his hat off the hat stand by the office door and reached for his coat. "I'm afraid not." He indicated I should go ahead of him into the corridor.

I waited as he locked the door behind us and walked with him to the foyer. "What about the situation with Mr. Clitheroe?" I whispered lest we be overheard by Mr. Hirst.

"There is no situation," he whispered back. "The fellow you saw must have indeed been Mr. Clitheroe. He does have a prominent nose. Besides, there's no reason for Mr. Hirst to lie."

Mr. Hobart really was naïve if he thought that. Indeed, now that I thought about it, the former housekeeper had stolen the silverware from under his nose. If it hadn't been for one of the staff telling him directly that it was missing, and if Mr. Armitage and I hadn't investigated, the former housekeeper would have got away with it. For some reason, that naivety only made me like Mr. Hobart more. But it didn't help solve crimes.

"There's one way to solve this definitively," I said. "You must point out Mr. Clitheroe to me. I'll be able to tell you immediately if he's the same man I saw that night."

Mr. Hobart gave me an apologetic look. "I'm afraid Mr. Clitheroe checked out today. So that's the end of that."

I doubted it, but bit my tongue. Perhaps I could involve Mr. Armitage in the case again. He didn't need his uncle's approval to investigate. He could make discreet inquiries of the staff or follow Mr. Hirst when he left the hotel. Indeed, it was a good compromise. If he wouldn't share the Pearl Westwood case with me, perhaps he would consider the Hirst one.

I headed up to my room and, using the speaking tube, asked the kitchen to bring up a cup of tea. To my surprise, Harmony brought it along with two cups.

"Shouldn't you have finished for the day?" I asked her.

She set the tray down in the sitting room and poured tea into the cups. "I've been waiting in the kitchen for you to get back. I thought if you didn't order tea straight away, I'd soon hear you were back from Goliath."

"Am I really that predictable?"

She handed me a cup and saucer then eased herself down on the sofa with the other. "Lord, my feet ache."

"Put them up on the table. I don't mind."

"Lord no! This is a sitting room in one of the Mayfair's best suites!"

I couldn't help smiling. "You're such a snob when you want to be."

She pouted. "This table looks expensive and it shouldn't have feet on it."

"Then kick your shoes off and recline on the sofa."

She considered this a moment then undid the laces on her shoes. She sighed with contentment as she leaned into the sofa's end, her long legs outstretched beside her. "Mrs. Short had me running all over the hotel today, up and down, fetching this or that. I think it's a test."

"For what?"

"To see how agreeable I am. She's been doing it to all of us. Those who complain get the pointy end of her sharp glare." She sipped then put down the cup. "So what did you learn today?"

I told her about the funeral this morning and the anonymous gentleman paying his respects, as well as the conversations I'd had at the memorial service at the Playhouse. "Everyone agrees that Pearl was frivolous and liked the nice things Lord Rumford gave her, but there were differing accounts of jealousy. Her understudy says no one was jealous of Pearl or Rumford, yet another actor said men adored her and would have liked to be in Rumford's place."

"And if she'd rejected one, he might have become angry and violent?"

"Precisely." I sipped my tea as I thought. "Perhaps I should ask Danny for his opinion of the actor. Mr. Alcott says he knew Danny, and I suspect that knowledge was of an intimate nature."

"I'll ask him," Harmony said. "He'll be honest with me."

"Why wouldn't he be honest with me?"

"Because you're a Bainbridge."

"I'm a Fox," I said snippily. "I'm also very friendly and accepting of people, no matter who they're intimate with."

"You're also related to his employer."

She was right. No matter how much I didn't like it, the fact was, most of the staff treated me differently and always would. Mr. Armitage had been right about that. "*You* don't seem to care that I'm Sir Ronald's niece."

She flashed me a smile as bright as the electric bulb hanging from the ceiling. "That's because I'm different to most folk."

"You certainly are, Harmony."

Her smile vanished and she once again became serious. "So what should we do now?"

"I have an idea, as it happens. Mr. Culpepper the theater manager suggested that Lord Rumford was actually going to end the affair with Pearl because he didn't believe she loved him completely."

Harmony screwed up her nose. "Is that a good reason to end it with a lover who's much younger and more attractive than yourself? I mean, didn't he already know she didn't love him and was just with him for the gifts?"

"Perhaps he was blind to her true feelings."

"Stupid, more like."

"Whatever we think, if there's even the slightest chance Pearl could have killed herself, we must consider it. We aren't positive she was murdered yet."

Harmony drained her teacup and set it down. "So you think we should ask Rumford if he was going to end it with her?"

I shook my head. "Not ask. Would he even give us a direct answer? He won't want us to think he was responsible for her throwing herself off the balcony."

"If Pearl wasn't in love with him, she wouldn't have thrown herself off the balcony if he was going to end it with her. She'd be relieved she could move onto someone else."

It was what I'd thought too. "Mr. Culpepper thinks she liked the gifts too much and if she was having financial difficulty, she might be worried about losing Rumford."

Harmony sat up straight, putting both feet on the floor. "This is all backward, Cleo."

If she realized she called me Cleo instead of Miss Fox, she gave no sign, and I didn't correct her. I didn't want to. It felt right that we were on a first name basis. "I still think we need to rule it out if it will prove Mr. Culpepper was lying and deliberately putting the idea into my head."

She slipped her shoes on and bent to tie the laces. "And how are we going to do that?"

"I'll enter Lord Rumford's room when he's not there and look for clues. There might be some correspondence from Pearl or details about this holiday they're going to take together in the autumn."

The idea didn't shock her in the least. She finished tying her shoes and looked up. "We'll need his key. I don't do his room and I don't want to ask the maid who does. The fewer people who know what we're up to, the better. We could get Peter to let us into Mr. Hobart's office and use his spare key."

I'd learned in my last investigation that Mr. Hobart kept spare keys for all the rooms, as did the housekeeper. I'd also learned that the keys were kept in a locked drawer in Mr. Hobart's office and he kept that key on his person, and another with the assistant manager. Mrs. Short's spare keys were also kept in a locked box in her office. There was only one person I knew who could get into all those locks. Victor. There was also just one door that needed to be unlocked.

"We'll bypass Mr. Hobart's office and his spare keys and break into Rumford's room," I said. "Victor will do it."

"And be glad to, knowing him." She frowned. "What do you think he did before he came to work here?"

"I'm not sure. I thought you knew."

"Something wild, I expect. He's a no-good character, that one."

"What makes you say that?"

"It's written all over his face."

"If you mean his scars, that's a little unfair. Without them, he'd have quite a sweet, babyish face."

She stood suddenly and peered down at me. "Victor is neither sweet nor good, and you should remember that. He's trouble."

I smiled.

"What's so amusing?"

"Nothing," I said innocently. "Now, you go and get some

rest. I'll see what I can learn about Lord Rumford's movements."

She gathered the teacups onto the tray and picked it up. "I'd better speak to Victor before I go and let him know our plans for him."

"That won't be necessary. You don't have to speak to him if you don't want to."

"I don't want to, but it must be done." She indicated the tray. "Besides, I've got to return this to the kitchen."

She strode towards the door, back straight. I smiled, until she suddenly turned around when she reached the door. She scowled at me, and I expected to be scolded for smiling again. But she simply opened the door and marched out.

* * *

ACCORDING to Peter at the check-in desk, Lord Rumford had ordered a hotel carriage to take him to the theater then on to his club. He'd asked for the coachman to collect him there at three AM. It gave us plenty of time.

I went in search of Victor in the kitchen and spotted him at one of the long central benches. The *chef de cuisine* stood at a stove, breathing down the neck of a red-faced youth stirring a pot. The head chef had a fierce reputation and I didn't like venturing into his domain, but this time it was necessary.

I darted into the kitchen and was immediately enveloped by the heat. It pulsed around me like a living, breathing thing, as if it were trying to warn me to get out. Chefs eyed my progress; some shook their heads in warning. The operatic one momentarily stopped singing until I signaled that he should continue.

Victor glanced up from his station and raised his brows.

I mouthed "midnight." Hopefully he'd spoken to Harmony and understood me.

"YOU!" The bellow, spoken with a French accent, cut through the hot, dense air of the kitchen. "What are you doing?"

"I just lost my way," I said.

The *chef de cuisine* barreled towards me like a bulldog. He was a short man with a ridiculous curled mustache, but I wouldn't dare mock him for it. He looked as though he'd throw one of the knives from his belt at me. "I do not care who you are! Get out! Get out!"

I turned and fled.

* * *

I DINED with Flossy and Floyd in the dining room that evening. Aunt Lilian kept to her suite, and Uncle Ronald had gone out to a gentleman's club with friends. It made for a relaxing evening, despite having to keep up appearances for the guests. Some still approached our table and greeted my cousins by name, but their number was fewer than when my uncle was present.

For once, Floyd didn't rush off after dinner. He ordered a glass of port while Flossy and I drank coffee, and sighed with contentment as he sipped. "Good stuff, that."

"Did you order the most expensive?" Flossy asked.

"Who knows how much it costs?"

"Father."

"He doesn't check the accounts that closely, so he'll never know it was me who ordered it. If he does see it, he'll assume it was one of the guests."

Her gaze lifted to the steward, standing by the lectern where he noted down the names of guests as they entered. "Mr. Chapman will know."

"But he'll never tell Father."

"Why not?"

Floyd gave her a smug smile. "Because I'm going to take over one day and Chapman might like to keep his job."

"That's a long way off. Father could live for years. Sometimes I think he'll be here forever." She said it without much feeling, as if discussing the demise of a mere acquaintance. "And anyway, who's to say he won't leave his majority share to someone else? Someone *he* thinks is more capable of running the show."

"I am bloody capable."

"I know that, Floyd, but you know what Father's like."

Floyd hunched morosely over his glass while Flossy looked as though she regretted mentioning it at all.

"That was an excellent meal," I said to break the tension. "I enjoyed your company this evening. To what do we owe the pleasure, Floyd?"

"I'm staying in tonight. I'll entertain some friends in my suite later."

"Who?" Flossy asked.

"The usual set."

Her gaze narrowed, and I thought she'd press him further, but she simply said, "Make sure they're quiet when they leave. Don't wake Mother."

"They'll be very discreet. Don't worry about me, Floss. I'm an expert in sneaking in and out of the hotel at all hours." He finished his glass of port and rose. "Think I'll rest up before my guests arrive. Goodnight, ladies."

We watched him go. He seemed cheerful tonight, which I suspected had a lot to do with his father's absence. Floyd had a carefree manner, much to his father's consternation. Uncle Ronald wanted a son like himself, serious and business-like with the hotel always at the forefront of everything he did, every friend he made. But Floyd just wanted to have a good time.

"I wish I could entertain friends in my suite whenever I wanted," Flossy muttered. "It's not fair that he can and I have to be stuck here until Mother or Father let me out, and even then I have to go out with Mother or a hotel maid as chaperone. I want to be free, Cleo. I want to see whomever I want whenever I want. You're so lucky your parents are dead." She winced. "Sorry, but you know what I mean."

"You ought to tell them you'd like a little more freedom. Start small. Ask if you can meet a friend for lunch or coffee."

"They'll tell me to meet my friend here. The Mayfair has the best afternoon tea and lunch in London, after all." She sighed. "Don't mind me. I've just got a touch of melancholy. It'll pass."

She might not look like her mother, but in that moment, she reminded me of Aunt Lilian in one of her low moods. I wondered if Flossy's parents ever saw the likeness, or if they were too keen for her to live the same sort of life they'd had at her age—one where she was expected to associate with the right sort and only under the watchful eye of a parent.

* * *

THE FOURTH FLOOR corridor was quiet at midnight. I heard the distant thud of a door closing on another level, but otherwise the building was silent. I didn't even hear Victor's footsteps on the stairs, and I only saw him emerge from the stairwell because I was watching it.

"Harmony said you had a task for me up here," he whispered. "Am I right in assuming I'm picking a lock?"

"Lord Rumford's suite." I led the way along the corridor and stopped at the door numbered four-fifteen.

Victor dropped to his knees and went to work with the slender tools he'd brought with him. He didn't have his knife belt on him, nor did he wear his chef whites. He must have returned to the staff residence hall and changed after his shift.

He hadn't asked me why I needed to look through Lord Rumford's suite. Indeed, he took the exercise in his stride, as if this were no more unusual than turning up to work.

The lock finally clicked, and Victor opened the door. I entered while he kept watch. I flicked the light switch on and headed straight for the sitting room. I looked through the desk but there was no personal correspondence among the hotel stationery. I looked through his belongings in the bedroom, but also found nothing. After a half hour, and a thorough search, I slipped out of the suite and rejoined Victor.

He crouched down to relock the door. At the same time, a door further along the corridor opened and Floyd all but fell out of his suite along with two women in bare feet, their hair in disarray and their clothing askew. One of the girls giggled and Floyd shushed her with a finger to his lips.

Then he spotted me standing beside Victor, still crouched in front of Lord Rumford's door.

CHAPTER 6

I froze. Floyd froze. The girls did too, but only after they giggled again.

Victor was the only one who moved. He finished locking the door and stood. With a tug on his cap, he bid me good-night and departed level four via the stairs.

Floyd finally came to life. He spoke to the girls in whispers and they disappeared back into the suite, returning a moment later with coats and shoes. When they stopped at the lift, and one of them went to push the button to summon it, he ushered them towards the stairwell instead.

Once they were gone, he returned to his door and, after making eye contact with me, disappeared inside.

I slunk into my room and leaned back against the door, eyes closed. How was I going to explain what I'd been doing to my cousin?

* * *

Harmony listened to the story of our nocturnal encounter with a glowering frown. My hair forgotten, she shook her head at my reflection in the mirror.

"Victor should have been keeping watch."

"It's not his fault. I was already in the corridor, and he'd started re-locking the door, when Floyd emerged. It was completely unavoidable."

She resumed brushing my hair and asked me if I'd found anything in Lord Rumford's belongings.

"Nothing to indicate he was either going to keep Pearl around longer or break off their arrangement soon," I said. "He's very careful. There weren't even any letters from Pearl amongst his things."

"So what will you do next?"

"I still have the keys to Pearl's flat. There were some letters from Lord Rumford in her dressing table that I didn't read the first time. I'll go back and look through them for an insight into their relationship over these last few weeks."

She pinned up sections of my hair in silence, seemingly lost in thought. It was only once she'd finished, and I was admiring her handiwork in the mirror, that she revealed what she was thinking. And it was nothing to do with our investigation.

"Were the girls whores?"

I turned to look at her properly. She was utterly serious. Indeed, she looked somewhat concerned. "I don't know, but they certainly weren't well-bred ladies who'd escaped their chaperones for the evening."

She shook her head. "Sir Ronald won't like it. It's one thing for the guests to bring their mistresses here, but it's quite another for a family member to do it. This is the Bainbridge family home."

"I suspect Floyd doesn't plan on my uncle or aunt finding out." I opened the dressing table drawer and looked for my tan leather gloves. "Has my cousin done this sort of thing before?"

"Not that I'm aware. You'd have to ask the footmen and doormen. They know more about what goes on here at night than anyone."

Harmony left and I followed soon after with the keys to Pearl's flat in my purse. Just as I locked my door, Floyd emerged from his room. In a repeat performance of last night, we both froze.

Floyd was the first to move. He pocketed his key and joined me. He glanced around and, seeing no one in the corridor, leaned closer. "About last night."

I suddenly felt hot and cold all at once. Floyd may have

had whores in his room, but he was a young man, and young men were allowed their indiscretions. I was in a guest's room with one of the cooks beside me. My predicament was much worse, particularly if seen through the eyes of my uncle.

"Yes?" I whispered.

"I will agree to mind my business if you agree to mind yours."

I let out a long breath. "I think it serves both our interests not to mention what we saw to anyone."

He looked relieved. "Good, good. So do I need to get all cousinly and worry about what you were up to in Rumford's room with that fellow?"

So he hadn't recognized Victor as a hotel employee. That was a relief. I didn't want to get him into trouble. "It's part of my investigation into Pearl Westwood's death."

He frowned. "Your what?"

I put my finger to my lips and shushed him, just as he had shushed the girls last night. With a little wave, I hurried off to the stairwell, leaving him staring after me.

* * *

PEARL'S FLAT was as cold as ice. I wondered what Lord Rumford would do with it now. Did it have too many memories of happy times spent with Pearl and he wanted to sell it because he could never step foot in it again? Or would he keep it for his next mistress?

I sat at the escritoire with the stack of letters in front of me and huddled into my coat for warmth. I set aside the ones I'd already read and steeled myself for some very personal reading.

By the time I reached the end of the stack, my face was hot. Some of the things the couple had written to each other made me feel as naive as a school girl for never having even contemplated such things, let alone read about them. Lord Rumford certainly hadn't been shy in voicing his desires to his lover.

The letters talked mostly of what he wanted to do to Pearl when they next met, and very little about their plans for the future. There was one mention of the holiday in a letter dated

December fifth, with Lord Rumford saying he couldn't wait to see Pearl living as carefree as the local French ladies in Nice. I had no idea what that meant.

I bundled up the letters and slipped them back into the drawer. I was glad there was no evidence in them of their relationship cooling. I didn't want to think that Lord Rumford might be responsible for Pearl's death, even inadvertently by making her want to end it all. It meant I was no better off than before, however.

I closed the drawer a little too hard and the escritoire shook. A pen fell out of the holder and rolled onto the floor before I could catch it. I bent to pick it up and was about to straighten when I spotted a piece of paper under the glass display cabinet filled with ceramic knick-knacks.

Down on hands and knees, I reached underneath and pulled it out. It wasn't a piece of paper but a photograph. The table full of framed photographs was nearby. Pearl must have dropped this one when she'd removed it from a frame and never retrieved it. It was quite dusty and must have been under the cabinet for some time.

I blew off the dust and held it to the window to get a better look. A couple stared back at me. I recognized Pearl instantly. She was dressed in evening clothes and sported a large necklace at her throat. She rested her hand on the shoulder of the gentleman beside her in a pose that was almost identical to the photograph on display where she stood beside Lord Rumford. But this man wasn't Rumford. At first I thought I didn't know him, but on closer inspection, I recognized the man from the cemetery. He had no warts on his face, however. Indeed, he was handsome, although somewhat older than Pearl.

I tucked the photograph into my purse and locked up the flat. When I reached the hotel, Frank, standing on the pavement, greeted me with a smile.

"How was your morning, Miss Fox?"

"Somewhat productive. And yours?"

He seemed surprised that I would ask. "Very good, miss, very good. I can't complain." He looked past me as a carriage pulled up. "Sir Lawrence Caldicott. Excuse me, Miss Fox."

Frank approached the carriage with the distinctive red

coachman's seat and wheels. He opened the door and welcomed Sir Lawrence to the hotel. "Mr. Hobart will greet you in the foyer, sir, and take you up to Sir Ronald's office."

The gentleman hardly acknowledged Frank as he moved past him into the hotel. When Frank closed the door, I rejoined him.

"You still here, Miss Fox?" he asked. "Best to go inside before the weather turns."

I indicated the carriage, pulling away from the curb. "How did you know that was Sir Lawrence Caldicott's vehicle?"

He frowned at the carriage as the coachman drove it into the small gap between two hackneys, earning himself an angry shout from the driver of the rear one. "I'm familiar with the vehicle, I suppose. But I was also told to expect Sir Lawrence today. Mr. Hobart likes to keep me informed if important people are due to arrive. Sir Lawrence works at a bank and does business here with Sir Ronald from time to time."

"But you would know that vehicle even if you weren't expecting him?"

"I suppose I would. It's the red wheels. Not too many have them. Why?"

It was a wild shot in the dark, but I had to take it. The Mayfair Hotel hosted many wealthy guests and I suspected the gentleman with the blemishes on his face was well-off. There was a chance he'd walked through these very doors, and Frank had welcomed him. "Do you know of a brougham with dark green doors?"

Frank scratched his sideburns. "Green doors are unusual, certainly, but not that rare. I reckon I can think of three, off the top of my head." He stuck out his thumb. "Mr. Unley has one." He put up his forefinger. "Lord Hatfield." His third finger joined the others. "And the Mallorys."

I opened my purse and pulled out the photograph. "Is he one of the gentlemen you just mentioned?"

He began to shake his head, but stopped. "He's not, but he looks familiar. I can't think of his name, but I haven't seen him here in a long time. I don't know what color doors his carriage has, either. You should ask Mr. Hobart or Mr.

Armitage." He clicked his fingers. "Sorry, force of habit mentioning him in the same breath as his uncle. Ask Mr. Hobart. He's got a good eye for faces."

I spent the next half hour chasing Mr. Hobart around the hotel. Peter told me he was in Mr. Chapman's office, but when I got there, Mr. Chapman said I'd just missed him and he'd gone to the kitchen. The kitchen staff said he'd already left and was with Mrs. Short, but Mrs. Short hadn't see him yet and suspected he'd been waylaid by a guest.

I gave up and headed out again. The walk to Mr. Armitage's office did me good and allowed me to gather my thoughts. Not that there were many to gather, but I at least felt as though I was making progress.

Mr. Armitage's office door was locked but there was a handwritten note pinned to it that said he could be found in the Roma Café next door. I entered the café and was greeted with a hearty welcome from Luigi and nods from each of the two old men sitting on stools at the counter. They were the same men as last time.

"What a pleasant surprise!" Luigi said, throwing his arms wide. "It's good to see you, *Bella*. Come, sit with Harry and I'll bring you coffee."

Mr. Armitage watched me approach with a scowl. He'd been reading the newspaper but he now folded it up and tossed it onto a nearby table. "Let me guess," he said. "The beak-nosed man is stealing jewels from the guests' rooms."

"No, and I don't think you should joke about it. It might very well be true." I sat and placed my purse on my lap. "I see you're working hard."

"I don't have any work yet, so I might as well come here for the company and coffee."

I eyed the elderly men on the stools and Luigi grinding the beans behind the counter. "You were reading the newspaper, keeping your own company. And what if someone comes to your office and finds you not there?"

"That's what the sign is for."

"It's not very professional."

"Is there a point to your visit, Miss Fox, or are you just here to find fault with me?"

I tilted my head to the side and gave him an arched look. "It's very difficult to find fault with you, Mr. Armitage."

He blinked rapidly back at me and his mouth opened and closed without uttering a word. It seemed I'd caught him off-guard.

"And well you know it," I added.

He laughed softly. "I knew you complimenting me was too good to be true."

I smiled back, pleased with his reaction. There weren't many ways to disarm him, but I was learning how to crack his frosty façade whenever he put it up. I still had some way to go before he'd forgive me completely, however, and treat me with the same open friendliness from before the debacle that saw him dismissed from the hotel.

"I need your help, as it happens," I said.

His gaze narrowed. "Is this your way of getting me to agree to share the murder investigation?"

"Of course not. I'm not offering to share with you anymore. You made it quite clear that you were offended by the idea."

His gaze narrowed further. "So…?"

"So I've come to ask for your help but am not giving you a thing for it in return. Except my company over a cup of Luigi's excellent coffee, of course," I added with a smile for Luigi as he set a cup down in front of me.

"Excellent coffee? Ah, *Bella*, you make me a very happy man to hear you say that. Very happy indeed."

"I'll even pay for the coffees today," I said to Mr. Armitage, once Luigi left us alone. "So what do you think? Will you help me?"

He sighed and sat forward. "How can I resist such an offer? So how can I help?"

I removed the photograph from my purse and slid it across the table to him. "Do you know this man?"

He studied the photograph and nodded. "It's Lord Wrexham." He passed the photograph back. "He and Miss Westwood were lovers?"

"I think so. What do you know about him?"

"Very little. He came to the New Year's Eve ball two years in a row, but that was at least two years ago. He was never a guest at the hotel. That either means he stayed at another hotel when he was in London or he has his own townhouse. I'm going to assume the latter. If he's a regular guest at another hotel, he's less likely to come to the Mayfair's ball, although it's not unheard of."

I studied the couple in the photograph again. Pearl looked so fresh faced and beautiful and Lord Wrexham's skin was clear. "Did Lord Wrexham have lesions when you saw him?"

He frowned. "No. Does he now?"

I told him about seeing him at Pearl's funeral and indicated where on his face he sported warts or sores. "I'm surprised he hasn't grown a beard to cover them up."

He sipped his coffee thoughtfully. I studied him over the rim of my cup, and allowed myself to be distracted from the task at hand by his handsome face. Good looks didn't last, so Mrs. Larsen told me. Beauty might not last forever, but it certainly helped a woman in Pearl's line of work get ahead, although I wasn't sure it mattered as much for men. In my experience, powerful and wealthy men got what they wanted. Sometimes the clever and enterprising ones did too. It didn't matter what they looked like. Being handsome was more likely to make a man complacent in his youth and enjoy the attention too much, but it rarely had a long-term effect.

Mr. Armitage was not the usual sort of man, however. He might not be powerful and wealthy, but he was enterprising and clever. His good looks could be an asset in gaining business from wealthy women if he coupled it with his charm.

"I wonder when they were together," he said, setting down his cup. "Before Pearl was with Rumford or during?"

"And was he upset enough to kill her out of jealousy," I added.

"What will you do now?"

"Question Lord Wrexham, I suppose."

He *humphed*.

"You have something to say?"

"Good luck with your questioning."

"Thank you." I finished my coffee and rose. "And thank you for your help."

He stood too and buttoned his jacket. "My uncle could have answered these questions for you."

"I couldn't find him. I did try. I would certainly rather speak to him in the warmth of the hotel than come all the way over here in the cold."

He smirked.

I decided not to ask him why he was smirking, as I suspected that was what he wanted me to do. What I needed was another reason to call on Mr. Armitage that would convince him I had to come here and not wait for Mr. Hobart. "There was one other thing, as it happens, and this is something I couldn't ask your uncle. It's a somewhat awkward matter. Also, your uncle is not at the hotel overnight, but you were when you lived there."

"Are you going to say something to make me blush, Miss Fox?"

"That depends on how delicate your sensibilities are." I glanced towards the counter where Luigi spoke in Italian to the two customers. I lowered my voice so they couldn't overhear. "Did my cousin Floyd often bring back…women to his suite without my uncle's knowledge?"

Mr. Armitage leaned down a little and matched his tone to mine. "You hesitated before saying women. Are you not sure?"

"I was about to say whores, but decided to give them the benefit of the doubt."

"Whores?"

"Overt ones, not the elegant mistresses like Pearl or the one on that Russian count's arm."

"Ah." He straightened. "While I can't be certain of everything your cousin got up to in private, I'm sure he didn't entertain women of any description in his suite. I would have heard about it if he had."

It was my turn to *humph*. "Surely the footmen and night porter didn't tell you all the comings and goings."

"Of course they did."

I rolled my eyes. "All managers think their staff confide in them."

"In my case, they did. You might find it hard to believe, but they actually liked and respected me. I had a good relationship with the staff."

I thanked Luigi and smiled at his customers who nodded

back. Mr. Armitage followed me outside to the pavement. He hadn't finished with me yet.

"Is Floyd's nocturnal adventures relevant to anything?" he asked.

"No."

"So you're just being nosy."

I opened my mouth to protest but had no defense. He was right. "I want to know everything about the people I'm related to. I still have so much to learn about them."

"Be careful, Miss Fox. If you snoop too much, you might learn something you wish you hadn't." He removed the key from his pocket and inserted it into the lock for his office door. "Let me know how you get on with Lord Wrexham." He sounded amused.

It would seem he doubted I'd get anywhere with Wrexham. I hated to admit it, but he was probably right about that too. I had to try, however.

* * *

FINDING where Lord Wrexham lived wasn't as difficult as I expected it to be. Mr. Hobart had the address on file so he could send him invitations to balls and other events held at the hotel. Since I was investigating on behalf of Lord Rumford, he was happy to assist me and handed over the address readily.

"How is the investigation coming along?" he asked.

"Slowly, but I have a suspect now."

He glanced at the card for Lord Wrexham. "Him?"

I nodded. "Out of jealousy when she left him for Lord Rumford. That's my theory, anyway. I might change my mind after I question him."

He returned the file to the cabinet and closed the drawer. He removed his spectacles to look at me. "He wasn't a guest here, so I never really knew him. But please be careful, Miss Fox. Men of standing like Wrexford think they don't have to answer to anyone. He won't like being questioned."

"Then he can just refuse to see me. There'll be no danger involved."

* * *

I CALLED at the Belgravia townhouse after luncheon, but the butler who answered the door said his lordship was not at home. He could not tell me when he would return but he did agree to give my calling card to his lordship.

Since I didn't have calling cards, I quickly penciled my name on one of the hotel cards I carried in my purse and handed it to him. "I'm Sir Ronald Bainbridge's niece," I told the butler.

The butler showed a spark of curiosity but it was quickly dampened. I didn't enlighten him as to the nature of my visit.

I headed back down the steps and glanced over my shoulder as the butler closed the door. The curtain in one of the front windows fluttered. Someone had been watching me.

I crossed the road to the small garden square opposite. It was a private garden, not for public use, and fenced off with the only access through the locked gates. I watched the townhouse from a safe distance for an hour before my fingers and toes grew numb from the cold. The only reward I'd had for my efforts was when a maid climbed the steps from the basement service rooms and headed along the street, a basket over her arm.

Fifteen minutes later, the rain started and I gave up. Whoever had watched me from the front window wasn't going to come out, and there was no sign of Lord Wrexham. I headed off, only to stop as a carriage with green doors pulled up outside the townhouse. Lord Wrexham must be arriving home.

Thrilled with my good fortune, I hurried back the way I'd come. But no one alighted from the carriage. Instead, the townhouse door opened and a gentleman emerged. He trotted with a springy step down the stairs and quickly climbed into the cabin. His face had been hidden behind his turned-up coat collar, but I was quite sure it was Lord Wrexham. He'd been home after all.

The carriage took off before I could so much as call his name.

I headed back to the hotel. Frank greeted me with a nod as he opened the door. "You've got a visitor, Miss Fox."

"Who?"

He didn't answer as he moved off to greet a new arrival.

Goliath, standing beside a trolley loaded with luggage near the check-in desk, signaled me with a jerk of his head. "There's someone waiting to see you in Mr. Hobart's office."

"Who?"

He didn't have an opportunity to answer, however, as the guests whose luggage he carried collected their key from Peter and headed in the direction of the lift.

"Room five-twenty," Peter told Goliath.

The porter pushed the trolley towards the service lift.

"Who is waiting for me in Mr. Hobart's office?" I asked Peter. "Is it Lord Wrexham?" Hopefully he'd been intrigued by my calling card. But why wait for me in Mr. Hobart's office when he could have enjoyed a cup of tea in the sitting room? Perhaps his disfigurement made him shy away from public spaces.

"Finally," said a familiar deep voice behind me.

I turned to see Mr. Armitage striding towards me. "You've been waiting for me? Why?"

"To see how you fared with Wrexham."

"Is that a suspect?" Peter asked, leaning on the counter in a most uncharacteristic casual pose. "Are you getting closer to solving the case?"

"I'm afraid not," I said. "Progress has been slow."

Mr. Armitage joined us. "Were you with Wrexham all this time?"

"I was watching his townhouse."

His lips curved into a smile. "He wouldn't see you?"

"Given I'm a stranger, that's understandable." I eyed Terrence, manning the post desk. "When I saw him depart, I left too. Perhaps he came here and left a message for me."

"He didn't," Mr. Armitage said.

"How do you know?"

"Terence told me."

I bristled. "You made him give you my messages?"

"No, I simply asked if you had any and he said no. That's not the same thing."

"It almost is."

"But it's not."

We both looked to Peter. He straightened, hands in the air in surrender. "Don't expect me to referee your match."

Mr. Armitage's gaze suddenly lifted to a point behind me and he stiffened. His lips pressed together.

I turned to see Uncle Ronald striding towards us. My heartbeat quickened. The last time these two men had met, Mr. Armitage had just helped arrest a murderer, but not even that service was enough for my uncle to forgive him for lying about his criminal record. My uncle felt he'd been betrayed. He'd forgiven Mr. Hobart, in a fashion, but he couldn't bring himself to forgive Mr. Armitage.

Mr. Armitage had never once begged to be reinstated to his former position of assistant manager, and I suspected that was part of my uncle's problem with him. He now knew Mr. Armitage was a formidable character, someone who stood up for himself on principle, and that was something my uncle didn't like in an employee.

He marched up to me, eyes flashing, his jaw set just as hard as Mr. Armitage's. "Cleo. A word." He moved into the center of the foyer, expecting me to follow.

With a glance at Mr. Armitage and Peter, I did. "Yes, Uncle?"

"What's he doing here?"

"Calling on me."

"Why?"

I didn't want to tell him about the investigation, but if I didn't, I would have to come up with an excuse as to why Mr. Armitage was visiting me. And I could think of nothing that would meet with Uncle Ronald's approval. "He's assisting me with an investigation I'm conducting on behalf of Lord Rumford."

His nostrils flared. "Why wasn't I informed about this?"

"It has nothing to do with you. Sir," I added for good measure.

"It has everything to do with me! Rumford is a guest in *my* hotel."

This was going to require all the patience I possessed and as much diplomacy as I could muster. But at least I was prepared with an answer. "I heard his lordship express his doubts about the verdict into Miss Westwood's death. He didn't believe she killed herself and suspects she was murdered. He wanted someone to look into it so I offered since I have experience in such matters."

"Experience! Stumbling over some clues and almost getting yourself killed does not give you experience in investigative techniques." He'd expelled a considerable breath along with his words so by the time he finished, his face was quite red. His chest expanded like a bellows as he refilled his lungs.

I chose to ignore his insult and focus on something that would get him to calm down rather than anger him further. "Lord Rumford was very grateful that someone was prepared to take on the case."

Uncle Ronald drew in another deep breath, somewhat mollified. Lord Rumford was a very important guest and my uncle would never deny a guest anything. The Mayfair's reputation for servicing the needs of guests was legendary. He couldn't very well order me to stop investigating if Lord Rumford had expressly asked me to. I was immensely glad I was able to keep Mr. Hobart's name out of it—and Harmony's.

"I promised his lordship I'd be discreet, of course," I assured him. "Neither his name nor mine will be attached to any scandal or to the solving of the case, if I am able to solve it."

"See that it doesn't." He jutted his chin towards Mr. Armitage. "Why do you need *his* help?"

"I'm sorry, I'm afraid I can't tell you."

He glanced sharply at me.

"The promise I made Lord Rumford about discretion means I can't tell even you what paths I'm pursuing. I am sorry, Uncle. If it weren't for his lordship, I would have told you everything from the beginning."

He grunted but seemed to believe me. "He can't stay out here."

"We were just about to go into the sitting room."

"No."

"Why not?"

"Cleo, I know you have a kind heart and feel sorry for him, but you must remember he's a former employee. There are lines that cannot be crossed, particularly in front of the guests. Imagine how it would look if that man was sipping tea with my niece in the sitting room of the hotel where he used to work."

I bit my tongue. How things looked to the guests mattered to my uncle. I'd learned that very quickly. But I couldn't bring myself to give verbal acquiescence to his order so I simply gave a curt nod. "Is that all, Uncle?"

He eyed Mr. Armitage, who eyed him right back, unperturbed. "For now."

He slapped his hat on his head and strode off, his footsteps loud on the tiles.

I rejoined Mr. Armitage and Peter. "Now, where were we?" I said cheerfully.

Mr. Armitage frowned. "You don't have to order Goliath to throw me out?"

"Of course not. My uncle is perfectly fine with your presence here in the hotel."

He smiled. "Excellent. Shall we talk over tea in the sitting room?"

My face fell.

Mr. Armitage's smile turned cynical. "I didn't think so."

I looked to Peter for help, but he simply stood there, listening and watching as if he was front row at the theater. "We'll talk in Mr. Hobart's office," I said.

"No need. What I have to say won't take long. I came to offer you some advice if you failed to secure a meeting with Lord Wrexham."

"Good, I could do with some advice. I suspect he's sensitive about his disfigurement and doesn't wish to see people, particularly women. Will you call on him instead? He might be prepared to face another man."

Mr. Armitage shook his head. "I doubt he'd be prepared to see me, either. I think you should return, but knock on the door to the staff entrance this time. Someone will talk for a few coins."

Peter agreed. "You can find out all sorts of things from staff. Trust me, we've had some tattlers work here, haven't we, sir?"

"Call me Harry. And yes, we have. Once I learned who

spoke to the journalists, they were quickly dismissed. Go back to Wrexham's house tomorrow with a full purse and see what you find. I suggest trying the stables too. Coachmen have a wealth of knowledge about their master's movements."

"Thank you," I said. "That's a good suggestion. But you could have given me this advice when we spoke earlier."

"And miss my opportunity to see Peter again?"

Peter suddenly straightened. "Nice to see you too, sir. I mean Harry."

Mr. Armitage picked his hat up from the counter where he'd left it. "I'll leave you to your sleuthing, Miss Fox." He gave me a nod and headed for the door.

I raced after him. "Just a moment, Mr. Armitage. There's one more thing."

He stopped. "Yes?"

"Will you accompany me?" The idea had occurred to me while we were talking. It was an excellent way to involve him. Even better, if he learned something useful, he'd have to accept part payment. I was determined to share this case with him, whether he agreed or not.

"You want me to talk to the coachman and stable hands?" he asked.

"I thought I'd speak to them while you question the maids. You have a way with women that I suspect will encourage them to say more than they would to me."

"Is that so?"

"There's no need to look so surprised. You know very well how most of the hotel maids act coy in your presence."

With a small smile, he placed his hat on his head and tilted it at an angle that oozed arrogance. "Just the maids?" He turned and walked off. "I'll be back at ten tomorrow morning," he tossed over his shoulder.

I watched him go, not sure whether I wanted to laugh or roll my eyes.

CHAPTER 7

When Harmony came to do my hair in the morning, she brought Victor. She didn't look happy about his presence, however. She scowled at him from the moment they walked in.

"He insisted on speaking to you himself," she said, arms crossed over her chest.

"I didn't want the details to get lost in the chain of communication," he said.

"You think I can't deliver a message accurately?"

"If you don't believe me then you must think I insisted because I want to see Miss Fox in her dressing gown." He shook his head sadly. "It disappoints me that you think that of me, Harmony."

She adjusted her arms higher, no longer looking so prickly. "Don't twist my meaning. This is not only irregular, it's dangerous. If you're seen coming or going, Miss Fox will get into trouble with her family."

"I'll say he delivered my breakfast tray this morning." I nodded at the empty plate and cups on the table. "Apparently there were no footmen available at the time and he didn't want it to get cold."

Harmony clicked her tongue. "You shouldn't encourage him."

Victor sat on the sofa without being invited, which only made Harmony's lips purse tighter. She frequently sat in my sitting room without being invited, and had taken to sharing my morning pot of tea or coffee, also without being invited. I liked her for it. I liked Victor for being relaxed around me enough to do it too, although I suspected his reasons had more to do with irritating Harmony than any friendship we'd built.

I suppressed my smile. "What did you want to tell me, Victor?"

He already wore his chef's whites, even though I knew he didn't start in the kitchen for some time yet. It seemed he'd wanted to catch me before I left. "I heard from Goliath that you suspect Lord Wrexham of Miss Westwood's murder."

"It could be a case of jealousy. I need to question him to learn more. I'm going there today, in fact, to try and get answers from his staff."

"That's why I wanted to speak to you. I reckon I know someone who'd be willing to help, for a fee."

"Of course," Harmony bit off.

"He's someone I used to know but haven't seen in years. About the time I came to work here, he found work in Lord Wrexham's household as a footman, and we lost touch. When I thought you might like to speak to someone there, I called 'round first thing."

"You called on your friend at his place of work after not seeing him for years?" I said. "He must have been happy to see you."

Victor took a moment to answer. "He was surprised." He glanced at Harmony but she was studiously not looking at him.

"What did he say?" I asked.

"He couldn't spare me much time, but he did say he goes for a drink during the hour he has off between five and six. He says if you want to ask him questions, you'll find him in The Nag's Head then. His name's Adams. Thomas Adams."

"Thank you, Victor. That's a considerable help. You've saved Mr. Armitage and me from blundering about, hoping to find a servant willing to talk."

"Glad I could help." He rose. "If you need me to break into Wrexham's house, you know where to find me."

"Victor!" Harmony stamped her hands on her hips. "Miss Fox will not be breaking into a lord's house."

"Why not? She broke into a lord's hotel suite."

That knocked the wind out of her sails. With a flash of her dark eyes, she stormed off into the bedroom.

Victor smiled and saw himself out.

* * *

"THERE'S BEEN A CHANGE OF PLANS," I told Mr. Armitage when he arrived. "Victor has a friend who works for Lord Wrexham. We're going to meet him later at The Nag's Head."

"I know the place," Mr. Armitage said.

We met in Mr. Hobart's office to avoid my uncle seeing Mr. Armitage in the foyer. Mr. Hobart was elsewhere but had been fine with me meeting his nephew there.

"Is he the coachman?" he asked.

"Footman."

"I'd still like to talk to the coachman."

I agreed it was a good idea. As he had said the day before, coachmen knew their masters' movements better than anyone. "I'll go now."

"I'm coming with you," he said.

"I thought we decided that I'd speak to the coachman and you'd talk to the maids."

"I never agreed."

I swept past him as he held the door open for me. "You did."

"I'm coming with you to speak to the coachman, and that's final."

I didn't argue the point. For one thing, it fitted nicely with my plan to involve him more in the case. And for another, I would enjoy the company.

I managed to keep up with Mr. Armitage's long strides as we walked past Green Park and headed for the intersection at Hyde Park Corner. The air was cold but it wasn't raining. I'd brought an umbrella with me, in case.

"So you're involving the staff in your sleuthing now?" he asked as we passed Apsley House.

"They insist. In fact, I'm sure they discuss it behind my

back. I think they're a little bored with their day-to-day tasks and investigating adds a little excitement."

"Mind it doesn't get as exciting as the last murder investigation."

"You mean don't let the murderer drag me into a storeroom and try to kill me?"

We stopped to cross the road and his gaze slid to me. "I'd appreciate not having to rescue you again."

"You must admit it made the evening more interesting."

He stared at me, hard.

I spotted a gap between the traffic and stepped onto the road. "Come along, Mr. Armitage, or you'll get left behind."

* * *

WE FOLLOWED a carriage into the narrow mews behind the grand homes on Wilton Place. Lined with coach houses and stable blocks, with residences for servants above, it was the invisible artery used by the outdoor staff and tradesmen. Invisible to the masters and mistresses, that was. We passed The Nag's Head, where we'd be meeting Thomas Adams later, and continued along the curved section of the mews as it followed the course of Wilton Place and Wilton Crescent.

A pair of coach house doors opened for the carriage and the coachman maneuvered the vehicle through, but not before the horse had left a steaming deposit behind on the cobbles. Mr. Armitage asked the stable hand where we could find Lord Wrexham's coach house and he pointed to the red brick building with the white doors.

I knocked on the side door and a spotty faced lad opened it. "Is the coachman for the Wrexham house in?" I asked.

The lad's gaze lifted as Mr. Armitage moved up behind me. I didn't need to see him to know he was there. I could feel his presence. "Yes, sir."

"It's ma'am, actually," I pointed out. "*I* asked the question."

He looked a little confused, but opened the door and invited us inside. "Mr. Bull, sir!" he shouted in my ear. "There's a bloke here to see you. And a woman."

"I'm in here!"

We followed the bellow into the coach house proper. A man looked up from where he'd been polishing the green door of the brougham. It gleamed to a high shine, even in the dull light of the coach house.

"May we speak to you in private?" I asked.

"What about?" Mr. Bull was a balding fellow with a thick beard and bushy eyebrows. He was rather stout and hunched even after straightening.

"We'll tell you in private." I glanced at the stable boy who stood by, listening.

"Off with you, lad," Mr. Bull said in an Irish accent. "Go check on Rosie."

"But I already have."

Mr. Bull's glare was enough to send the youth off to the adjoining stables. The coachman picked up a cloth from the workbench and wiped his hands. "So what's this about?"

"We're investigating the death of Miss Pearl Westwood," I said.

He stopped wiping his hands. "Do you work for the police?"

"We're private detectives. A friend of Miss Westwood's commissioned us to look into her death as he didn't think she killed herself."

He resumed wiping his hands, slowly. I could almost see his mind ticking over, putting the pieces together. He certainly knew who Pearl Westwood was, but that didn't mean anything in itself. She was famous. "And what's this got to do with me?"

"Lord Wrexham knew her," I said.

He returned the cloth to the workbench and picked up the lid to the pot of polish. "Did he?"

"You drove him to her funeral yesterday."

His hands stilled before he continued screwing on the pot lid. "Do you have any questions, miss, or are you here just to point out facts?"

"Did you drive Lord Wrexham somewhere on the afternoon of Monday the fifteenth?"

"I can't recall."

"I'm sure you can. It was only four days ago."

"Nope. Don't remember."

Mr. Armitage set down some coins on the bench in Mr. Bull's line of sight. "Do you remember now?"

Mr. Bull put the pot back on a shelf above the bench and picked up the coins. He held them out to Mr. Armitage. "Lord Wrexham's a good master and the pay's reasonable. It's hard to find work like this in the city nowadays, so I won't do anything to jeopardize my position." He dropped the coins in Mr. Armitage's palm. "There's no point asking the lad, either. He doesn't know anything." He turned away. "See yourselves out."

I led the way back to the street. "Well? What do you think?"

"I think he's hiding something."

"So do I. If Lord Wrexham did not leave the house that afternoon, Mr. Bull would have simply said as much."

Mr. Armitage glanced at the opposite side of the street. The doors on that side belonged to the rear entrances to the townhouses on Wilton Crescent. It allowed the indoor servants to quickly pass on instructions to the coach house if a vehicle was needed around the front. "Perhaps we'll have better luck with the maids."

I felt a little irritated for not getting anywhere with the coachman and wanted to redeem myself by questioning the maids. I decided to leave it to Mr. Armitage as agreed, however.

The maid who answered his knock had the reddened, chapped hands of someone who has them plunged into hot water for a considerable amount of time. She took one look at Mr. Armitage, smiling on the doorstep, and buried them in her apron. She blinked up at him with wide eyes and seemed to have stopped breathing.

"My name is Harry Armitage, and this is Miss Cleopatra Fox." He smiled. "And you are?"

"Betty Proud, sir. Pleased to meet you." She didn't even look past him at me. Her eyes were firmly fixed on his face. At least she was breathing again and the blinking had stopped.

"Miss Fox and I are from the Piccadilly Playhouse."

Her eyes widened even further. So did mine. What was he up to? This was not planned.

"Are you actors?" Betty asked.

"No, nothing like that." Mr. Armitage chuckled. "The actors are still asleep, getting their rest for tonight's performance. They're resuming *Cat and Mouse,* but without its star, Miss Westwood."

Betty gave him a sympathetic look. "I read about her death. I'm so sorry for your loss, Mr. Armitage. You must all be devastated."

"We are. Losing her at such a young age is a tragedy."

I eyed him sideways. He looked quite distressed. He was good at this.

"That's actually why I'm here," Mr. Armitage went on. "I have a message for Lord Wrexham about Miss Westwood."

For the first time, Betty looked at me. She was confused by this turn of events. "Why would there be a message for him about her? He didn't know her."

"How long have you worked here?" I asked.

"Eleven months. What's your message, sir? I'll see the master gets it."

"Perhaps I'm mistaken," Mr. Armitage said. "Someone at the theater thought they saw Lord Wrexham there on the afternoon of Pearl's death."

She wrinkled her nose. "I doubt it."

"Betty? Betty, who're you talking to?" A woman with gray hair pinned into a bun muscled the maid aside and fixed a glare on Mr. Armitage. "Who're you?"

"Mr. Armitage, and this is Miss Fox. We work at the Piccadilly Playhouse." He smiled and gave a shallow bow. "Am I speaking to the housekeeper?"

"You are. I'm Mrs. Gardiner. What do folk from the Playhouse want with my scullery maid?"

"They've got a message for his lordship," Betty said. "It's about Miss Westwood, that actress who died."

Mrs. Gardiner squared her shoulders. "Go, Betty."

"But—"

"Get back to work." Mrs. Gardiner waited until Betty's footsteps had receded. "What do you want, Mr. Armitage?"

"I want to know where Lord Wrexham was on the afternoon of Monday the fifteenth."

She crossed her arms beneath her considerable bosom. "That's none of your business."

Mr. Armitage pulled out some coins from his pocket.

"Put that away," she growled. "Neither me nor my girls are willing to jeopardize their position for a few bob." She thrust out her chin. "You're not really from the theater, are you?"

Mr. Armitage pocketed the coins. "We're private detectives, commissioned by a friend of Miss Westwood's to make inquiries into her death."

"What has that got to do with this house?"

"I think you already know."

She stared at him, unblinking. "No," she finally said.

"Miss Westwood was a particular friend of his lordship."

The muscles in her jaw bunched and her glare sharpened. There was no surprise in her reaction, however.

"Miss Westwood might not have killed herself," he went on. "If there's a chance she was murdered, we should find out who did it. She deserves that, at least."

"Does she?" she spat.

Mr. Armitage's charm was working as well as mine had on the coachman. It wouldn't hurt if I cut in. This encounter couldn't deteriorate further than it already had.

"We know Lord Wrexham cared for her," I said. "I saw him at the funeral. He was upset."

She grabbed the edge of the door. "You people disgust me," she hissed. "Raking up all this filth when it should be left in the gutter where it belongs. You should be ashamed of yourselves." She slammed the door in our faces.

I stepped back. "I was about to commend you for your acting skills until the housekeeper came along."

"As disappointing as it was, it's nice to see loyalty still exists. Hopefully the footman can tell us something of use later."

"We did learn something from that exchange," I said as we headed back the way we'd come. "The housekeeper clearly knew about Pearl's relationship with Wrexham but the maid didn't."

"So the relationship definitely ended more than eleven months ago, the length of time the maid has worked for

Wrexham," he finished. "But why murder her *now*? Surely if he was wracked by jealousy, he'd have acted when the relationship finished."

"According to Mr. Culpepper from the theater, Pearl was with Rumford, and only Rumford, for two years, so her relationship with Wrexham must have ended before that."

It must have been nostalgia that made Lord Wrexham attend Pearl's funeral. Just because they hadn't been together for some years didn't mean he wouldn't want to pay his respects.

We parted ways outside the hotel with a promise to meet again later. I greeted Frank as he opened the door for me, and I waved to Peter, handed the umbrella to Goliath, and headed for the lift. The door slid open the moment I pressed the button and Flossy and Aunt Lilian stepped out.

"There you are, Cleo," Aunt Lilian said breezily. "I'm so glad we found you. You must join us for luncheon in the dining room. You won't be needing your coat in there." She signaled to Goliath who strode over.

"Yes, ma'am?"

"Take Cleo's coat." She assisted me to remove it then handed it to Goliath.

He folded it over his arm and carried it to the luggage room.

"I'm delighted to have lunch with you both," I said. "Isn't it a little early?" According to the clock on the wall behind Peter, it wasn't yet midday.

Flossy opened her mouth to speak, but her mother got in first. "It is, but Lady Caldicott prefers to luncheon early."

"Caldicott?" I asked. "Is she related to the banker?"

"Sir Lawrence, yes. She's his wife. You *are* well informed, Cleo. Good for you. I'm so pleased you're taking an interest."

Flossy sighed, so I suspected that was a slight aimed at her.

We followed Aunt Lilian through the vestibule to the dining room where Mr. Chapman greeted us with a smile. "You'll be served by Richard today, assisted by Gregory and Francis."

The three men stood behind chairs at the family's regular table, positioned in the center of the room. They all wore black ties as part of their uniform, but Richard, the head waiter, was the only one without an apron. He pulled the chair out for Aunt Lilian while Gregory and Francis did the same for Flossy and me.

Aunt Lilian was in one of her lively moods this morning as she conversed with the sommelier and Richard about the menu. She must have taken a dose of her tonic, which meant this wasn't an ordinary lunch. If it was important, I ought to be prepared.

"Is Sir Lawrence my uncle's banker?" I asked Flossy while her mother was occupied.

"Yes. He has two sons, both unmarried and in their twenties, and an older, married daughter. She and her mother are coming today."

"Is this meeting intended to butter Lady Caldicott up so that she can speak to her husband on your father's behalf?"

Flossy gave me a blank look. "It's about Lady Caldicott meeting me. Mother wants me to marry one of her sons, so I must give a good impression."

I pulled a face. "Oh. Sorry."

"Save some of that sympathy for yourself. Now that you're here, you'll be considered for the other son."

Ugh. So it was going to be *that* sort of lunch. "Any particular son or do I just get the one you don't want?"

Flossy suppressed a giggle. "You're wicked, Cleo. Be sure not to let it show during lunch. Lady Caldicott and her daughter have no sense of humor."

"Then I can tell you I probably wouldn't want to marry one of her sons."

She leaned closer. "Me either. But we mustn't disappoint Mother. She's gone to a lot of effort to arrange this lunch."

The two guests arrived and I was introduced as the niece from Cambridge. Lady Caldicott and her daughter, Mrs. Mannering, both commented on how much I looked like Aunt Lilian, and expressed their sympathies over the recent loss of my grandmother.

Both women wore the latest fashions, like my aunt and cousin, and if they thought my black dress somewhat plain and out of date, they were polite enough not to show it. It wasn't until sometime during the dessert course that I noticed

Mrs. Mannering watching me from beneath lowered lashes. I thought she'd been listening in to her mother and Aunt Lilian gossiping, but it seemed not. I waited for her to say something, but she didn't.

"Oh, I almost forgot to tell you about Lady Rumford," Lady Caldicott said to my aunt.

The name had me turning sharply towards them.

"What about her?" Aunt Lilian asked.

"Do you know Mrs. Preston-Lowe? She told me she saw Lady Rumford at the opera last week."

Aunt Lilian looked up from her Bavarian cream. "She must be mistaken. If Lady Rumford is in London, she'd be staying with us."

"While her husband is here grieving for his late mistress?" Lady Caldicott sounded triumphant, as if she knew Aunt Lilian was attempting to hide that fact. Lady Caldicott was reveling in spreading her gossip. "Come now, Lilian, don't look so surprised. Almost everyone knows he kept that actress, even Lady Rumford."

"So sad about her death," Mrs. Mannering said.

"I doubt Lady Rumford is sad. I heard she and Rumford had blazing rows over his interest in Miss Westwood. Not the affair itself, you understand, but the expense of keeping her." Lady Caldicott positively glowed with delight at imparting such salacious news. The three glasses of wine probably had something to do with the glow too.

"Mother," Mrs. Mannering chided.

"Is Lady Rumford still in London?" I asked.

Everyone stared at me. Considering it was one of the few times I'd spoken throughout lunch, perhaps their surprise was warranted.

"I don't know," Lady Caldicott said. "Mrs. Preston-Lowe's sighting is the only one I've heard."

"Perhaps she was mistaken," Aunt Lilian said. "Doesn't she wear spectacles?"

"For reading, not for watching the opera."

"Let's leave such gossip alone in the presence of the young ladies," Mrs. Mannering cut in.

"I don't mind," Flossy said.

Mrs. Mannering ignored her. "Mother, weren't you going to ask Lady Bainbridge and her family to dine with you?"

A discussion about dinner plans followed, and a suitable date settled. Mrs. Mannering and her husband were invited, of course, and Sir Lawrence and Lady Caldicott's two sons would be there. Lady Caldicott insisted all of us should attend too. I'd hoped to be left out, but it seemed I was firmly a part of the Bainbridge family for such events.

I couldn't decide whether I would feign illness that day or not. I had a week in which to consider my options.

I met Harmony and Victor in the staff parlor after lunch. It was a busy time for the front-of-house staff, but the maids had all finished for the day, and Victor was taking a break between lunch and dinner.

I told them about the sighting of Lady Rumford at the opera. "If it's true and she is in London, then she's a suspect."

"Most definitely," Harmony said as she picked up her teacup.

Victor sat forward on the chair and rested his elbows on his knees. He cradled the teacup between his hands and looked up at me. "But did she care enough about the affair to kill?"

Harmony looked at him as if he were stupid. "What woman wouldn't feel jealous that her husband keeps a mistress?"

"Some women wouldn't. Humiliation, maybe, but not jealousy. Most toff marriages are for the sake of convenience, not love. She might like him to be occupied elsewhere, if you get my meaning."

"I do but I don't understand why any woman would give up on love," Harmony said, matter-of-factly. "I'd never marry anyone unless I was in love with him and he in love with me."

"Lucky fellow."

Harmony narrowed her gaze at him, as if trying to determine if he was teasing her. Victor's face was utterly serious, which didn't necessarily mean he was being serious. Her look was lost on him, however, as he was staring straight ahead at the wall.

"Actually, you're right, Victor," I said. "According to Lady

Caldicott, Lady Rumford was only upset about the expense of keeping a mistress, not the fact he had one."

"Rightly so," he said. "Rumford paid for Miss Westwood's flat, but his wife stays at a hotel when she visits London."

Harmony bristled. "And what's wrong with the Mayfair? Why wouldn't she prefer to stay here? There's an army of staff at hand, an excellent dining room, and the location is superb."

"You ought to write the advertising copy," I said, smiling.

She sniffed. "The Mayfair doesn't need to advertise."

Victor glanced at the clock then drained his cup and rose. "Seems like you've got an extra suspect, Miss Fox. But how are you going to find Lady Rumford?"

"If she's not staying here, there are few other places she'd be," Harmony said.

Between them, they rattled off the names of four other suitable hotels where someone of Lady Rumford's status would stay. I would have to visit them all individually and somehow find out if Lady Rumford had stayed there and if her visit coincided with Pearl's death. When I told them I wasn't looking forward to such a task, Harmony's face lit up.

"Leave it with me," she said, jumping to her feet. "I'll put the boys to work on their afternoon off tomorrow."

"The boys?" I asked.

"Peter, Goliath and Frank."

"They get so little time off," I said. "Don't give them this extra task."

"None of them have anything better to do. Well, Peter visits his parents, but Goliath and Frank are always looking for a distraction." She was so enthused by her idea that she left ahead of Victor and me.

"Lucky you don't have the afternoon off tomorrow," I told him as we left together.

"I wouldn't mind. I reckon Harmony would come with me to investigate."

"Oh? Why do you think that?"

"Because I'd run some questions past her as practice and she'd think they were so bad she'd just have to help me."

I smiled. "Would they be bad on purpose?"

He walked off, whistling.

* * *

The Nag's Head was an unremarkable pub, befitting an unremarkable street. It was small, dark, and filled with men talking quietly or sitting alone, nursing tankards. Tucked away as it was in the mews, the patrons were the servants of the large townhouses nearby—footmen, coachmen and stable hands. Butlers wouldn't deign to drink with their inferiors. There were only three women, all dressed in maid's uniforms complete with mob caps, but without their aprons.

The man who must be Thomas Adams lifted his tankard in greeting when we entered. A cigarette burned in the ashtray in front of him. He picked it up, put it in his mouth, and shook Mr. Armitage's hand. After a slight hesitation, he also shook mine.

We slipped onto the booth seat opposite him and I made the introductions. "Thank you for meeting us, Mr. Adams."

Mr. Adams was a slightly built man aged in his early twenties. Like most footmen for great households, he was good looking and well-groomed with his dark hair parted down the middle and jaw cleanly shaved.

He drew on the cigarette and leaned back, his arm draped across the back of the seat. "Victor says you're investigating the death of that actress," he said in a Cockney accent. "I reckon you'll be interested in what I have to say, but it'll cost you."

I placed my purse on the table. The coins inside jangled. "The amount depends on the information."

He'd addressed his financial statement to Mr. Armitage but now he looked at me with renewed interest. His gaze raked over me and his lips stretched into a smile. "I see why Victor wants to help you."

Mr. Armitage rested his forearms on the table. "Where was Lord Wrexham on Monday afternoon?"

"I don't know but he wasn't at the house. He rarely goes out, so that day was an exception."

"That won't earn you much."

Mr. Adams drew on the cigarette and blew out a puff of smoke. "Lady Wrexham went out too, but she caught a cab, since his lordship had the brougham. She also doesn't leave the house much usually, so something must have been important."

"Is there a reason she rarely leaves?" I asked.

"She's unwell. Doctors are always coming and going from the house, and her dressing table's full of bottles of tonic and jars of creams, so the maid who cleans it tells me. His lordship's got some lumps here." He indicated his mouth. "He doesn't go out because he doesn't want to show his face. Some of the creams are for him, I expect. Doesn't seem like they work."

He eyed the purse. I was about to remove some coins when Mr. Armitage placed his hand over mine to stay it.

"That wasn't worth much," he told Mr. Adams.

Mr. Adams leaned forward and blew smoke at me. "What I tell you next is going to be worth a quid."

"It had better be good for that amount," I said, removing a sovereign from my purse.

"Oh, it is, Miss. It's real good."

CHAPTER 8

Mr. Adams took the sovereign and sat back, pocketing the coin. He plugged the cigarette back into his mouth and took a long drag. With a tilt of his head, he blew the smoke towards the ceiling.

"We don't have all night," Mr. Armitage snapped.

Mr. Adams smiled. "Pearl Westwood came to the house a few weeks back."

Both Mr. Armitage and I leaned forward.

Mr. Adams drew on his cigarette. "Thought that would get your attention." Smoke billowed out of his nostrils like an angry dragon. "I can't remember when it was exactly, but it was between Christmas and New Year."

"Did she call on Lord or Lady Wrexham?" I asked.

"Lord. She spoke to him in his office."

"What did Lady Wrexham think of that?"

"I don't know. Want me to ask her for you?"

"Yes please." He gave a sneering laugh. "Oh. You were joking."

He tapped the cigarette end and ash fell into the tray. "She might not have known Miss Westwood was there."

Mr. Armitage sat back with a shake of his head. "We spoke to one of the maids this morning and she didn't mention Miss Westwood's visit. Even if she wasn't there at the time, it would have caused a sensation among the servants. She would have heard about it later."

"You calling me a liar?"

Mr. Armitage held the footman's gaze.

Mr. Adams grunted. "The butler threatened me with dismissal if I spoke about it. Only him, me and maybe the housekeeper knew. The only reason I knew is because I opened the door for Miss Westwood and I recognized her immediately. I saw her on the stage once at the Playhouse. Real pretty she was. Real pretty." He sniffed. "'Course, she was little more than a whore."

"So she didn't regularly call at the house?" I asked. "Not even when they were together, over two years ago?"

He shook his head as he stubbed out the cigarette butt in the ashtray. "I don't know about back then. I only got this job two years ago and Miss Westwood's never visited except this one time. Before that, me and Victor were busy avoiding coppers."

"How long did she stay?" Mr. Armitage asked.

"No more than ten minutes."

"How did she seem?"

"Hard to say. She didn't speak to me. Didn't even look at me." His jaw firmed and his top lip curled into a sneer. "She thought she was better than us. Maybe that's what got her killed. She ignored the wrong person and they murdered her." He wagged a finger at me. "You can have that opinion for free."

"The only opinion I'd like from you is the one about Lord and Lady Wrexham," I said. "What are they like?"

"He's all right, compared to some toffs." He removed a tin cigarette case from his inside pocket and flipped it open. "It's Lady Wrexham you got to watch out for. She acts all pious and good, but she's got a temper. She's thrown things at his lordship, twice. Once it was a vase, and the second time a little statue of a dog. Lucky for him, she's got bad aim."

"What did they argue about?" Mr. Armitage asked.

Mr. Adams shrugged. "Don't know. That's the thing. They always argue in low voices so as we can't hear. I reckon it's a skill they learn in the cradle in them big houses." He removed a cigarette and reached for the box of matches beside the ashtray. "Anything else? Only I've got to get back soon and I'd like to enjoy this in peace."

I rose and thanked him. Mr. Armitage rose but did not say a word. Once outside, I clasped the collar of my coat tight at my throat as the cold wind whipped along the street. It had grown dark while we were in the pub, but the street lamps were all lit and I was surprised by how many there were. The gentlemen of Belgravia didn't want their expensive coaches damaged because the lighting in their mews was poor.

"I cannot believe he and Victor were friends," I said. "What a revolting man."

"You're a terrible negotiator," Mr. Armitage said. "He would have settled for less."

"But he gave us excellent information. I think it was worth it."

He huffed a humorless laugh. "Don't get into business without hiring someone else to handle the transactions or you'll find your customers taking advantage."

"Thank you for the unwanted advice. So what do you think of the information? I think Pearl needed money and asked Lord Wrexham for it. According to Mrs. Larsen, Pearl was fine on Christmas Day. She seemed her usual carefree self and had no financial troubles. But within days, something changed, and Pearl hoped Wrexham could help her."

"But why call on her former lover and ask for money? Why not ask her current lover, Rumford?"

"She felt ashamed?"

Mr. Armitage didn't seem convinced. "By all accounts, she hadn't seen Wrexham in years. Why go to him in her time of need? And so brazenly too when Lady Wrexham was at home."

"It's certainly odd timing," I agreed. "It could have ended disastrously if Lady Wrexham threw her out." Pearl must have been quite desperate. Or perhaps she didn't care.

"Just because Pearl and Wrexham ended their liaison, doesn't mean she stopped caring about him, or he her," Mr. Armitage said thoughtfully. "Her arrangement with Rumford could have been entirely financial, on Pearl's part, but her heart remained with Wrexham."

My own heart sank and it occurred to me that I had to speak to Lord Rumford again. I needed to know if he knew about Pearl's visit to Lord Wrexham. If he did, he could be a suspect, after all. Except for the fact that this investigation was entirely his idea.

We walked on in silence, each lost in our own thoughts. I finally broke it as we turned onto Piccadilly. "We need to speak to both Lord and Lady Wrexham, but not together. We have to find out why Pearl visited, and we need to know where both of them were the afternoon of her death because apparently neither was at home."

"*You* need to do that," Mr. Armitage said.

"Pardon?"

"Not 'we.' You. This is your investigation, not mine. My part is finished."

I stopped, but Mr. Armitage kept going. I had to hurry to catch up to him. "But…why did you come with me today if you don't plan to continue helping?"

"I didn't want you visiting the servants alone. Considering the sort of fellow Adams turned out to be, I'm glad I went along."

"That's very gallant of you."

"Not at all. My uncle would have throttled me if he found out."

I watched his profile. The jaw might be firm, but I was quite sure I detected the hint of a smile. "You've come this far, you might as well continue to help me."

"No, Miss Fox."

"Why not? Do you have another case?"

"Not yet."

"Then what could you possibly have to do that's more important?"

"I was thinking about designing a pamphlet announcing my agency's services."

He could do that in his spare time. It wouldn't take long. He was searching for excuses, and coming up with terrible ones. "You're just proud."

He looked down at me, his face quite serious. "Pride isn't a bad thing, Miss Fox."

"It is when it gets in the way."

"In the way of what?"

Of us becoming friends, I wanted to say. But instead, I said, "Of you taking on your first case, albeit a shared one."

"Pride has nothing to do with it, Miss Fox." He looked away and added in a mutter, "Believe me."

I sighed. I couldn't think of what to say to get through to him. The damsel in distress card might get him agreeing to help, but I didn't want to play it. *My* pride was stopping me from doing that.

We walked the rest of the way to the hotel in awkward silence. He entered the building with me, but only to meet his uncle who was waiting in the foyer, hat and umbrella in hand. Mr. Hobart had been speaking to Mr. Hirst but broke away on our arrival to greet us. Mr. Hirst frowned at the exchange.

"Ready, Uncle?" Mr. Armitage asked.

Mr. Hobart put his hat on his head. "Ready. You must be looking forward to a home cooked meal."

"I've dined with my parents three nights this week. Didn't my father tell you?"

"We don't live in each other's pockets." It was said somewhat defensively.

Mr. Armitage warred with a smile that his uncle didn't see. "Good evening, Miss Fox, and good luck. I hope you get the answers you're after."

I bade them good evening and turned to go as they left the hotel. Out of the corner of my eye, I noticed Mr. Hirst's frown deepen.

* * *

After dressing for dinner, I knocked on Lord Rumford's door, hoping to catch him before he left. A gentleman of his standing would have an invitation to dine with friends or at a club, so I suspected he wouldn't leave quite this early. It was only seven-thirty.

He answered the door in his evening suit of stiff shirt and collar, with a white bow tie and waistcoat. "You've found her killer?"

"Not yet, I'm afraid. I needed to check something with you."

He did not invite me in, which was quite all right with me. Without Harmony or another chaperone, it would not be appropriate. What I had to say would be brief anyway.

"Actually I have two questions. Both might be a little painful for you to answer, but I hope you understand that I have to ask them."

"Of course," he said carefully. "If you think they'll help."

"According to witnesses, Pearl called on Lord Wrexham just after Christmas."

His jaw went slack. "Oh."

"Did you know?"

He shook his head.

"Do you know why she would see him?"

Another shake of his head, but this one was more thoughtful. "I don't understand." He glanced down the corridor then met my gaze. "I'm not such a fool to think she loved me. Not the way I loved her. I do like to think she cared for me, however, and certainly more than she cared for Wrexham."

"You knew they were together before she took up with you?"

"It was common knowledge in certain circles. The thing is, Pearl told me he was somewhat mean and selfish. He gave her gifts, of course, but nothing extravagant. He didn't put her up in her own place, and didn't care that she lived in a god-awful room in the worst part of the city. He never visited her there, of course. They went to hotels to be alone. That's ultimately why Pearl left him."

"Do you know how Lord Wrexham took the rejection?"

"She didn't say."

I almost told him it was Lord Wrexham I'd seen at Pearl's funeral but decided against it. "What about Lady Wrexham? Do you know what she thought of her husband's relationship with Pearl?"

He gave me a cynical smile. "She probably accepted it as well as any man's wife would."

It was the perfect lead-in to my next question, but my mouth suddenly went dry. I didn't want to ask it. This man was old enough to be my father; he was a distinguished lord. And I was going to ask him a very personal question.

But it had to be asked. "Do you know if Lady Rumford is in London?"

"My wife?" he blurted out. "Of course she's not. Why would she be?"

"I don't know, but I heard a rumor that she was seen at the opera a few nights ago. I'm sorry, but I had to check. The witness must have been mistaken."

He no longer seemed to be listening. The moment I mentioned when she'd been seen, the crease across his forehead deepened. He stared down at the floor between us.

"That's all," I said. "Goodnight, my lord. Enjoy your evening."

He rallied, his gaze refocusing. "Actually I'm dining with you and your family. I was at a loose end and Sir Ronald was kind enough to invite me."

I smiled. "Then I'll see you down there."

"May I escort you?" He checked his pocket watch. "I'll collect you at eight."

"I'd be delighted."

At precisely eight, Lord Rumford knocked on my door. With a warm smile, he offered me his arm. We waited at the lift together and were soon joined by Flossy, who gave me a suspicious look.

Downstairs in the dining room, we were greeted by Mr. Chapman who bowed at his lordship before indicating the family table. Uncle Ronald and Floyd were already there, although neither were seated. They spoke to two other men. Or, rather, my uncle spoke and Floyd looked on. The two men departed upon our arrival.

My uncle gave Lord Rumford an enthusiastic greeting, but once again, I was given the oddest look. Floyd merely smirked and winked at me when no one was looking.

Uncle Ronald gave my aunt's excuses for not joining us, then the men fell into conversation about my uncle's plans for the hotel's expansion. I listened until Flossy caught my gaze. She mouthed something at me, but I couldn't work out what. Caught on the opposite side of the table to one another, we would have to endure the men's conversation all night.

The sommelier arrived and poured the wine while Richard explained the evening's menu, for Lord Rumford's sake. Once they departed, my uncle resumed telling his lordship about the new restaurant he wanted to build.

After a dutiful period of time, his lordship changed the subject. "We must be boring the ladies."

My uncle blinked at his daughter then me as if he'd just noticed us. He looked disappointed.

"Not at all," I said. "I enjoy hearing about the hotel's plans for the future. I can see how a public restaurant, positioned facing the street, will attract a new clientele and not just hotel guests. This room can then be turned into a permanent ballroom."

"All the best hotels have a restaurant for non-guests," Flossy pointed out.

"But ours will be different," Floyd told her.

"How?" Lord Rumford asked.

Floyd glanced at his father.

Uncle Ronald picked up his wine glass and saluted us with it. "Because it will be better."

I watched Lord Rumford over the course of dinner. He was polite and listened attentively, even when my uncle talked incessantly about the hotel. He always gave an opinion when obliged to do so and drew Flossy and me into the conversation when possible. Indeed, because my uncle tended to ignore his children and me, and address only his guest, it was rather noticeable when Lord Rumford spoke to us.

Despite his politeness, he seemed lackluster. It was as if he were keeping up his side of the conversation merely because it was expected. Not knowing him from before Pearl died, I wasn't sure if he was always like this in polite company or if it was something new and a result of her death. It must be hard to pretend to be cheerful when he'd just lost someone he cared about.

He made his excuses immediately after the dessert course. He bowed to Flossy and me then went on his way. Uncle Ronald also departed, but only from the table. He drifted around the dining room, greeting guests and stopping to talk to those who dined alone.

Floyd finished his dessert wine and rose too. I thought he'd follow in his father's wake and greet guests, but he bade us goodnight then hurried out of the dining room. He eyed Uncle Ronald all the way, but with his back to us and the door, Uncle Ronald didn't notice.

Flossy moved to sit next to me. She hailed one of the

waiters and ordered tea. "Now, Cleo," she began as he walked off. "We need to talk. Just because the position of his mistress is available, doesn't mean you should fill it."

I stared at her. Then I burst out laughing.

She pouted. "What's so amusing?"

"You thinking I'm interested in Lord Rumford in that way."

"I'm not the only one thinking it. I saw the look on Father's face, and Floyd's. They think it too."

"That's absurd. Why would you assume I'd want to be his mistress?"

"You came in on his arm which means you clearly know one another already. You have also declared that you're not interested in marrying anyone, so the family thinks you want to be a kept woman, like Pearl Westwood. Not Mother, of course. She still has hopes that you'll marry. I assumed Father thought that way too, but now I'm not sure."

I followed her gaze to where her father sat at a table with a gentleman. "Do you all talk about me?"

The waiter arrived with a pot of tea and two cups. Flossy poured the tea and milk and added a lump of sugar to a cup before handing it to me. "Shall we go shopping tomorrow, Cleo?"

Goliath, Peter and Frank were calling on the other luxury hotels tomorrow to find out if Lady Rumford was staying at one of them. Until I could think of a way to discover Lord and Lady Wrexham's movements on the day of Pearl's death, I had nothing to do, and I would just be twiddling my thumbs waiting for their return. I might as well go out. But I didn't want to go shopping.

"I thought I'd visit the British Museum tomorrow," I said.

"But you dragged me there last week. Why do you want to go again?"

"Because I haven't seen everything yet. You don't have to come."

She eyed me over the rim of her cup. "You'll go alone? I'm not sure Mother would approve."

"Flossy, I'm twenty-three and not an heiress. While I'm appreciative of everything your parents have done for me, I am free to do as I please. Besides, it's just the museum."

"But men can go there."

"Scandalous, isn't it?"

She gave me a withering glare. "There's no need to be prickly." She sighed. "Very well, I'll come with you. At least the British Museum is better than the Natural History Museum where one can't turn without bumping into a dead creature."

The last person I wanted with me in any museum was Flossy. The last time, she'd been completely disinterested in any of the exhibitions and continuously asked when we were leaving. I'd rushed through my visit just to be rid of her. I liked her, but our interests were not aligned. "You don't have to come," I told her again.

She sipped her tea.

"Flossy, I am not going there to meet Lord Rumford or any other man. I give you my word."

She lowered her cup. "Very well. You can go alone, and I'll go shopping. But if Mother asks, we both went to the museum."

It was my turn to narrow my gaze. Perhaps *she* was going to meet a man. I wasn't sure if I should be worried or not. Unlike me, Flossy was an heiress. She was also quite unworldly. If a man was after her money, she might not be able to tell.

* * *

MY WALK around the museum not only proved to be educational, it was also cathartic. It gave me time to think as I wandered around the collections. By the time I arrived back at the hotel in the mid-afternoon I'd decided to be upfront with the Wrexhams and ask them what they were doing on the day of Pearl's death, and also the reason why she called on Lord Wrexham. I would not tell them who I worked for, however. Indeed, by the time I arrived home, I realized I would have to lie if I were to get any answers. Lying for good reason was acceptable and this was a very good reason.

Or so I told myself.

Terence from the post desk waved me over when I entered

the hotel and handed me a letter. "It's from Harmony," he said.

"Should you be reading my messages, Terry?"

"It wasn't sealed," he said defensively. "If Harmony didn't want me reading it, she would have sealed it. She knows I read everything that isn't sealed."

I must remember to seal all my letters before giving them to Terence to send.

I unfolded the letter and read. Harmony asked me to meet her at the Aerated Bread Company's Oxford Circus teashop at three-thirty. I glanced past Terence at the clock.

"You'd best get a move on if you want to make it on time," he said. I suspected he wanted to know why I was meeting Harmony away from the hotel. If she hadn't told him then I wouldn't either. The fewer people who knew about my investigating, the better.

The ABC's tea shop near Oxford Circus was a busy place filled with mostly women chatting and drinking tea at the tables, and four men. Three of those men were with Harmony. They looked like they'd rather be in a pub.

I sat and welcomed the cup of tea Harmony poured for me from the pot. The woman behind me bumped my chair as she got up to leave and some of my tea sloshed over the sides of the cup. "Next time we should meet at the Roma Café. It's much quieter and the coffee is excellent."

"I know the place," Peter said. "But I've never been inside."

"I don't like coffee in the afternoons," Harmony said.

I wiped the cup's sides with a napkin. "I'm sure Luigi will make you a pot of tea."

She managed to instill both a question and disapproval into the arch of her brow. "Luigi?"

I chose to ignore her and concentrate on the task at hand. "How are your inquiries going at the hotels?"

"No luck," Goliath said. "We all spoke to one or more staff, but no one recalled seeing Lady Rumford."

"Cost me a copper to get the doorman to talk," Frank grumbled. "And then he had nothing useful to tell me."

I reached for my purse. "Let me compensate you for your trouble." I handed out coins, hoping it covered their expenses.

Harmony handed hers back without a word. "I'm convinced the sighting of Lady Rumford was false."

"It would seem so."

Goliath picked up the teacup in one giant hand, the delicate handle pointing away from him. "So what're you going to do now, Miss Fox?"

"I've decided to confront Lord and Lady Wrexham. I can see no other course forward." I told them what Mr. Armitage and I had learned from the Wrexham servants and the theories we'd developed. "I think Pearl asked Wrexham for money to pay off her blackmailer. But I don't know why she'd go to him when Rumford was her current lover. It doesn't make sense."

"She asked Wrexham first, right?" Peter pointed out. "She only asked Rumford when Wrexham wouldn't cough up."

"But why ask Wrexham at all?"

Harmony sat up a little straighter. "Perhaps the blackmailer had proof of her relationship with Wrexham but not Rumford, and threatened to expose it. Even if their relationship ended some time ago, it would be humiliating if it became public."

It was an excellent theory and I told her so. Harmony sat back, satisfied with herself.

We finished our tea and went our separate ways. Since all four of them had the day off, I was the only one who returned to the hotel. I arrived there at the same time Flossy alighted from a hotel carriage. One of the porters rushed forward to help with her parcels. There were several, proving that she had been shopping, after all, although she still could have met with someone before or after. She'd not taken a maid to act as her chaperone.

"You're back very late," Flossy said as we headed for the lift. "You can't possibly have been at the museum *all* day."

"I met some friends for tea afterwards."

She gasped and stopped me with a hand to my arm. "You have friends here in London? Are they down from Cambridge?"

My heart sank at my error. I couldn't tell her about meeting the staff. She would be shocked and ask me not to do it again. I didn't want to start an argument with her although

I felt awful for not standing up for my friends, if I could call them that when I hardly knew them. "They're already heading home again."

"Next time invite them here for afternoon tea. I'm sure they'd love the Mayfair's sponge cake."

I smiled and nodded. I was such a coward.

* * *

As much as I was dreading confronting Lord and Lady Wrexham, I was looking forward to finally getting some answers. I felt certain I would today. My tactic couldn't fail.

Thomas Adams, the footman, answered my knock. His face fell upon seeing me. "Bloody hell. Not you again. What're you doing here?"

I straightened my shoulders. I didn't have to answer to him. "Are Lord and Lady Wrexham at home?"

He pressed his lips together, huffed out a breath that smelled of cigarettes, and said, "He is, she isn't, but he won't see you. Go away."

"I'm not leaving until he agrees to see me." I folded my arms.

The butler appeared by Mr. Adams's side. I'd met him on my first visit when I'd left him a hotel calling card with my name scrawled on it. "Is there a problem, Thomas?"

"Er. No, sir."

I gave up on Mr. Adams. It was the butler I had to get past. He looked rather more formidable, however. Mr. Adams might be younger and more physically intimidating, but the butler had an air of command about him. I imagined entire armies would quake in their boots if he looked at them down his nose like he looked at me. I felt like something he'd stepped in and wanted removed from his shoe.

"I'd like to see Lord Wrexham, please. Be so kind as to tell him I'm here."

"He's not in."

"He is, and I'd like to see him."

The butler's censorial gaze slid to Mr. Adams. "He's too busy to see visitors at this moment. Would you like to leave your card again, Miss Fox?"

"He didn't contact me after I left it last time so I expect this time will be no different. So no, I don't wish to leave my card. I want to see him."

The butler's gloved hand curled into a fist at his side. "And as I said—"

"He'll want to see me. I have something to tell him about Pearl Westwood. Something that the police would be interested in if they found out."

The butler remained unmoved except for a flicker of interest in his eyes. Beside him, Mr. Adams crossed his arms, an observer rather than a potential obstacle.

Still, my tactic of mentioning the police did not get results as I had hoped. Time to change course again. "What I have to say is something of a scandalous nature that journalists would delight in reporting."

The butler's fingers uncurled and he released a breath. "Thomas, see if his lordship will receive Miss Fox."

The footman disappeared. The butler blocked my entry until Mr. Adams returned. "He'll see you in his study, Miss Fox. I'll show you the way."

It would seem scandal in the newspapers was more of a threat than the police. Good to know for future reference. I smiled sweetly at the butler. He scowled at me as I passed.

The footman led the way up the marble staircase. Our footfalls were deadened by a thick crimson and gold carpet. A chandelier with dozens upon dozens of crystal teardrop pendants hung in the stairwell, but it wasn't lit. There was enough light coming through the large front windows that the gas ones weren't needed. Once we were out of sight of the butler, Mr. Adams glanced at me over his shoulder. "I'm impressed. Would you have followed through on your threat?"

"Of course," I lied.

He smiled. "Pity you weren't Victor's friend back when he and I were conning the toffs. We could have done with a girl like you."

"This *girl* is not interested in conning anyone," I bit off.

"Is that right?" He indicated the door ahead. "Tell that to his lordship after you get the information you want out of him."

He knocked and Lord Wrexham bade us enter. Mr. Adams announced me then discreetly closed the door again, leaving me staring at a man seated at the desk, writing in an appointment diary. With his head bent I couldn't see his face. I schooled my features so that when he finally looked up, I showed no shock at the sight of the disfiguring lesions.

Now that I was up close, I could see the red-brown lumps were sores, not warts. Lord Wrexham would have been a handsome middle-aged man without them, despite his receding blonde hair. His eyes were extraordinarily blue and piercing.

"What do you want?" he snapped.

"I have a few questions I hope you can answer."

"I mean what do you want in exchange for not printing your filth?" He opened the top drawer of his desk and removed some bank notes. He smacked them down on the desk. "This is all I have. Take it and go."

I steeled myself. "I don't want money. My price is answers. I'm writing about the life and death of Pearl Westwood and I think you can fill in some gaps for me. In exchange I will keep your name out of the article."

He sat back and settled his clasped hands over his paunch. He regarded me levelly, without a hint of self-consciousness over his appearance. "Hasn't interest in her waned yet? She was just an actress, for God's sake."

"The public's interest in her life is insatiable, more so now than when she was alive."

"You'll be writing entire books about opera singers and actresses next." Lord Wrexham indicated I should sit then he handed me a piece of paper. "I want an assurance that my name will not appear in any article you write, nor alluded to in any fashion. Is that clear?"

I wrote the statement, signed and dated it.

He read it before setting it aside. "What do you want to know?"

This could be easier than I expected. "You were at Pearl's funeral. Why?"

He blinked in surprise. "I cared for her once. I wanted to say goodbye."

"When were you together?"

"We began seeing one another early ninety-five and the relationship ended nearly two years later."

"Who ended it?"

"I don't remember."

I waited, but he didn't add to his answer. "When did you last see her?"

"When our liaison ended."

"That's not true."

He bristled. "Are you calling me a liar?"

"Pearl Westwood called on you between Christmas and the New Year."

His nostrils flared but he didn't deny it.

"What did you talk about?" I asked.

"That's none of your business!"

I glanced at my handwritten declaration. "We have an agreement."

His jaw worked in an attempt to stamp down on his rising fury. "We talked about the weather."

"Did she ask you for money?"

His lips parted with his silent gasp. He was surprised I knew that much. But he didn't answer.

"Did she tell you that someone is blackmailing her over her relationship with you?"

He gave a humorless laugh. "You are a fool, Miss Fox."

It was my turn to be surprised. Why would he think that? Then it occurred to me. If someone knew about his relationship with her, they wouldn't blackmail Pearl; they'd blackmail Lord Wrexham. He had more to lose and more money to pay.

So the blackmailing attempt had nothing to do with her relationship with Wrexham or, for the same reason, with Lord Rumford. Then what was it about?

I couldn't answer that unless this man admitted she asked him for money. "What was the money for?" I pressed.

"She didn't come here for money. She came to reminisce."

I scoffed. "That's absurd. She visits her former lover in the middle of the day when his wife is at home simply to reminisce with him? I am not *that* much of a fool, my lord."

He simply smiled at me. The sores on his face made it look sinister.

I wasn't going to get an answer about the meeting, and I doubted I would get an answer for my next question, too, but it had to be asked. "Where were you last Monday, the day Pearl died?"

He frowned. "Why?"

"It's just a question."

"An unnecessary one, in my view. She killed herself. What has that got to do with my whereabouts?"

"Even so, can you tell me where you were?"

He sniffed. "I can't recall."

I pointed at the open diary on his desk. "Why don't you check?"

He slammed it shut and placed his hand on the cover. "Which newspaper do you work for?" The ice-cold edge of his tone made me shiver.

I glanced at the piece of paper I'd signed. "We have an agreement."

"I asked you a question."

"And I asked you—"

He smacked his hand down on the diary.

I stood abruptly to hide my flinch. It was time to go anyway. I wasn't getting anywhere.

I turned to leave, but Lord Wrexham was surprisingly fast and reached the door before me. He blocked it.

"Who do you work for, Miss Fox?"

"Let me out," I said with a calmness I didn't feel.

He smashed his fist against the door. "Answer me, or by God you'll regret coming here."

CHAPTER 9

I gritted my teeth. "Let me out or I'll scream."

His lips curled with his cruel smile. "I'm the master of this house. Do you think the servants will dare go against me?"

"They might not, but your wife will. I doubt she'd like to deal with the repercussions if any harm came to Sir Ronald Bainbridge's niece in this house."

The mention of my uncle's name had him staring at me. It would seem the butler hadn't informed him who I was.

"Step aside, please," I said sweetly.

His chest rose and fell with his deep breaths. "Why is Sir Ronald's niece writing salacious articles for the papers?"

Someone knocked on the door. "Is everything all right, sir?" called the butler.

"Does Sir Ronald even know you're here?" Lord Wrexham asked me.

I swallowed.

The knocking continued. "Sir?"

Lord Wrexham's smile stretched. He stepped aside and opened the door. "See that Miss Fox finds her way out."

I swept past him and found myself between the butler and Mr. Adams as I descended the stairs. The door to Lord Wrexham's office slammed shut, the sound reverberating around the house.

On the second floor landing, movement in an adjoining

room caught my eye. A woman stood in the drawing room, her skirts swishing as if she'd just risen from the sofa.

"Wait," she said.

I halted, as did my escorts. The butler looked caught, unsure what to do. Obey his master or his mistress?

"We were just seeing Miss Fox out," he said.

The woman moved to the door but didn't leave the room. She wore dark purple with white bows on the sleeves and a large sapphire ring on her finger. She was a plain looking woman and much younger than her husband. From what Mr. Adams had told us about her reclusiveness, I'd expected to see a similar disfigurement on her face as her husband, or signs of illness, but she looked perfectly well to me. "And who are you, Miss Fox?"

The lie about the newspapers had ultimately failed with Lord Wrexham and, although I thought about using it again, I didn't want to. "I'm investigating Pearl Westwood's death. It may not have been suicide."

"A woman detective? You don't work for the police then."

"I do not. Did you ever meet Miss Westwood?"

Her hand began to shake. When she saw I'd noticed, she tucked it behind her. "Why would I have cause to meet an actress?"

I glanced at the butler standing stiffly beside me. "May I talk to you in private, my lady?"

Lady Wrexham's eyelashes fluttered. She gave a small nod.

I joined her in the drawing room and she closed the door. The furnishings reminded me of those in my hotel sitting room—elegant, expensive and all matching, as if all the pieces had been purchased together rather than over time. She moved the embroidery hoop she'd set aside on the sofa cushion and signaled for me to sit.

"I have some very personal questions to ask you, and I want to apologize in advance for asking them," I said. "But they are necessary to find out who killed Miss Westwood."

She settled her clasped hands on her lap. One of them still shook slightly. "I read about the actress's death. It was a tragedy, but I can't say I'm sorry for her. I know why you're here, Miss Fox. I know you're trying to find out if my husband killed her." She lifted her gaze to mine. "Or if I did."

Her directness was more unsettling than Lord Wrexham's fury. Ice ran through her veins, where fire heated his blood. "You say you never met her. But you knew of your husband's relationship with her."

She inclined her head in a nod.

"Miss Westwood called here between Christmas and New Year."

Her eyelashes fluttered again and I realized it was a tic, but whether it was a nervous one or not, I couldn't tell. "I believe so, but I didn't see her. She spoke to my husband in private. I don't know what they discussed."

"Was that the first time they'd seen one another since their relationship ended?"

"As far as I am aware, yes."

"What did you think of her coming here that day?"

She gave me a wry look. "What do *you* think, Miss Fox?"

"I think you hated her."

"Ah. So you *are* accusing me of her murder. If you think I did it out of jealousy then you're wrong. Their affair ended years ago. Why would I kill her now?"

"Because they were going to resume it."

She barked a laugh. "Were they? I doubt it. From what I can glean, Miss Westwood was getting more out of Lord Rumford than she did from my husband."

"You're well informed about her life."

Lady Wrexham stiffened. "Is there anything else, Miss Fox?"

"Where were you on the afternoon of Monday the fifteenth?"

"The day she died?" She frowned in thought. "I was shopping at Harrod's. I'm afraid no one can vouch for me, however. I didn't purchase anything and I caught a cab there and back as my husband had the carriage. If you're a very good investigator you could probably track down the driver."

I thanked her and rose.

She reached for the bellpull beside the armchair but hesitated. "Despite what you may think, I don't blame Miss Westwood for her liaison with my husband. I sincerely hope you find her killer."

She tugged on the tasseled cord and the door opened immediately. The butler glared at me until I exited, and I felt his glare all the way down the stairs and out the front door. It slammed behind me.

I hurried home, mulling over what I'd learned. It amounted to very little. My two suspects had proved evasive, which in itself was suspicious. But perhaps most suspicious of all was that Lady Wrexham had not once looked surprised when I said Pearl was murdered when the police ruled it was suicide.

* * *

I WENT in search of Harmony after eating lunch alone in my suite and found her on the third floor, cleaning one of the rooms. I slipped past her cart, parked near the door, and entered. "There you are."

She spun around with a gasp which quickly turned into a look of relief when she realized it was me. She might have been facing away from me, but I'd seen her tuck something into the large pocket on the front of her apron. "You scared me."

"Did you think I was Mrs. Short?"

She scowled and resumed dusting the desk. "How did it go with the Wrexhams?"

"As well as can be expected."

"That bad?"

I sidled up to her and peered into her apron pocket. I smiled. "What's the book about?"

Her scowl deepened. "You shouldn't snoop."

"I can't help it now. It seems to have become something of a habit."

She pulled out the book and handed it to me. It was a gothic novel with a creased spine and well-thumbed pages. "I bought it from a used bookseller at the Leather Lane Market."

I read the description. "It looks interesting. Can I borrow it when you're finished?"

She plucked it out of my hand and returned it to her pocket. "You won't like it."

"Why not?"

"It's not written for people like you."

I bristled. "What do you mean 'people like me?'"

She returned to the cart and hung the duster on the hook on the end. "Smart people."

"That's ridiculous. For one thing, you're smart and you're reading it." I was rather pleased with my retort. She couldn't possibly argue with it.

"Educated people," she shot back.

I crossed my arms. "Why can't educated people read it?"

"They'd find it too silly."

"Can I not be the judge of whether I'd like it or not?"

She removed folded white sheets from the cart and marched back into the room. "What did Lord and Lady Wrexham say?" she asked as she unfurled the bottom sheet.

I gathered the other side and began spreading it over the unmade bed.

Harmony straightened. "What are you doing?"

"Helping you. Or can't educated people make beds properly either?"

"I'll reserve my judgement until the end."

We made the bed together then Harmony fixed my side, tucking the sheets in tighter and making sure there was not a wrinkle in sight before laying the bedspread over the top. By the time she'd finished, I'd told her everything that had transpired at the Wrexhams' house.

"I have no idea what to do next," I finished.

Harmony perched on the edge of the dressing table and rested her hands either side of her. "Could you speak to the coachman again? You can offer him more money to tell you where he took his lordship that afternoon."

I shook my head. "He values his job too much. The same with the butler." I clicked my fingers. "I could offer Victor's friend money to look at his lordship's diary. It's better than my other idea."

"Which is?"

"Something that carried too much risk." I'd considered breaking into the townhouse and getting my hands on that diary, but it was far too dangerous. I might be able to weather the risk if I got caught, but Victor couldn't and I needed his lock picking skills to get in.

His friend, Mr. Adams, worked there and had proved he could be bought, however.

"Miss Fox!"

I swung around to see Mrs. Short standing in the doorway, a thunderous look on her face. Built like her name, she stood at less than five feet and was as round as a barrel. Her gray hair was drawn back into a tight bun, pulling her eyes into a squint. Her mouth pinched with disapproval.

"What are you doing here?" she asked.

"I was just talking to Harmony. I wasn't distracting her. She continued to work the whole time."

Her brow creased. "*Why* are you talking to Harmony?"

"For company."

"Miss Fox, I'd appreciate it if you did not distract my maids while they're working."

"But—"

"Do I need to speak to Sir Ronald about this inappropriate behavior?"

"We were just talking."

"She needed a clean sheet," Harmony blurted out.

Mrs. Short and I looked at her.

"She just came in to ask me if I had a spare. I was about to check." She cleared her throat and waited for Mrs. Short to move aside to let her through to the cart.

I followed, squeezing past the scowling Mrs. Short.

Harmony bent to check the contents of her cart. "I can spare one. No need to go to the linen cupboard." She straightened. "I'll be up in a moment to change the bed, Miss Fox."

Mrs. Short put out her hand for the sheet. "I'll do it."

Harmony hesitated then went to pass her the sheet. I snatched it off her before she could.

Mrs. Short's brows arched so steeply they almost joined her hairline. "What are you doing?"

"Changing my bed, and if you ask me why, I'll need to speak to my uncle about your inappropriate interest in my personal affairs. Good day, Mrs. Short."

It was immensely satisfying to see the housekeeper's jaw

slacken and eyes widen. My satisfaction dissolved after hearing her scold Harmony for fraternizing with a member of the Bainbridge family.

* * *

AFTER LEAVING the clean sheet on my dressing table, I spent some time browsing the library. The small room off the main sitting room was packed full of tomes the discerning guest would like, but there wasn't a single medical text among them. It didn't really matter anyway, as I doubted I'd find what was wrong with Lord Wrexham's face by searching for the symptom. It would be a near-impossible task.

I was careful when leaving the library to check the sitting room and make sure my aunt and cousin weren't present. I didn't want to be invited to afternoon tea. Not when I had somewhere to be by five.

Fortunately I didn't recognize anyone, and was able to leave without being stopped. With hat, gloves and coat already in hand, I headed for the front door, only to change my mind and divert to Peter. The front desk was quiet at this time. New arrivals had already checked in for the day and most guests were either taking tea or out.

He smiled upon seeing me. "Any advances in the investigation today?"

Goliath entered the hotel and loped over. "Frank's in a mood."

"When is he not?" Peter muttered.

"True enough. How's the investigation coming along, Miss Fox?"

"Slowly, but I'm glad you're both here. Do either of you know someone who can follow Lady Wrexham for a few days? I'd pay all travel expenses and a small daily wage."

"My little brother would do it," Peter said.

"Shouldn't he be in school?"

"Try telling him that."

"I have a cousin who'd do it," Goliath said. "Big strapping lad who can look after himself."

Peter rolled his eyes. "Well that's no good, is it? He'll stand out like a giraffe." He turned to me. "You don't want someone who'll look out of place on a Belgravia street. My brother shines shoes when he's not making trouble. He can set up a stand near the house."

"And if Lady Wrexham leaves when he's got a customer?" Goliath asked.

Peter shrugged. "He's quick on his feet. He'll think of something."

I gave Peter the address then headed out, waving at Frank as I passed him. I reached The Nag's Head at five past five and spotted Mr. Adams seated alone at the same booth as last time. He looked up when I slid onto the seat opposite.

"You're here without your chaperone, Miss Fox. Is that wise?"

"We're in a popular pub filled with people. Why wouldn't it be?"

He drew on his cigarette and blew the smoke towards the ceiling. "You made my master very angry today. Perhaps he'll set someone on you to teach you a lesson."

Was he threatening me? Warning me? Or simply toying with me? What would Harry Armitage say if he were here? I wasn't sure, but I knew he wouldn't be baited. I gathered up all my bravery and leveled my gaze with Mr. Adams'. "I have a task for you. Do you want to know what it is?"

"It'll cost you."

"I'm well aware that you do nothing unless there's a reward."

He smiled around the cigarette before removing the short stub with his thumb and forefinger. "I can't afford principles." He blew out smoke, not bothering to direct it away from me. "So what task do you have for me?"

"Lord Wrexham keeps an appointment diary in his office. I caught a glimpse of it today. I want you to look through it and see where he was on the afternoon of Monday the fifteenth."

He contemplated his cigarette before drawing on it again. "I don't go into his office. The maids clean it, and Wrexham sends the butler if he wants something fetched from there."

I gathered up my purse and rose. "Then I'll ask one of the maids."

His hand shot out and grabbed my forearm. "Sit."

I sat.

He let me go. "I can do it, but it'll cost you more than last time."

I plucked a sovereign coin out of my purse and slid it across the table. "I'll give you the same. If you don't like my terms, I'll ask a maid. I believe they get paid less than you and do more work, so I'm sure I'll find a willing spy. Probably a friendlier one, too."

"You don't want someone friendly. You want someone devious." He pocketed the coin which I took to mean he accepted my terms.

"Report back to me here at the same time tomorrow." I rose. "I expect a good return on my investment." I strode out of the pub, feeling much better about this encounter with Mr. Adams than the last one.

* * *

The following morning, Harmony arrived to do my hair. She was not alone; Danny accompanied her.

He hovered at the entrance to my bedroom, looking uncertain as to whether to proceed. It was understandable, considering I wore my dressing gown with my hair tumbling past my shoulders.

Harmony had no such qualms. She grabbed his arm and pulled him into the bedroom. "Danny's got something to tell you."

Danny studied the dressing table as if he'd never seen anything so interesting. "My friend, Perry Alcott from the Playhouse, wanted me to tell you he found something that might interest you."

"Oh? What is it?"

He cleared his throat and his gaze quickly met mine before he looked away again. "He was cleaning out Miss Westwood's dressing room at the theater and found a letter which he thinks proves she was with someone else."

"Someone other than Rumford? Now that is interesting. Thank you, Danny. Do you know if Mr. Alcott is at the theater this morning?"

"He'll get there late morning, I expect. Do you want me to send a message letting him know you'll meet him there?"

"Yes, please. Make it eleven."

I managed to fill in my time with Flossy until it was time to leave for the meeting. She wanted to know where I was going and if she could come. She changed her mind when I said I was off to the Natural History Museum.

The main entrance doors to the Piccadilly Playhouse were locked, but a side door opened at precisely eleven and the debonair Mr. Alcott beckoned me.

"What a pleasure to see you again, Miss Fox. If only it were for happier reasons."

"Danny tells me you found a letter."

"I did. It could be a clue." He spoke in hushed tones even though we were alone as we crossed the foyer.

Some of the memorabilia from Pearl's memorial service remained, although most had been removed. The posters advertising *Cat and Mouse* still showed her face although a strip bearing Dorothea Clare's name had been stuck over Pearl's. I asked Mr. Alcott about it.

"Dotty hates that Pearl still features on them," he said in a low voice. "She's been on and on about it to Culpepper but he's refusing to have new posters made."

We passed through a door labeled STAFF ONLY and entered a long corridor. There was no one about, although I could hear hammering in the distance. We walked quickly past closed doors, some labeled, others not, our footsteps muffled by the carpet. Finally we reached a door with a piece of paper stuck to it. "Miss Clare" it read in neat handwriting. Mr. Alcott lifted the paper to show me Pearl's name painted on the door underneath.

"Another thing Dotty hates," he said.

"Why hasn't Pearl's name been painted over?"

"Pearl was adored around here. It's hard to let her go."

He pushed open the door to reveal the lead actress's dressing room. As with Pearl's flat, much of it was upholstered in dusky pink, from the sofa to the chair and cushions. The scent of perfume hung in the air, but it didn't completely hide the smell of cigarette smoke. A privacy screen painted with spring blossoms separated a corner of the room. A cream silk dressing gown hung over it and a pair of slippers had been positioned nearby.

I felt like I was intruding. "Should we be in here?"

"Dotty's not in yet. She's been asking Culpepper to clear out Pearl's things for days but she finally gave up and asked me to do it, since I was Pearl's closest friend at the Playhouse. I started yesterday, and that's when I found this."

He disappeared behind the screen and emerged carrying a box. He set it down on the dressing table beside a vase filled with coral peonies and roses. The box appeared to be full of women's underclothes and other personal items—a hat, handkerchiefs, combs and brushes, a hand mirror, and many cards.

I opened one and read. It was from an admirer of Pearl's confessing his undying devotion. It was signed with his full name and address. The next card was similar. "Did she know these men?"

Mr. Alcott shook his head. "They were strangers, people who watched her on stage and fell in love with her. Or thought they did. They're not all from men either. Some are from women."

"Why did Pearl keep them if she didn't know the senders?"

He shrugged. "A reminder of her popularity, I suppose."

"Did she need reminding?"

"We all do, from time to time. Actors and actresses thrive on adoration. Without it, we're just ordinary." He smirked. "And if we're just ordinary, what's the point?"

He said it with a light tone, but his words saddened me. Did Pearl wonder what the point was? Did she kill herself after all because she felt the adoration was waning? Looking at the dozens of cards, it was hard to imagine that she could feel ordinary and unloved, but sometimes it wasn't the quantity of love but the quality that waned.

"Here." Mr. Alcott handed me a folded piece of paper, but he held something back in his hand. "Read it."

It was a letter, but not addressed to anyone and not signed. Indeed, it appeared to be a draft, with words crossed out and punctuation missing. It was a love letter, of sorts. It began with the author's confession of love for the unnamed recipient and went on to plead for them to be patient and to wait just a little while longer before they could be together openly. It finished mid-sentence with "I do not love R, I love you, but he must think…"

R most likely referred to Lord Rumford. "Pearl wrote this?"

"That's her hand. I know it well."

"Who do you think she was writing to?"

He took back the letter. "I don't know. It's taken me by surprise. I thought she told me everything, but it seems she kept the name of her true love from me. I had no idea she cared for anyone but Rumford. She hid it well. But there's more."

He opened his palm to show me what he'd held back. It was a man's square-set black onyx ring with a plain gold band. "This was inside the folded letter, and both were buried under her unmentionables in the left drawer." He indicated the dressing table with its central narrow drawer and deep ones on either side.

"The letter could have been written some time ago. How long has she had this dressing room?"

"Years. The entire time I've known her, she's had it." He looked around and sighed. "It doesn't seem right for Dotty to use it so soon after, but she insisted. She and Culpepper argued about it, and it seems she won."

"I imagine if she walked out now, the production would be in jeopardy."

"Lord, yes. Her understudy isn't up to snuff yet. But Dotty better tread more carefully if she wants Culpepper to keep her on long-term."

"Perhaps she doesn't plan on staying long-term. Perhaps she's hoping a man will come along and whisk her away to another life."

He narrowed his gaze. "You mean she wants more than Pearl's job? She wants her benefactor too?"

The door opened and Dotty Clare paused on the threshold upon seeing us. She stared at me a moment, as if she couldn't place me, then entered. "You're in early, Perry."

"I wanted to finish up in here before you arrived, but I see you're early too."

"I had a meeting with Mr. Culpepper."

Mr. Alcott motioned to me. "You remember Miss Fox from Pearl's memorial."

"How do you do?" She dropped her bag on the dressing table and threw her coat onto the sofa. "Have you come to help Perry?"

I nodded. "Yes."

"Thank God." She flounced onto the chair and peered at herself in the dressing table mirror. "I want it all gone. Every single thing. Gone. I don't want to see so much as an eyelash of hers in this room."

"I'm not your servant, Dotty," he said with a steely edge to his tone.

"I know you're not, darling, but I'm finding that woman's things everywhere. It's very upsetting."

"You can say her name. Or are you afraid if you say it, she'll come back to haunt you?"

She pulled a face at her reflection. "Don't even joke about such a thing. I swear I can feel her presence in here." She waved a hand at the box. "That's why I want it all gone. Hopefully her spirit will leave with her things. God knows there are enough memories of her at every turn in this place, I don't need more."

Mr. Alcott discreetly tucked the letter and ring back inside the box and picked it up. "She was a star here for a long time, Dotty. You can't erase her a mere week after her death."

"I don't want to erase her, Perry, but Culpepper is being excessive. He's just doing it for the publicity, you know."

"Doing what?" I asked.

"Keeping her things around. Her picture on the posters, photographs in the foyer, her name on my door. While the newspapers are still talking about her, he'll continue to associate her with the Playhouse. Ticket sales have been good since she died. Did you know that?" She looked at me over her shoulder before turning back to the mirror. "The seats have been full, whereas they were half empty before."

Mr. Alcott rested the edge of the box on the dressing table and glared at her reflection in the mirror. "Are you suggesting Culpepper killed her for publicity?"

She lifted a shoulder. "I never said that. But let's be honest with one another. Her star wasn't going to be rising for much longer. She only had a few years left before her looks began to fade. When that happened, the public would move on and Mr. Culpepper would need a new star to attract the audiences again. The lovers would disappear too, of course."

"Lovers?" I asked. "Plural?"

Dotty looked up at me through her lashes and smiled. "She'd be a fool to have just one."

"Wouldn't that invoke jealousy?"

"Yes! But isn't that the fun of being beautiful? Come now, Miss Fox. Don't look so shocked. I'm sure Pearl had a lot of fun, but she also knew it couldn't last forever. She'd be the first to admit that her life was better off ending now at the height of her fame."

"Dotty!" Mr. Alcott cried.

She removed a hairpin and a tendril of blonde curls fell past her shoulder. "Although I'm sure she would have wished to die in a different manner." She shivered. "Her scream as she fell was blood-curdling."

"You were here in the theater when she died?" I asked.

"Of course. We all were. We had a show that night."

"Where were you?"

"In the privy, if you must know. I'd just come out when I heard her scream. Then there was silence. It was very strange. Unnatural, almost."

"It took everyone a few moments to work out where the scream had come from and what it meant," Mr. Alcott said quietly. "Then Pearl was found and…it was chaos."

"Who found her?"

"Culpepper was first on the scene," Dotty said. "He shook her as if he couldn't believe she was gone. Then when it did sink in, he held her in his arms."

Mr. Alcott wiped away a tear. "I can't talk about this anymore. Forgive me, Miss Fox, but I think we're finished here."

I followed him out and we walked back along the corridor together. "What will you do with her things?" I asked.

He studied the box in his arms. "Give them to her sister, I suppose."

I was about to ask him if I could keep the letter and ring

for a while when the door we were passing by suddenly opened and Mr. Culpepper almost bumped into me.

"It's Miss Fox, isn't it?" He frowned. "What are you doing here?"

"She came to see me," Mr. Alcott said before I could speak. He indicated the box. "I've been cleaning out Pearl's dressing room."

"I'll take that." He reached for the box.

Mr. Alcott drew it away. "I was going to give it to Mrs. Larsen."

"I'll pass it on to her after I go through it. Property belonging to the theater should remain here."

Mr. Alcott handed the box over and we continued along the corridor. Once we were out of earshot of Mr. Culpepper, he said, "I hope he doesn't destroy the letter."

"So do I."

It wasn't a complete disaster if he did, however. I'd recognized the ring.

CHAPTER 10

I carried the key to Pearl's flat in my purse so I didn't need to return to the hotel to retrieve it. Her flat was exactly the same, with all her things in the same place, as if Pearl had just stepped out. It made my task easier.

I went straight to the table with all the photographs and bent to study them. In the one I wanted, Pearl stood in the center, dressed in the sleeveless and belted *stola* of a Roman noblewoman, a gold band in her hair and another around her upper arm. On one side of her, with a hand resting on her shoulder, was a man dressed in a Roman gladiator's costume. I recognized him from the posters in the Playhouse's foyer as the lead actor in *Cat and Mouse*. On Pearl's other side stood another man, his hand also resting on her shoulder. He was not in costume but wore a pinstripe suit. On his smallest finger he wore a ring with a dark square gem.

I took the framed photograph with me and returned to the Playhouse, just a short walk away. The side door was still open and I slipped inside and made my way along the corridor that led to the offices and dressing rooms.

I stopped at Mr. Culpepper's door and knocked quietly before I changed my mind.

"A moment!" His voice sounded thick, muffled.

I waited and several moments later, the door opened. I think I was as shocked to see Mr. Culpepper as he was to see me. While I'd certainly expected him to open the door, I hadn't expected him to have swollen red eyes. He'd been crying.

It took the wind out of my sails. I was no longer sure how to begin.

"What are you still doing here?" he asked.

At least he didn't invite me in. I didn't want to enter his office. If I was going to confront him with what I knew, I preferred to do it in the corridor. I glanced along it, left and right, but there was no one about.

"I have some questions to ask you," I said.

He clutched the edge of the door and leaned into it, as if it were the only thing holding him up. "Are you still trying to suggest Pearl was murdered?"

"Why are you so sure she wasn't?"

He sighed. "Because I believe Rumford drove her to take her own life. It's obvious. Something happened between them, they fought, he was going to give her up...something like that."

"You don't really believe that, Mr. Culpepper."

He looked down at the carpet.

"You don't believe that because you know she wouldn't kill herself because of Rumford. She wasn't in love with him."

His Adam's apple bobbed with his hard swallow. "What makes you say that?"

"She was in love with you."

He looked up. His eyes brimmed with sorrow and something else. Remorse?

"Mr. Alcott showed me the letter Pearl wrote expressing her love to the unnamed recipient. She never got a chance to give it to him, which is a tragic shame."

He swallowed again. "I just read it myself. It was very moving. Why do you think I am the man she was writing to?"

"The ring wrapped up with the letter is your ring, isn't it?" I showed him the photograph. "Did you give it to her as a token of your love?"

He closed his eyes and tipped his head back. He expelled a shuddery breath before looking at me again. "All these years of hiding our relationship, and a complete stranger uncovers it." He huffed a humorless laugh. "Pearl would have found that amusing."

"You loved her, and that's why you can't bring yourself to clear out her dressing room or change the posters."

He pressed his lips together, but it didn't stop them trembling.

"Tell me about your relationship. When did it begin?"

He stepped aside, inviting me into his office.

"Let's talk out here."

His frown deepened before clearing in understanding. "You think *I* killed her and will kill you too for discovering our secret?" He shook his head. "Pearl really would find that amusing. I didn't kill her, Miss Fox. I loved her. You even said so yourself just now."

"You must have been jealous of her relationship with Lord Rumford." When he didn't respond, I forged on. "I imagine this is painful for you, but if you want me to believe you didn't hurt her, you have to talk. But I'll be staying right here."

He stroked his thumb and forefinger over his thin moustache. "I wasn't jealous of Rumford. I had no reason to be. I knew she didn't love him. That letter proves it."

"But you never received the letter."

"I didn't need to read it to know. Look. Pearl and I had been together for a few years. When she left Wrexham, I thought we'd finally be together. I'd hoped it would be just the two of us, and I even asked her to marry me. She said she would, but not yet. She was at the height of her career and didn't want to give it all up. Then shortly after Wrexham, she took up with Rumford. She said she missed the gifts and attention. He paid for a nice flat, took her to expensive restaurants, and they attended balls and parties together. She met princes and dukes because of Wrexham and then Rumford." He sounded as though he was in awe of the life she was able to lead, not jealous that he couldn't give her those things.

"It must have stung that she promised to be with you but took up with Rumford instead." I recalled something Mr. Alcott had said. "You argued about it, didn't you?"

"We fought about that and other things. We had a volatile relationship." He gave a hollow laugh. "There was never a dull moment." He must have realized how that sounded, because he quickly shook his head. "I never wanted her dead.

Our fights only showed how much we loved one another. If we didn't fight it would have meant we were indifferent, and indifference is the end of a relationship."

I believed him when he said he loved her and didn't wish her dead, but that didn't mean he hadn't done it in the heat of the moment, perhaps accidentally causing her to fall to her death. "Where were you when she died?"

"Here at the theater."

"I mean where precisely. You must have been nearby if you got to the body first."

He frowned. "I didn't. Perry Alcott was already there when I reached her."

If that were true, why hadn't Mr. Alcott corrected Dotty when she claimed Mr. Culpepper was first on the scene? "Can you show me where?"

"I don't have time."

"Please, Mr. Culpepper. This is for Pearl. If she was killed, she deserves justice."

His eyes filled with tears. He nodded. "Follow me."

He led the way along the corridor, past the dressing rooms and a store room where a staff member was polishing a candlestick. He pushed open a door and we emerged into the ground floor seating area. Four actors on the stage looked up from their scripts.

"Miss Fox?" said Mr. Alcott. "You've returned."

"I had some questions for Mr. Culpepper," I said without stopping. Mr. Culpepper's strides weren't long but they were purposeful and quick.

Mr. Alcott and Dotty Clare exchanged glances then Mr. Alcott jumped off the stage. He assisted Dotty down then they both followed us up the aisle.

Mr. Culpepper stopped eight rows back. "Here." He pointed along the row. "Seats seven to ten." He swallowed and looked away.

"What time did it happen?"

"Three-thirty?" He looked to the others and they nodded.

Dotty took his hand. "Is this necessary, Miss Fox?"

"Can you all point out where you were when you heard Pearl's scream?"

Mr. Alcott clutched his throat but was the first to answer.

"I was behind the stage curtain. When I heard her, I came out here and looked around. When I didn't see anything, I jumped off the stage and started checking the rows."

"You were the first one to reach the body," I said, watching him closely.

"Was I?" He shrugged. "I can't recall. It was all so chaotic. So horrible."

"Was anyone backstage with you?"

"No."

"Did you see anyone out here?"

He nodded at Mr. Culpepper. "He came out of that door." He nodded at a side door further back. There was a matching one on the other side of the theater. The words FIRE EXIT were painted on both.

"I was in the actress's privy," Dotty said. "I think I'd just come out when I heard Pearl's scream. I tried to follow where I thought it had come from and emerged through that door." She indicated the door at the back of the theater through which the audience would come and go. "I saw Perry and Mr. Culpepper standing here. I didn't realize what had happened until I came over to see." She pressed the back of her hand to her trembling lips.

"Thank you," I said. "I know how difficult this is for you, but I'm sure it will help."

Mr. Culpepper excused himself and hurried off, but not before I saw his eyes fill with tears.

One of the actresses on the stage called Dotty's name. "I need help with this scene."

Dotty sighed. "She'll never do." Hands on hips, she headed towards the stage.

Mr. Alcott watched her go. "The girl is Dotty's understudy. She's quite good, but Dotty hates admitting it. I think she's worried."

"Thank you for your help today," I said. "Finding that letter was a revelation."

"I thought it would be important. I wish I knew who it was meant for."

"You have no inkling?"

He shook his head. "I'd best be off too. Good day, Miss Fox."

I tipped my head back to look up at the balcony of the dress circle. It seemed unlikely that anyone could fall by accident, but I wanted to see the balcony's height for myself.

I continued up the aisle but instead of going all the way to the back of the stall seating and exiting through the door Dotty said she'd used, I glanced to the stage to see if anyone was watching, then pushed open the fire exit. Just as I assumed, there were stairs.

I lifted my skirts and headed up, pushing open the door on the second tier. I emerged into the dress circle seats. I peered over the balcony. It reached my waist, and from what I could gather from Pearl's clothes in her wardrobe, she was about my height. No one could accidentally trip and fall over. Pearl was either pushed or she jumped to her death.

I headed back to the hotel, my mind awhirl as I went through what I'd learned. There were holes in all three stories I'd just heard. Any one of them could have been upstairs in the dress circle, pushed Pearl over the balcony, and come back downstairs without anyone seeing. Mr. Alcott was alone backstage but no one had seen him so he couldn't prove it. He'd also been the first to reach the body, although had apparently forgotten that fact when Dotty initially mentioned it. Was that because he hadn't wanted me to know that he was closest and so assume he was the killer?

In Dotty's case, she hadn't used the nearest door to the ladies privy. We'd passed the actress's privy in the corridor and it was nowhere near the entrance she said she'd used. That entrance conveniently gave access to the dress circle and upper circle.

And I'd just proved the emergency fire exit also gave access to the upper levels. It would have been very easy for Mr. Culpepper to push Pearl over the balcony and race downstairs upon hearing her scream. Not only that, of the three of them, he had the strongest motive: jealousy. It was hard to believe his claim that he wasn't jealous of Pearl and Rumford. No man liked to share his lover, and it must have galled him that Rumford could give her what she wanted when he couldn't—a luxurious lifestyle mingling with the cream of society.

Instead of heading back to the hotel, I caught an omnibus

to the Natural History Museum, partly so I wouldn't have to lie to Flossy about how I spent my day and partly because I found museums both inspiring and soothing. Walking around the exhibits gave me time to think. It also filled in the rest of the day until it was time to meet Mr. Adams at The Nag's Head.

"Don't bother taking a seat," he said as I approached his booth. "This won't take long."

I slid onto the seat anyway. From the look on his face, I guessed he'd been unsuccessful. "If you weren't able to get into his office, I'd like my money back."

"I got in." He squared his shoulders, thrusting out his chest. "There's not a lock in London that can keep Thomas Adams out."

"Did you find the diary?"

"I did." He sat forward, elbows on the table, and removed the cigarette dangling from his lips with his thumb and forefinger. Smoke billowed from his mouth as he spoke. "But the relevant page was missing."

"Missing?"

"Torn out. Only a jagged edge remained. It wasn't in the waste basket, drawers, nowhere." He shrugged. "Sorry, but you're not getting your money back. I did what you asked, at great risk to myself, and found nothing."

"Thank you," I muttered.

I left, but my despondency didn't last all the way home. If nothing else, that missing diary page told me Lord Wrexham didn't want me to find out where he was on the day Pearl died.

* * *

I TOSSED and turned for much of the night, unable to sleep. All the clues I'd gathered so far jumbled together in my head until they began to make no sense. At three, I gave up and threw on a dressing gown and headed downstairs. The library would be unlocked, as would the sitting room through which one had to cross to access it.

I turned down the gas on my lamp so that the light wasn't too bright, but bright enough for me to traverse the stairs safely. The hotel was quiet, my footsteps sounding disembodied within the stairwell. When I reached the third floor landing, I realized my footsteps weren't the only ones on the stairs. It sounded like several sets moving rapidly below me and going down.

"We want what we're owed," came a woman's voice in a Cockney accent.

"We know you've got our money, you thieving prick, so give it," said another woman.

"Let's get out of here first," a man said. "I ain't hanging 'round. Last time, we nearly got caught by the owner's niece."

I stopped and turned off the lamp. My heart hammered in my chest and I hardly dared move. Moments later, the footsteps receded altogether and I found the courage to continue, albeit in the dark.

When I reached the ground floor, I peered around the corner. The light was dim in the foyer, but I could discern three men. The one closing the door was the night porter, James, who did all the duties of the front-of-house staff overnight. He must have just let someone out of the hotel. The women?

The second man was Mr. Hirst. He accepted what appeared to be paper money from a third man whose face I couldn't see. That man touched the brim of his cap and moved away. He also handed something to James before exiting the hotel. James had not held the door open for him.

If only I'd seen his face. While he'd dressed like the beak-nosed man I'd seen a few days ago, and had a similar build, it was impossible to know if they were one and the same. I was quite sure it wasn't Mr. Clitheroe, the guest Mr. Hirst had claimed I'd seen that time and who also had a prominent nose. For one thing, he'd checked out, and for another, I'd never heard a hotel guest speak with a Cockney accent.

Mr. Hirst disappeared into the senior staff corridor and James roamed the foyer. I thought about asking him who'd just left but decided against it. The stranger had given him something, and if it was money in exchange for turning the other cheek, James wouldn't tell me.

I abandoned my plan to get a book and headed back up

the stairs, feeling my way with a hand on the rail. The women and man had emerged onto the stairwell on the second floor so I walked along that corridor. All was silent. If they'd been in one or more of the rooms, those occupants were most likely asleep now.

Unless the rooms had been empty.

* * *

I MANAGED to finally get a few hours sleep, only to be awoken by Harmony holding my breakfast tray at eight. I let her in and crawled back into bed.

She followed me into the bedroom. "This was waiting for you in the corridor." She set the tray down on the dressing table. "Why haven't you eaten yet?"

"Because I couldn't sleep and now I'm tired."

"You won't solve the case by lying in bed all day."

"I don't want to lie in bed all day, just for another hour."

"I have to do your hair before I get on with my chores."

"I'll do it myself today."

She stood with a hand on her hip. "I've got something interesting to tell you."

"Write me a letter and leave it on the desk. I'll read it later."

With a shake of her head, she reached for the curtains.

"Don't!"

She wrenched the curtains back letting in the dull light of a wintry London morning. It could have been the sunniest day as far as I was concerned. I pulled the bed covers over my head.

Harmony jerked them down. "Come on, Miss Fox. You'll feel better once you eat and splash water on your face."

"If you throw water over me I'll never share my breakfast with you ever again."

She smiled. "I know it's hard to get up when you haven't slept much. Believe me, I do. But you really need to hear the gossip I have to tell you. It will wake you up."

I sighed and sat up. "You know there's no better way to get my attention than the promise of juicy gossip. So what have you heard?"

She picked up the breakfast tray and positioned it across my lap then sat near my legs and helped herself to a cold slice of toast. "Goliath told me that his friend at the Savoy Hotel said he'd overheard a guest gossiping about seeing Lady Rumford at the theater."

"That's a rather tangled grapevine. Should we trust the information?"

"The woman claimed to be a friend to Lady Rumford. You would think she'd know what her own friend looked like. It's worth following up, which is why I told Goliath to tell his friend to find out more."

"Excellent idea. That leaves me free to follow up other clues."

"Such as?"

I sighed as I peeled the shell off a boiled egg. "I don't know yet. Perhaps inspiration will strike by the time I finish breakfast."

Inspiration did indeed strike, and I left the hotel feeling buoyed. This investigation might prove complicated, with so many suspects compared to the last one, but it was better to have too many than none at all. That's what I told myself, anyway.

The events of the previous night also occupied my thoughts. Indeed, they were getting in the way of the murder investigation. There was only one way to stop that—pass the information onto someone else. It was fortunate that the person I planned to see could help me with that as well as give advice on what to do about the sightings of Lady Rumford who, according to her husband, should not be in London.

I poked my head into the Roma Café and smiled at Luigi and his two regular customers.

"He's not here," Luigi told me.

I headed up the stairs next door and knocked on Mr. Armitage's office door. He beckoned me in, looking somewhat disappointed to see me and not a potential customer.

"How is business coming along?" I asked cheerfully as I took a seat.

"I'm run off my feet."

A newspaper was spread out in front of him but his desk

was otherwise neat. His jacket hung alongside his coat and hat on the stand by the door, which meant he wasn't expecting anyone. "Quite," I said, trying not to let him see that I knew he was lying.

He folded the newspaper and set it to one side. "Do you require my services to accompany you to The Nag's Head again?"

"No, thank you. I've already spoken to Mr. Adams twice since we last met." I spread out my arms. "As you can see, I came to no harm."

He leaned back, elbow resting on the chair arm, and stroked his top lip with his finger. "You've made progress. Well done. I knew you would."

"I haven't solved it yet, but I do need your help."

"I ought to start charging you."

"Or you could just agree to make me your partner and we can halve the fee."

He laughed. "You don't give up, do you?"

"It's an annoying habit, so I've been told." I opened my purse. "Since you won't agree to become my partner, yet, I'm happy to pay you for your time."

He shook his head when I tried to hand him some money. "Put it away, Miss Fox. That was a joke. I don't want payment for accompanying you when you speak to dubious characters. What kind of man do you take me for?"

"One who thinks I'm attacking his pride." I dropped the money back into my purse. "I don't want you to accompany me anywhere, this time. I want your opinion."

My retort about his pride had stung him into silence and I wished I could take it back. Sometimes I needed to check myself before saying whatever came into my head.

"I'm sorry," I mumbled. "But I really do want your opinion on something. Two things, actually. As someone who worked in a luxury hotel for many years, I think you can offer a unique and valuable perspective."

"Apology accepted. There's no need to lay it on too thickly."

I gave him a withering glare. "I wasn't." I adjusted my position in the chair, suddenly feeling uncomfortable as he stared back at me. "It's about Lady Rumford. Two separate people have now mentioned seeing her, one at the opera, the other at the theater. But she isn't staying at any of the premier hotels. Lord Rumford doesn't have a London residence, so she must be staying somewhere."

"With a friend?"

"But wouldn't Lord Rumford have been informed by that friend?"

"A friend to her, but not to him, perhaps."

That was certainly a possibility, although it seemed odd that no one seemed to *know* where to find her. "If she was staying with a friend, wouldn't she have caught up with other friends while in London? So far, we only have the occasional secretive sighting, which is causing everyone to gossip."

He steepled his fingers and tapped his thumbs together. "There's one other possibility. Something that, if true, means she doesn't want her friends to know she's here."

"Because she came to London to commit murder." I sat forward. "Go on."

"She could be staying at a hotel under an assumed name."

"I suppose she could. If she came here with the intention of killing Pearl, she wouldn't check in using her own name. That's a brilliant deduction, Mr. Armitage."

"For what it's worth, I think you're barking up the wrong tree."

I looked up. "Why?"

"If she killed Pearl, she'd be foolish not to leave London immediately. But even more importantly, what does she gain by killing her?"

"The removal of her rival for her husband's love, of course."

He *humphed*.

"What's so amusing?" I asked, defensive.

"You. I hadn't pegged you as a romantic."

I wasn't sure if he meant it as an offense or not, so I remained silent.

"You said there were two things you wanted to discuss with me," he went on. "What's the second?"

I told him what I'd seen and heard on the stairs and in the hotel foyer last night. He listened attentively, a small crease forming across his forehead. But not for the reason I suspected.

"Why are you here, Miss Fox?" he asked when I finished.

I blinked. "To tell you about the man who appeared to be paying Mr. Hirst and the night porter."

"You have no evidence of any wrongdoing, just suspicions and speculation. Added to which, you could have taken your suspicions and speculation to my uncle."

I bristled. "Next time, I will. I just thought you would be interested in investigating it further. I see I'm wrong. And anyway, my other reason for coming was to ask your opinion about Lady Rumford. You were actually quite helpful in that regard."

"You would have worked that out yourself. Or, again, talked it through with my uncle. He has more experience when it comes to hotel guests than me." He sat forward and crossed his arms on the desk. His smile was positively wicked.

Something inside me flipped. He'd managed to unnerve me with one little smile. I wasn't sure I liked it.

"So why did you come here, Miss Fox?"

"I'm no longer sure."

He laughed softly.

"Are you making fun of me?"

He put up his hands in surrender. "I wouldn't dare."

I stood. "Good day, Mr. Armitage. Thank you for your assistance." I turned and walked out.

How had that meeting deteriorated so quickly? Mr. Armitage was being deliberately provocative and I couldn't fathom why. We'd been getting along well, and I'd hoped we could become friends. Clearly he had no interest in doing so if he was going to sabotage our fledgling friendship like that.

I put Mr. Armitage from my mind and considered my next step in the investigation. I needed to narrow down my suspects. There were too many. Jealousy and hurt over a possible rejection were looking like strong motives for a number of my suspects, both former and current lovers, their wives and even Pearl's understudy, Dotty Clare. Both Lord and Lady Wrexham and Mr. Culpepper had known Pearl for several years, and someone who might be able to give me a better insight to those older relationships would be Pearl's sister. She claimed she didn't know Pearl all that well anymore, but she must have an opinion on the people from Pearl's past.

I fished out the paper on which she'd written her address from my purse. I wasn't sure of the area so I caught a hansom. Some fifteen minutes later, the driver deposited me at the entrance to a court surrounded on three sides by indistinguishable tenements. Small children played a chasing game and a woman hung out washing, although I couldn't see how it would dry in this weather.

I nodded at her as I passed and felt her gaze on me as I approached Millie, sitting on a stoop. The little girl was humming to herself and staring straight ahead, her body rocking to the rhythm of her tune.

"Good morning, Millie," I said.

She stopped humming and lifted her face, although she didn't look directly at me.

"Do you remember me? I'm Miss Fox. I met you at your aunt's home."

She began humming again.

"Is your mother inside?"

"You won't get no answers from her," the woman said from the washing line. "She's not deaf, she just don't talk much. If it's Mrs. Larsen you're after, she's inside."

"Thank you." I knocked and, as I waited, thought of a question for the neighbor. "Did you ever see Mrs. Larsen's sister here?"

"The actress? Aye, I saw her at Christmas. She only ever came Christmastime."

"How did she seem?"

The woman shrugged. "Fine to me, but I only caught a glimpse. She was real pretty, and so fancy looking with her fur coat and matching hat."

The door opened and Mrs. Larsen smiled in greeting. "This is a surprise."

"I want to ask you some questions about Pearl."

"Come in." She clicked her tongue at Millie, blocking the way. "Let Miss Fox past."

Millie continued to hum and didn't move.

"Millicent! Move!" She rapped Millie's shoulder with the back of her hand and Millie shifted to the side.

I squeezed past her.

"Forgive me, but I'll have to receive you in the kitchen. We're having some work done in the parlor." She led me along the corridor, past closed doors and the staircase, until we reached the warm kitchen. A pie baking in the oven filled the entire house with its delicious smell. "You remember my husband from the funeral?"

Mr. Larsen stood. He nodded at me before gathering up the boot he'd been fixing along with his tools, and left.

"He's a man of few words," Mrs. Larsen said, somewhat self-consciously. "Tea?"

"Thank you, that's very kind."

I sat and watched her fill teacups from the teapot warming on the stove. The kitchen was a sizable one with a large central table that Mrs. Larsen had been using as a place to knead dough. A large pie had been set aside, ready to be baked in the oven when the other one finished. It was too much food for the family of three. Perhaps Mrs. Larsen baked them for neighbors or sold them.

On the wall above the table was a shelf full of neatly labeled jars and above them hung a wooden cross. A pink glass vase stood empty by the window, as if waiting for the first signs of spring to fill it with flowers. It was a very pretty vase and looked out of place in the drab kitchen. It was more to Pearl's taste than her sister's.

Mrs. Larsen must have taken it from the flat that day I'd met her there. I wondered what else she'd removed, and how much of it she'd already sold.

She handed me a cup and saucer. "I'm so sorry, but I don't have cake today."

"It's very good of you to receive me. I do apologize for calling on you without notice."

"How may I help you?"

"What can you tell me about Pearl's—*Nellie's*—prior relationships? The ones before Lord Rumford came on the scene. And the ones during."

Her lips pinched. This wasn't a conversation she wanted

to have. "I know very little. As I told you, my sister and I weren't close. She rarely confided in me."

"What do you know?"

"She was with another lord before Rumford. I can't recall his name. She didn't like him much, and when I asked her why she would ruin her reputation over someone she didn't like, she got angry with me. She told me she needed him if she was to get anywhere in life." She stared down at the teacup, held in both her hands. "Nellie wasn't satisfied with the life she had. She wanted more glamor, more amusement. She hated being bored so she'd make trouble, just to entertain herself."

"What kind of trouble?"

"All kinds. Like seeing one man when she already had another."

"For example…?"

She regarded me over the teacup. "You said it yourself. You wanted to know about the man or men she saw *while* she was seeing Rumford."

"Can you give me their names?"

She contemplated her tea. "I don't like naming names. I'm not a gossip. But you should ask that theater manager. They were close."

"Close enough to be jealous of her seeing other men?"

"I wouldn't know."

I let her mull that over for a few moments, but when she didn't elaborate, I decided to change tack. "Did Nellie ever mention the wives of her benefactors?"

She snorted. "If Nellie cared about them, she never showed it."

"You don't think she considered their feelings?"

"No. It's not all her fault, mind. The lords have to take some of the blame. Most of it, I suppose." She sighed and put down the teacup. "Nellie just did what came naturally to her. She flirted and smiled her way through life, taking all she could while she could. I suppose one of her lovers ended her life out of jealousy." She shook her head sadly. "So very, very selfish."

I wasn't sure if she was referring to Pearl or the murderer.

Silence weighed heavily on us, each of us lost in our thoughts. It was only broken by Millie's humming.

The girl approached along the corridor, her hand running along the wall. She stopped when she reached the kitchen. "I'm hungry."

"Not now, Millie, we have a guest."

Millie seemed to consider this. "Will I eat at school?"

Mrs. Larsen clicked her tongue. "Enough! I'm tired of hearing about that place." She took her daughter's shoulders and turned her around to face the corridor. "Go back outside." When Millie didn't move, she gave her a little shove. "Go!"

Humming to herself, Millie headed off.

"She seems a content child," I said.

"She's simple." Mrs. Larsen sat down again. "Simple children are often content."

"Is that why she's going to school at a young age? I hear that can be good for children who have difficulty learning, to give them the best start. How old is she?"

"Four this March."

She didn't answer my other question, and I wondered if she was sensitive about Millie being slower to develop compared to other children her age. But that wasn't what intrigued me about the girl.

I put down my teacup and watched Mrs. Larsen very carefully. I wanted to see every flicker of her lashes, every flinch, when I said what was on my mind. "She looks like her mother."

Mrs. Larsen's gaze sharpened and a muscle in her cheek twitched. "We have the same shaped face, and I was blonde too, at her age."

The twitch gave me enough of a hint that I was onto something with my line of questioning. I pushed forward, even though it was one of the most uncomfortable questions I'd ever asked anyone. "She's Nellie's daughter, isn't she?"

She almost dropped the teacup. It clattered in the saucer. "She's *my* child. If she weren't, do you think I'd keep her? I'd give her back to her mother, even if that mother was my own fool of a sister."

Her harsh words did not sound like a mother's. Or, rather,

they didn't sound like a *loving* mother's words. There was a ring of truth to them, however. I couldn't imagine Mrs. Larsen taking in a simple child that was not her own. She didn't seem to have a kind enough heart for it. That destroyed the theory brewing ever since seeing Millie walk down the corridor—that Pearl had asked for her daughter back and Mrs. Larsen had killed her to stop her taking Millie.

"I'm sorry for asking," I said. "I must look at all possibilities."

Mrs. Larsen's lips pursed. "More tea, Miss Fox?"

"No. I must go." I rose and saw myself out.

Mr. Larsen stood by a cart with Millie sitting on the back of it. He was teaching her a clapping game which required her to copy him then add something to the sequence, which he then repeated. He had a lot of patience and Millie quickly picked up the rhythm. A moment later, she'd changed it to something equally rhythmic yet different.

He smiled at her then caught sight of me. He nodded. I nodded back and left the court behind.

A few minutes ago, I'd had two potential candidates for Millie's father, based on her age—Lord Wrexham and Mr. Culpepper. After watching Mr. Larsen with her, I now had a third.

Despite Mrs. Larsen's protests, I was absolutely convinced that she didn't give birth to Millie. Her sister had. But for some reason, Pearl—Nellie—couldn't, or wouldn't, raise her.

CHAPTER 11

Mr. Culpepper wasn't in his office at the Piccadilly Playhouse. I followed the corridor towards the dressing rooms and quickly realized mid-afternoon was a busy time of day in the theater. Actors and actresses were beginning to arrive, squeezing past me in the narrow corridor to reach their dressing rooms. A man's voice filled the cramped space as he performed vocal exercises, and a group of women talked loudly to be heard over him—and each other. Backstage staff hurried past me carrying props, costumes and stage pieces. None seemed to care that an extra person was in their midst, and I wasn't stopped.

I knocked on Dotty Clare's dressing room door. When she didn't respond, I continued my search and found her in the main women's dressing room. The door stood open even though one of the actresses wore only her corset and wide-leg bloomers.

"Miss Fox?" came the familiar voice of Mr. Alcott from behind me. "What are you doing here?"

"I'm looking for Mr. Culpepper."

"I haven't seen him. Did you try his office?"

Dotty joined us, wearing a silk dressing gown and slippers. She leaned against the doorframe and languidly lifted an arm and pointed towards the door that led to the stage. "He's out there with my understudy. That girl requires work. Honestly, I think he should get someone else."

"It's too late to get another," Mr. Alcott said. "There's no time for a new girl to learn the lines. What if you got ill tomorrow? Or you had an accident?"

"Going to push me off a balcony too, Perry?"

He gasped.

Dotty turned to me, a satisfied smile on her lips. "Have you seen my show yet, Miss Fox?"

"*Your* show?" Mr. Alcott scoffed.

"Find Miss Fox some tickets, will you, Perry?" She patted his cheek. "Good man." She walked off, her hips swaying seductively and the silk gown fluttering around her ankles.

Mr. Alcott shook his head. "She's getting more unbearable every day. She'd best be careful or someone might push her off the balcony. *Her* understudy perhaps."

I made a small sound of shock and he gave me an arched look.

"You seem disturbed by our little spats, Miss Fox. Clearly you haven't spent much time around actors."

"It's always this nasty?"

"That's not nasty. Not that Dotty and I are friends, either. I have made great friends in the theater though. Pearl, for example." He released a shuddery breath and blinked back tears. "It's beginning to sink in that she's never going to walk out on that stage again."

Mr. Culpepper emerged through the stage door then stopped upon seeing me. "I don't have time for your questions." He strode past me.

I raced after him. "This won't take long."

"Not now, Miss Fox." He paused outside his office door. "I'm too busy. Good day."

There was only one thing to do—tell him here and now in the corridor. "Pearl had a child."

His jaw slackened.

"The child was adopted by her sister and brother-in-law, the Larsens. They're bringing her up as their own."

His gaze shifted away and he frowned in thought. After a moment, as if he'd been wound up, he invited me inside. He closed the door behind me, but I remained near it while he rested his hands on the desk.

He lowered his head. "I've never seen the girl. I don't even know her name."

"It's Millie. She'll be four in March."

He sat heavily on the desk chair and rubbed his chin. The fingers of his other hand lightly tapped the desk. He was calculating Millie's birth year and perhaps when she must have been conceived. His fingers stopped tapping and he swallowed heavily.

"Pearl stopped working for a few months over the winter of ninety-six. She told me she was ill and went to convalesce at her sister's home."

So I'd been right. Millie was Pearl's child. A niggling doubt had lingered after Mrs. Larsen denied it. "You never saw Pearl during that time?"

"She didn't want to see me. She wrote saying she was too ill and illness made her look ugly." He almost smiled, but it didn't quite eventuate. "She was always worried about how she looked, even with me." He passed both hands over his face. When they drew away, he glanced up at me. "My God. You've shocked me, Miss Fox. I—I can't believe she wouldn't tell me!"

I couldn't quite believe it either. But if Mr. Culpepper was lying, he was a very good actor.

"Is the girl mine?" he asked.

"I hoped you could tell me."

He lifted a shoulder. "The timing fits. We were certainly together then, but..." He squeezed his eyes shut.

"But she was also with Lord Wrexham," I finished.

He gave a small nod. "She would have told me if the child was mine. Wouldn't she?" He seemed to be asking himself, or perhaps the ghost of Pearl. His gaze grew distant. "When she returned to work, she was as happy as she'd ever been. She and Wrexham went to a lot of parties then. She was always careful not to mention them around me, but I heard. It was almost as if she decided to make the most of what was on offer, and there was a banquet spread out before her."

That didn't sound like someone who'd just given up her baby. Unless she hadn't wanted that baby.

"Why didn't she tell me?" he muttered.

I bit the inside of my lip. The only reason she wouldn't

have told him was because she knew, or suspected, the child wasn't his.

I went to open the door at my back, but thought of one more question. "Did Pearl ever ask you for money?"

He'd been rubbing his hand through his hair and when he stopped, his hair stuck out at odd angles from his head. "No."

"Not even quite recently?"

He shook his head. "She knows I couldn't give her anything. Besides, Rumford gave her everything she could have wanted. What did she need more for?"

I thanked him and slipped out, leaving him staring vacantly after me. I was glad I'd spoken to him. His answers were a revelation. And yet some things didn't ring true. How could he have not known that his lover had a baby? Surely he would have noticed the swell of her belly when they were together before her self-imposed confinement. And surely he wouldn't simply have accepted her excuse that she was ill. If he loved her, he would have tried to see her during her illness.

I also didn't believe that he had no money. He was the manager of one of London's premier theaters. Even if he didn't have enough on hand for whatever Pearl needed, he could get a loan. If nothing else, Pearl would have gone to the man she loved first before going to Lord Wrexham.

If she had asked Mr. Culpepper for money so she could take back her child, he must have become angry that she'd never told him about Millie. Perhaps they argued and he killed her during a confrontation. Perhaps the entire conversation I'd just had with him was a fabrication, an act. He might not be an actor himself, but that didn't mean he couldn't perform when necessary.

The more I thought about it, the more I warmed to the idea. Ever since realizing Millie was Pearl's daughter, I couldn't stop thinking about it. What other reason could there be for Pearl to want money? She was going to pay off her sister and raise Millie herself.

Which pointed to *Mrs. Larsen* as the murderer. She could have killed Pearl out of fear that she was going to lose the girl she'd raised as a daughter for almost four years.

"Miss Fox! Wait!"

Mr. Alcott hurried along the corridor behind me, waving some strips of paper in the air. As he drew closer, I realized they were tickets. He handed them to me. "They're for tonight's performance. Best seats in the house."

"Thank you. I look forward to it."

He leaned forward and whispered, "Dotty's performance won't be as good as Pearl's."

The mention of Pearl reminded me just how close they'd been. "May I ask you a very personal question about Miss Westwood?"

"This sounds serious. What is it?"

"Did she ever mention that she'd had a child?"

"Bloody hell," he murmured. "No, never. When was this?"

I didn't like spreading gossip, but I needed answers and this man might be able to give them to me. "The child will be four in March. Pearl's sister and brother-in-law have been raising her as their own."

He shook his head. "I'm flabbergasted. Not only did Pearl never mention her, but…" He shook his head.

"Go on."

"But as I said, I never had an inkling. Even now that you've told me, I can't think of a single time Pearl even hinted at that child being hers. There were no photographs of her in her dressing room, no children's drawings. I don't even know the girl's name."

"Millie."

"She bought her a gift at Christmas, of that I'm sure. It was a teddy bear. She asked me if I thought it was a good gift for a toddler, but you're saying the girl is almost four." He shook his head over and over. "How could she not have told me?"

The more he spoke, the more he threw cold water over my theory. "So there were no times you thought she seemed sad? As if she regretted giving the child away?"

"Pearl was never sad. She was always happy. She had everything she could ever want, as far as I knew—men who adored her, a generous benefactor who lavished her with gifts. If she regretted anything, she never showed that side to me, and I was her best friend."

A best friend who hadn't known about Pearl's relationship

with Mr. Culpepper. So perhaps he hadn't known Pearl's true feelings about the baby, either.

But everything in the picture he painted of her was the same that others painted. Pearl was happy. She enjoyed her life. She didn't act like a woman who missed her child and wanted her back. Surely if she had, her lover and friend would have known, or at least seen some small sign.

But Pearl seemed to have no regrets, no sorrows. She had not showered her little girl with gifts, and when she did buy her a Christmas gift, it wasn't what a girl her age would want. Indeed, according to the Larsens' neighbor, Pearl only visited once a year, at Christmastime. That wasn't a woman who missed her child and wanted her back. If Millie was Pearl's daughter, Pearl's heart was cold indeed.

Perhaps Mrs. Larsen was telling the truth and Millie was indeed her child, not Pearl's. If so, my theory that she'd killed Pearl to stop her taking Millie lay in tatters.

I headed back to the hotel with a heavy heart. It seemed like the more I learned, the further away from the truth I got.

* * *

THE PICCADILLY PLAYHOUSE looked different at night. With all lights blazing in the foyer and audience members dressed in their evening finery, it became a glamorous wonderland, much like the Mayfair Hotel. Mr. Alcott had given me five tickets, one for each of the Bainbridges and myself. Uncle Ronald had initially declined, but after discovering the seats were in the box on the second tier, he changed his mind. Mr. Alcott was right when he said they were the best seats, and my uncle wasn't going to give up an opportunity to be seen.

The show was a little dull, the story lacking something that I couldn't quite put my finger on. The performances were excellent, however, although Floyd didn't think so.

"Pearl Westwood was better." Seated between Flossy and me, thought he'd been enjoying the show, until he yawned.

Flossy nudged him with her elbow. "You're only saying that because she was more beautiful than Dotty Clare."

Aunt Lilian rapped Flossy on the shoulder. "If you're going to talk, be more subtle. People are watching."

Flossy pouted. "He started it."

"That's enough, Florence. You're a lady; act like one."

Floyd snorted, earning himself another jab from Flossy's elbow.

Uncle Ronald leaned forward. "I expect better from you, Floyd."

"I know," Floyd muttered in hushed tones so his parents couldn't hear. "I'm never good enough."

Flossy squeezed her brother's arm and gave him a sympathetic smile.

We received callers in our box during intermission as if we were royalty receiving courtiers. One couple remarked on our good fortune for securing a box. No one mentioned that I'd been given the tickets.

I was introduced to yet more friends. My family seemed to know everyone and I was surprised there were still people in London they hadn't introduced me to before now. They had a very wide circle. Everyone was so nice to me, too, inviting me to afternoon tea along with Aunt Lilian and Flossy.

"My word, look who it is," said one of my aunt's friends, peering over the balcony. "Come and look, Lilian. Isn't that Lady Rumford? The woman with the teal gown and feather in her hair."

I followed her gaze to the lady dressed in teal, seated in the stalls below.

Aunt Lilian gasped. "So it is. So she *is* in London. How odd that she's not staying with us."

Her friend eyed her sideways. "Come, Lilian. Is it really so strange considering who *is* staying there?"

Aunt Lilian fluttered her fan at her face as she continued to stare into the audience. "Who is she with?"

The woman appeared to be alone. She didn't speak to anyone else.

The bell to end intermission sounded and our guests departed except for a friend of Floyd's, whom I'd met at the hotel's New Year's Eve ball. Jonathon sat on the seat beside me and settled in for the second act.

"I've been hoping to bump into you again, Miss Fox."

I doubted that. He could have come to the hotel many times and seen me there. According to Flossy, the blue-eyed, blond-haired gentleman was something of a ne'er-do-well. He and Floyd both had a reputation with women and for attending parties hosted by a fast set. There was a charm about him, however, and I suspected there might be some substance behind his easy manner and flirtatious smile.

"It seems you succeeded," I said, not taking my gaze off Lady Rumford.

"Are you enjoying the show?"

"Yes. You?"

"Not particularly. This is my second time. I wanted to compare the performances of Miss Clare and Miss Westwood. So far, I have to say I'm disappointed."

"Why? Because she's not as pretty as Miss Westwood?"

He leaned closer. "You would think I was going to say that, but actually, she just isn't as good. She struggles to hit the high notes and her voice doesn't carry as well. Miss Westwood was an excellent singer. You could hear her clear as a bell, no matter where you sat."

"You sound like an admirer."

"I was." He spoke so softly that I turned to him.

"Did you know her? On a personal level, I mean."

"Of course not." His blustery tone told me otherwise. It would seem Dotty Clare was right, and Pearl had several lovers.

The lights dimmed and I could no longer see Lady Rumford. I watched the rest of the show and when the applause finished and the curtains came down and the lights came on, I immediately sought her out. She didn't speak to anyone as she left.

"I wonder if Rumford knows she's here," Floyd said, following my gaze.

"Does he care?" Jonathon asked.

Floyd flashed a grin. "I hear he's scouting for a replacement for Miss Westwood. Perhaps he should ask Miss Clare."

Flossy wrinkled her nose. "Honestly, Floyd, do you have to be so vulgar?"

"You sound like Mother." He got the attention of his friend. "What say you, Jonathon? Should Rumford cast Miss Clare in the role of his next mistress?"

Jonathon stood and put out his hand to me. "We shouldn't discuss such things in front of ladies."

Floyd looked to his sister then to his friend and followed Jonathon's warm gaze to me. He chuckled. "Come on, Flossy, we'll meet them downstairs."

My heart sank as Flossy followed her brother out of the box, knowing full well why he wanted to leave me in Jonathon's presence. Even my aunt and uncle left after seeing Jonathon put out his arm for me. My uncle looked pleased.

I took Jonathon's arm and allowed him to escort me out of the box and down the stairs. We joined the audience exodus heading for the foyer. I'd completely lost my family.

Jonathon noticed me craning my neck. "Don't worry, we'll find them." He patted my hand, resting on his arm. "And if not, I'll walk you back to the hotel. It's not far."

"What about your family? Didn't you come with them?"

"I did, but I'll let you in on a secret." He bent his head to mine. "I'm old enough to find my own way home."

"Very amusing."

"In fact, I'm even old enough to escort young ladies home."

"People will talk."

His eyes gleamed with humor. "Let them."

I didn't like the warmth in his voice. It was much too familiar, too hopeful. Our path joined with those coming out of the auditorium from the ground floor stalls. I searched the sea of heads, hoping to spot my family or even Lady Rumford.

"The layout of this theater is appalling," Jonathon said as we shuffled forward. "Do you have a ticket for your coat?"

I handed him my cloakroom ticket and he left me standing near the refreshment counter with a cluster of other ladies, also waiting. I stood on my toes but could not see my family. I resigned myself to a walk home with Jonathon; I was going to have a word with Flossy in the morning about not abandoning me in future when Jonathon was circling.

A familiar figure in the midst suddenly looked up and scanned the faces of the crowd. Mr. Armitage was so tall that he soon spotted me. He nodded in greeting and bobbed his head to speak to someone at his side. A moment later, he headed my way.

"Good evening, Miss Fox. Did you enjoy the show?"

"Yes, thank you. We had a good view of the stage."

"I know. I saw you up in the box like the royal family."

I laughed. "The tickets were free. Someone must have pulled out at the last moment and I was at the theater at the right time."

Mr. Armitage's parents appeared out of the crowd but remained a little distance away. I nodded and smiled at them both, and I received a smile from Detective Inspector Hobart in return and a curt nod from his wife. She still hadn't forgiven me for costing her son his job at the hotel.

"How nice of you to come with your parents," I said.

"It was my Christmas gift to them." Mr. Armitage stretched his neck to get a better view of the crowd. "Are you looking for the Bainbridges? Because they just left."

I sighed. "Tell your father there's going to be another homicide."

"What?"

"I'm going to kill Flossy when I see her."

He laughed softly. "I hadn't pegged you as being so dramatic." He thought about it then shrugged. "Actually, I take that back. The way you stormed out of my office this morning was a performance fit for the Playhouse."

I tilted my chin up at him. "I did not storm out. You were making fun of me so I thought it best to leave before our friendship crumbled any further."

"I wasn't making fun of you." His low, melodic voice held no hint of humor. It rumbled like the sound of distant drums, vibrating through me. "And our friendship is alive and well—if you want it to be."

I opened my mouth to retort, but it died on my lips. I didn't want to utter a trivial quip. I wanted him to gaze at me like that all night. Like there was no one else in the room.

"Your coat, Cleo." Jonathon's words burst the bubble surrounding us like a pin in a balloon.

I accepted the coat and cleared my throat. Since Mr. Armitage didn't immediately move off, I had to introduce them. Indeed, Mr. Armitage looked somewhat taken aback by the arrival of a stranger bearing my coat.

As it turned out, they weren't strangers to each other.

"You look familiar," Jonathon said. "Are you an acquaintance of the Bainbridges?"

"Something like that." Mr. Armitage bade us goodnight and rejoined his parents.

Jonathon helped me into my coat. "He's not a friend of Floyd's, or I'd know. Armitage, Armitage…" He shook his head. "Who is he?"

"He was assistant manager at the hotel until recently."

His hand paused at my collar. "I see." It was spoken darkly, as if Mr. Armitage were an ominous cloud one had to keep an eye on at a picnic.

Jonathon led me outside. There was no sign of Mr. Armitage but the Bainbridge carriage waited for me. It would seem I wouldn't have to murder Flossy after all.

* * *

THERE WAS ONLY one thing to do at this juncture of the case, only one course of action. Just because I didn't want to take it didn't mean I wouldn't. I steeled my nerves and forged ahead to Belgravia to call on Lord and Lady Wrexham.

I was so nervous that I couldn't eat breakfast. I managed to escape Harmony's ire for not finishing everything and headed out to Belgravia mid-morning. A lad had set up a shoe-shine stand across the way and was polishing the shoe of a gentleman who sat on the stool, newspaper in hand and cigar in his mouth as if he were in the hotel's smoking room. The lad must be Peter's brother.

Instead of trying my luck and knocking at the Wrexham's townhouse, I waited not far away. I'd brought a newspaper with me as a disguise, of sorts, and pretended to read it, all the while watching the house. I decided not to declare myself to Peter's brother when his customer departed. If I were seen by the household, I didn't want the boy to be chased off as well.

Thankfully the rain stayed away. I waited for hours, but my patience was finally rewarded when the carriage with the green doors pulled up outside the house. I waited for the townhouse door to open and Lord Wrexham to emerge then crossed the road. He swore upon seeing me.

"A word before you leave, please, my lord."

"I don't have time for this."

"I think you will when you hear what I have to say."

He thrust his walking stick into my chest, stopping me. "Get out of my way."

The door opened again and the butler emerged. "You! Leave or I'll summon the constables."

"Do it," I said to Lord Wrexham. "Call the police. I'd be happy to inform them that you are the father of Pearl Westwood's child."

Lord Wrexham slowly lowered the walking stick. His gaze did not leave mine, but his expression gave nothing away. I couldn't tell if he was shocked by the news Pearl had a child or that I knew he was the father.

"Sir! Do you want me to summon a constable?" the butler asked.

Lord Wrexham shook his head. "Leave us."

The butler seemed reluctant to go, but he didn't need to be told twice.

Lord Wrexham waited for the door to close before speaking. "What do you want, Miss Fox?"

"The same thing I wanted last time. Answers."

He stretched his neck out of his collar. "You seem to think I have them. I assure you, I don't. For instance, I don't even know if the child is mine."

"Why would Pearl lie to you?"

"Money." It was said without pause, but with a great deal of bitterness.

"Is that why she came to you that day after Christmas? She wanted money from you for Millie?"

He stamped the end of the walking stick on the pavement and folded both hands over the head. "Yes. It was the first I'd heard of a child. She said it was born almost four years ago. Her sister has been raising the child."

"Did she say why she needed the money now?"

"No."

"Was she intending to take the child back and raise her as her own?"

He picked up the walking stick. "I don't know. She didn't offer an explanation, and I didn't ask. She told me the child was mine and I had an obligation to finance its upbringing. But she could bring no proof, so I refused."

A rage swelled within me. It wasn't for his arrogance, although that was certainly galling. It was for his callous disregard for a woman he'd once cared about and who needed his help. But I was even angrier on Millie's behalf. She was his child, his responsibility. By refusing to believe Pearl, he was denying Millie the opportunity to live a comfortable life. He was pathetic and mean.

I gritted my teeth. "She's a girl, my lord, not a thing. Please refer to her as she, not it."

He climbed into the carriage and grabbed the door handle. "If you don't mind, I have an appointment."

I positioned myself so that he could not close the door. "Where were you on the afternoon Pearl died?"

"I was not at the theater. That answer will have to suffice."

"It does *not* suffice. Where were you?"

He pulled on the door, but I didn't move. "Drive on!"

The coachman peered around from the driver's seat and saw me standing there. "But sir—"

"I said drive on!"

The coachman gave me an apologetic look then urged the horses forward. I jumped back to avoid the wheel, tripped over the gutter and landed on my backside. If the coach had started off at a faster clip, I would have been run over. The coachman had spared me that.

The door to the townhouse opened and the butler stood there. He peered down his nose at me. "Lady Wrexham wishes to see you."

I glanced up at the second story window where I knew the drawing room to be. She must have been watching. I dusted off my skirts, picked up my umbrella and newspaper from where they'd fallen, and headed up the steps. I handed the butler my umbrella and newspaper with a smile.

He passed them on to Mr. Adams, the footman, as if they were dirty rags.

"Are you injured, Miss Fox?" Mr. Adams asked.

"Thank you, no. Very kind of you to ask." Rather surprising too, admittedly. I didn't think he liked me much, but it appeared he liked me somewhat more than the butler.

Going by the elderly fellow's disdainful turn of his mouth, that wasn't setting the bar very high.

He led the way up to the drawing room and announced me at the door before leaving us. Her ladyship did not ask him to bring tea, so I assumed this was not going to be treated as a social call. I prepared myself for a few rounds of parries and strikes.

But this time, I expected success. I'd come armed with information.

CHAPTER 12

Lady Wrexham sat like a statue on the sofa. Not even her chest moved with her breathing. It was as if she was holding herself together, trying to keep her composure from fracturing. Or perhaps moving caused her pain. If she were ill, it was possible.

She did not invite me to sit, but I sat anyway, and received a disdainful look for my impertinence.

"I see you spoke to my husband," she said. "What about?"

I'd initially felt sympathy for this woman, for having a husband who kept mistresses, but the more I saw of her, the less sympathy I felt. That made it easier to be honest with her. "I told him I knew that he fathered Miss Westwood's child."

A ripple of something crossed her face. Surprise, certainly, but not shock. She must have known about Millie. "My husband says you are a journalist. Did he offer you money to not write about it?"

So he still thought I wrote for the newspapers. It seems she did now too. "No. But rest assured, I have no plans to mention his name in my article. I just want to get to the bottom of Pearl's death. I'm convinced she didn't kill herself."

She fidgeted with the large ring on her hand. "Why does it matter? Miss Westwood is gone. Let her rest now." She sounded tired, as if the saga with Pearl had drained her.

"It matters to those who loved her. It will matter to her daughter, one day."

"I doubt that. The girl is simple."

"How do you know?" When she didn't respond, I pressed on. "You overheard Pearl telling your husband that day she called here after Christmas, didn't you? You would have also overheard her asking him for money to support Millie."

She didn't seem to care that I guessed she'd been eavesdropping. She simply continued to toy with the ring on her finger.

"Were you angry with your husband for fathering another woman's child?" I asked. "Did you get angry with Pearl? Enough to kill her, perhaps?"

She scoffed. "Don't be ridiculous. I never met her. I've never been in the same room as her."

"Perhaps she threatened to tell the newspapers that your husband fathered her child if he refused to give her money to support Millie."

"She made no such threats. He refused to believe the child was his and ordered her to leave. He gave her nothing, promised her nothing."

"And how did she react?"

She lifted her chin. "I wouldn't know."

"Of course you do."

"She left, Miss Fox. As you ought to do."

The last time I'd been here, she'd called me into this very room after I'd been in Lord Wrexham's study. Pearl would have had to pass it on her way out too. When the encounter in Lord Wrexham's office was over, perhaps Lady Wrexham raced back into the drawing room to avoid being caught eavesdropping, then called Pearl in as she passed.

I wondered how that conversation transpired. The childless wife and the mistress who abandoned her girl but now wanted money to take her back. A new idea occurred to me, although it sickened me.

"Did you offer Pearl money in exchange for Millie?" I asked.

Her entire body seemed to tremble with her reaction, from her lips down. "If you mean did I want to raise my husband's child, the answer is a resounding no. If you think that, you don't know how the world works, Miss Fox."

The vehemence of her denial struck me like a blow. I

admit that people from high society were like another species to me, but surely they had the same base human emotions as the rest of us. Surely this woman felt some jealousy that Pearl had a child by Lord Wrexham and she, Lady Wrexham, did not.

"Then explain it to me," I said.

"The child is already three years old, nearly four. It's too late to pass her off as ours. But I would be prepared to do it, somehow, if it weren't for the child herself being damaged."

"Damaged?" I blurted out. "I've met her, and she's very sweet."

Her nostrils flared and the grooves at the corners of her mouth deepened. If I thought her plain before, I thought her positively ugly now. "I'm glad the girl's not mine. If you ask me, it's God's way of punishing that whore. She deserved what she got."

I was so stunned by her outburst that it took several moments before I could speak again. When I did, I got to my feet and glared down at her. "If we all got what we deserved then Millie would have parents who loved her. You, however, got precisely what you deserved with a husband like Lord Wrexham."

Lady Wrexham's hand slapped over her mouth, but not before her horrified gasp escaped.

I strode towards the door, my skirts getting tangled around my legs in my haste to be out of her presence.

* * *

I HADN'T CALMED down by the time I reached the hotel. To spare everyone my moody presence, I locked myself in my suite and dined alone. I didn't see anyone except for the footman who delivered my meal until the following morning when Harmony arrived, bringing Victor with her.

As soon as the door opened, she pushed him in and closed the door behind her. "Go on," she prompted him. "Tell Miss Fox."

"Was that my breakfast tray outside?" I asked.

Harmony blocked the door. "Breakfast can wait. It won't take long for Victor to say his piece."

"I don't want it to get cold."

She crossed her arms. I sighed and followed Victor through to the sitting room. With his hand loosely grasping the knife holstered in his utility belt and his stance a little apart, he would have looked like a gunslinger from the American Wild West if not for his chef's whites.

"There's no need to hurry," he told Harmony who also joined us in the sitting room. "I've got time before my shift starts."

"But Miss Fox has work to do and you shouldn't be in here."

"Who's going to know?"

"Me!" She flapped a hand at him. "Proceed."

He gave a slight bow. "Yes, ma'am."

Harmony's gaze narrowed but she didn't retort.

"Thomas Adams called on me last night," he said.

That got my full attention. "And?"

"And he told me he spoke to Lord Wrexham's coachman, but subtly, like they were just having a conversation to pass the time at the pub. The coachman let slip that he often takes his lordship to a physician's clinic on Harley Street." He pulled a folded piece of paper out of his pocket and handed it to me. "Thomas wrote down the details and asked me to give them to you."

I read the paper and committed the address to memory.

"There's more," Victor said. "Thomas says the coachman took Wrexham to the clinic on the afternoon of the murder, but when Thomas tried to get a precise time out of the coachman, the fellow closed up and stopped talking."

"If he was at the doctor's that afternoon, he has an alibi for the murder." I sighed. "He didn't do it."

"Unless he went from the doctor's clinic to the Playhouse."

Harmony read the note over my shoulder. "There are a lot of physicians and doctors on Harley Street, many of them specializing in some ailment or other. Does this one have a specialty?"

Victor shrugged.

I tucked the paper into my purse. "I'll find out. Thank you, Victor, that's immensely helpful. I'd better pay Thomas a visit at The Nag's Head and thank him personally. He risked his job by speaking to the coachman and I didn't even ask him to do it."

"I don't reckon you should," he said. "You've got an admirer in Thomas."

I frowned. "I don't see how those two statements are connected."

"You don't want to get too close to him."

Harmony took more offense at the comment than me. "Miss Fox is hardly going to fall for the likes of your friend, Victor. She's far wiser than that and can do much better, thank you very much."

Victor shrugged. "I agree. I'm just saying, be careful of Thomas. You don't want him liking you too much, Miss Fox, if you know what I mean."

I didn't. Not really. "I think you're wrong about him. If he has offered me compliments, they've been heavily disguised."

"That's his way. But he likes you, make no mistake, or he wouldn't have gone out of his way to help with the promise of nothing in return."

"Then I'll pay him for the information so there can be no misunderstanding."

Victor rubbed his hand over the hilt of his knife. "Ordinarily I don't agree with paying someone who hasn't demanded it, but in this instance, I think it might be wise. Thomas is not someone you should give mixed messages to."

Harmony clicked her tongue. "I knew a friend of yours would be trouble."

"We're no longer friends."

She headed for the door. "You ought to have warned Miss Fox beforehand."

"I didn't know he was going to end up admiring her," Victor said, following her.

Harmony spun around, eyes flashing. "And why wouldn't he? She's got a lot of admirable qualities."

"That's not what I meant." For the first time since I'd met him, Victor looked ruffled. It was curious, and rather sweet, that Harmony was the one to upset his usually smooth feathers. "I just meant that I didn't know he was capable of admiring anyone. If they cut him open, I'd be surprised if they found a beating human heart in his chest and not a mechanical device."

I laughed, only to have Harmony turn her glare onto me. "I don't see what's so amusing. Thomas Adams sounds like a horrid character. I'm glad I don't have to deal with him. If you must visit him, Miss Fox, take Mr. Armitage with you again. I'll feel better if you have a man with you."

She led the way outside, picked up my breakfast tray, and stood aside for Victor to pass her. "Make sure no one sees you leaving this floor."

He saluted her and walked off.

She frowned after him. "He needs to learn his place."

"And what is his place?"

She closed the door and followed me to the sitting room where she set down the tray. "In the kitchen, far away from the maids."

I removed the lid and inspected the plate of sausages and toast. "Do they like him?"

"They find him interesting. It's the dangerous air he has about him with all those knives and scars. You know how silly some girls are around men like that."

I tried to keep a straight face. "Not you, though."

"Lord no!" She narrowed her gaze. "You're not one of those types, are you? You don't like dangerous men like that Thomas Adams?"

"Definitely not. I'm much too sensible."

"I thought so, but even sensible women fall for scoundrels and wastrels if they're looking for some excitement."

"Then we won't have a problem. My life is far too exciting these days for me to be bored." I offered the plate of sausages to her. "Now come and sit down and eat with me."

* * *

HARLEY STREET, Marylebone, must be the health center of London. There seemed to be more private physicians and doctors in that one street than in the whole of Cambridge. According to the brass plaques beside each door, there were dermatologists and ophthalmologists, obstetricians and even a nerve specialist. Several other plaques were simply labeled physician or general practitioner. The plaque for number twenty-nine was positioned beneath the brass doorbell. If it hadn't been labeled PATIENTS AND VISITORS, I would not have known it housed a doctor's clinic.

A middle-aged woman dressed in white with kind eyes opened the door. "Oh. I thought you were our next patient, but you're clearly not him." She smiled. "Do you wish to make an appointment?"

"No. I just want to know what sort of illnesses are treated here."

Her smile vanished. "I'm afraid I can't discuss that with you. Good day."

I thrust my foot through the gap to stop her closing the door. "But what if I want to make an appointment? Will you tell me then?"

"Why would you make an appointment not knowing what Dr. Martin treats? That's rather backward, Miss…?"

"Why won't you answer? It's just a simple question."

"Why are you asking the question at all?"

I sucked in air between my teeth. This woman was a good guard dog. A little too good. I tried to peer past her, but she blocked my view.

"I'm afraid I have to ask you to leave." She pushed the door into my foot, hard. My boot offered little protection and I hopped around, my teeth gritted against the throbbing pain.

The door slammed shut in my face.

"That was very rude!" I shouted.

The only response I received was from a woman walking past on the pavement. She clicked her tongue and shook her head in disapproval.

I limped down the steps and caught a hansom back to the hotel.

I greeted Frank at the door, but he frowned back at me. "Why are you limping?"

I tried to walk normally. "An over-zealous receptionist decided she didn't like my question."

He gave a knowing nod as he opened the door.

Mr. Hobart had been walking through the foyer, a leather folder tucked under his arm, when he saw me and stopped. "Good morning, Miss Fox. Have you been out this morning?"

"I had to visit a doctor in Harley Street."

"Ah. I thought you were limping. I hope he was able to help. Did you enjoy the show the other night?"

"It was very good, thank you. I saw your brother and his family there."

He smiled. "So I heard." He glanced around and took a step closer. "Speaking of the Playhouse, how is your investigation for Lord Rumford coming along?"

"I'm making progress."

"Excellent." He cleared his throat. "Not that I want you to rush to conclusions, but do you think you'll have a conclusion for him soon? It's just that he plans to check out on Sunday and would like to know who was behind Miss Westwood's unfortunate demise before he leaves London."

"I'll do my best, but I'm struggling to make headway. No one will talk to me, you see."

"Have you tried bribery?"

I smothered my smile. For some reason, hearing this upstanding and kind man encourage me to bribe people amused me. "Unfortunately lords and ladies aren't easily bribed."

"You could try blackmail."

"I am."

"Ask Harry to help again. He's very good at charming answers out of women."

I arched my brows. "Is that so?"

"Haven't you noticed?"

"I have but haven't experienced those charms first hand. He hasn't employed them on me."

"Perhaps he'd rather you saw the real him, warts and all."

Speaking of warts... "You know a great many things about this city, Mr. Hobart. Perhaps you can help. There's a doctor on Harley Street with no plaque on his door stating his specialty."

"Is he a general practitioner?"

"There's no plaque even mentioning that. His receptionist also wouldn't let me in unless I was prepared to make an appointment. When I said I just wanted to know what the doctor's medical specialty was, she slammed the door in my face."

He looked down at my boots. "Your face or your foot?"

"Both."

He hitched the leather folder higher. "In my experience, if a medical clinic is so secretive as to not advertise their specialty on the door and not even allow in visitors who are not patients, the doctor must be the sort who treats diseases of a sensitive nature." He cleared his throat and his cheeks pinked a little. "If you understand my meaning."

"I believe I do." What Mr. Hobart was trying to discreetly tell me was that the doctor treated patients suffering from ailments that affected parts of their bodies they'd rather not mention.

"I know the names of a great many specialists, some of whom have rooms on Harley Street. Sometimes guests ask me to recommend a doctor. Indeed, some even come to London and stay at the Mayfair while they're being treated. Perhaps if you tell me this doctor's name, I'll know what he does."

"Dr. Martin at number twenty-nine."

His cheeks flushed a brighter pink. "Ah. Now that is interesting."

"Go on."

He fidgeted with his tie and nibbled the inside of his lip. With a glance around, he leaned closer. "He's the pre-eminent doctor in the country for treating syphilis."

No wonder he was uncomfortable telling me. The sexually transmitted disease was not a topic one liked to mention in conversation. "I see. Thank you, Mr. Hobart. That's very helpful. Very helpful indeed."

I watched him walk off to the lift where he pressed the button and waited. I stood beneath the central chandelier for some minutes, thinking about what he'd told me. I knew two things about syphilis. It was contagious, but only passed between sexual partners, and that it was a dreadfully disfiguring disease with no cure. The disease must be the cause of the sores on Lord Wrexham's face.

"Penny for your thoughts." Goliath smiled one of his wide, open smiles.

"I was thinking about the case. What do you know about syphilis?"

That wiped the smile off his face. "Nothing! I swear."

"I hoped you might know more than me." I lowered my voice. "Do you recall that one of our suspects is Lord Wrexham, Pearl's former lover? He has the disease."

He pulled a face. "Horrid business, syphilis. I don't know much about it, but Peter might. His neighbor had it, so he once told me."

Peter was poring over the guest register at the check-in desk. There was no one at the counter, although a few guests lingered in quiet conversation at the post desk.

"Miss Fox wants to know about syphilis," Goliath said. "I told her you were the one to see about that."

Peter nodded, not embarrassed like Goliath had been. "My neighbor had it. He's dead now. The disease got him in the end."

I told him about Lord Wrexham's visit to Dr. Martin, including on the afternoon of Pearl's death, and the likelihood that he had syphilis. "I know there's no cure, so why would a man with the disease visit a doctor? What's the point?"

"It's often treated with mercury, but it doesn't work. At least, it didn't for my neighbor. He took mercury pills and just got sicker and sicker until he died." He leaned on the counter, his arms folded. "If that's why Wrexham is visiting the doctor, it won't do him any good. The doctor's just taking his money and giving him false hope, if you ask me."

"Wrexham doesn't seem particularly ill to me, except for the sores."

"Illness will come later. Maybe not for some years yet. It can be a long, slow, cruel death."

Goliath passed a hand over his mouth and jaw. "With disfigurement in the meantime."

"What's this got to do with the case?" Peter asked.

I tapped my finger on the counter, thinking. "If Lord Wrexham blames Pearl for the disease, then perhaps he killed her in anger or revenge. Could she possibly have had it but bore no sores or other outward signs?"

"I don't know, but I do know she didn't give it to him. Not unless they were, er, together, in the last couple of months." At my confused frown, he added, "The sores appear a few weeks after the disease is caught. If they ended their relationship *years* ago then she didn't give it to him."

"What if they didn't end it then?" Goliath asked. "Or what if they resumed their relationship recently?"

It was a possibility. She had been to see Lord Wrexham after Christmas. Could she have been asking him for money to treat the disease she'd caught from him? Or he from her? "There were medical bills in her flat. They don't say what she was being treated for, but it's not the sort of thing you'd write on a bill, is it?"

"Isn't Wrexham's visit to the doctor's clinic his alibi for the time of the murder?" Peter asked.

"We don't know the exact time he was there."

Goliath clicked his fingers. "What about his wife? What if she also has the disease? If she blames Miss Westwood, she could have killed her out of anger."

According to Thomas Adams, Lady Wrexham was ill, yet I'd seen no signs of that illness. If she'd caught syphilis from her husband, the disease might not be as advanced in her as it had been in him. Her sores might come later, or perhaps she had them now in places where they could be covered up with clothes.

If my husband had given me such a terrible disease as syphilis, I think I'd want to kill someone too. I'd certainly want to scream at the person who gave it to me. I'd probably scream at my husband, however, not his lover.

But I wasn't Lady Wrexham.

"Thank you both." I leaned across the counter and pecked Peter's cheek. Even when I stood on my toes I was still too short to kiss Goliath's cheek so I settled for patting his arm. "You've been a marvelous help."

Peter blushed and smiled.

Goliath followed me to the door. "Where are you going now?"

"I can't confront Lord and Lady Wrexham with this information. They've told me very little so far and are hardly going to tell me anything more now. I'm going to call on Detective Inspector Hobart at Scotland Yard. It's time for the police to take over."

He looked disappointed. "But it's your case. You should get the glory of solving it."

"I've progressed as far as I can on my own."

"So you're just going to waltz into Scotland Yard and hope he'll see you?"

I chewed my lip. It did sound somewhat silly to think he'd see me immediately. And what if he wasn't there? I didn't want to speak to a different detective. I wanted to talk to someone who knew me.

"I'll ask Mr. Armitage what to do," I said as he held the door open for me. "After all, who knows his father better than him?"

* * *

I FOUND Mr. Armitage in his office, painting the wall. Dressed in overalls with his sleeves rolled to his elbows and a dash of paint on his cheek, he somehow looked even more handsome, something I thought entirely impossible until now.

"What was wrong with the previous color?" I asked.

"It was too plain."

I looked around at the walls, nearly finished in the off-white color he'd chosen. "As opposed to this vibrant shade?"

"There was an old water stain in the corner that needed touching up."

"I didn't notice it."

"Then you're not very observant. It was an eyesore."

"Or are you just bored?"

"I'm very busy. I have inquiries coming in all the time from my newspaper ad."

I opened the appointment book on his desk while his back was turned. "You don't have a single appointment listed."

"I don't have a single appointment *yet*." He rested the paint brush on top of the can and wiped his hands on a rag. "Have you come to criticize the way I spend my time or do you need my help?"

"The latter. You can spend your time in any way you like. Although you should spend a little more time contemplating paint choices. You know, Flossy's got a good eye for color. You should have asked her advice."

He laughed. "Next time I want to paint a wall, I'll ask the daughter of my former employer who dismissed me. Thanks for the advice, Miss Fox."

I scowled. "She'd be happy to help you. She has a lot of respect for you."

He arched his brows in a challenge.

In truth, I didn't know what Flossy thought of Mr. Armitage. We'd never discussed him.

"Do you have clothes on under those overalls?" I asked.

He gave me a lopsided grin. "I can't believe we're having this conversation so early in our friendship."

"Very amusing. I'd like you to accompany me to call on your father at Scotland Yard. I want to tell him about my theory for Pearl's murder. I think either Lord or Lady Wrexham killed her but neither will reveal their secrets to me. Your father will know how to get answers."

"Why do you need me?"

"I thought your presence might be a persuasive influence."

"Why do you need a persuasive influence? Does your theory have holes?"

"It's a very good theory. Do you recall that Lord Wrexham has sores on his face? I believe they're caused by syphilis which he may have caught from Pearl."

"I thought they ended their relationship years ago. If he has the sores now, he caught it more recently."

"Perhaps they resumed their relationship."

"Perhaps? Do you know for certain?"

"Well, no."

"And do you know if Pearl had syphilis?"

"No. But there are doctor's bills in her flat."

"For doctors specializing in syphilis?"

"I didn't know, but—"

"So you have no evidence, only speculation." He unbuttoned the front of his overalls, revealing a shirt underneath. "Jumping to conclusions again, Miss Fox?"

It wasn't fair of him to dredge up the time I'd accused him of murder and thereby inadvertently cost him his job at the hotel. I tried to look defiant, but I suspected I failed. Indeed, I must have because he gave me a sympathetic look.

He stepped out of the overalls and folded them up. He wore only trousers, suspenders and a shirt with the sleeves rolled to the elbows. His tie and waistcoat were hanging on the stand by the door.

"Miss Fox? Are you listening?"

I realized I'd been staring at his forearms, admiring the way the muscles moved beneath the smooth skin on the underside of his arms. "Of course I am." I cleared my throat. "Refresh my memory."

He smirked. "I was saying that you need evidence if you want my father's help. For one thing, Pearl Westwood's death was deemed suicide, and you don't have enough evidence to suggest otherwise. For another, my father didn't oversee the investigation. If you want him to overturn a ruling made by one of his colleagues, you'll need something solid."

I sighed. "Which I don't have."

He gave me a flat smile. "Sorry."

"And I'm also unlikely to get it. Lord and Lady Wrexham are a closed book and I have no authority over them."

He sat on the edge of the desk near me. "Sit down."

I sat, curious as to why he was looking rather serious.

"I'm going to tell you a secret."

"You have my attention."

"I'm going to give you the secret as to how I earned the respect of the staff at the hotel, even though I didn't have the seniority of my uncle nor the status of Sir Ronald."

"If you tell me it's arrogance, I already know that from observing you." When he gave me a withering glare, I muttered an apology then pressed my lips together.

"To command respect, you don't actually need to have any authority at all. You have to pretend to."

"I don't understand."

"You have to talk and act like you're above them. You even have to think you are, at times. When you're intimidated, don't show it. When they talk down to you, stand above them, metaphorically speaking. I think you'd be rather good at it. You have a certain confidence about you already. You just need a little more composure."

"If you're talking about keeping a lid on my temper, I'm afraid that might be impossible. I got quite angry with Lady Wrexham yesterday."

He rolled down the sleeve on his left arm. "It's something to practice, anyway."

I stood. "Thank you for the advice, but I don't think it will work on the Wrexhams. No matter how much pretending I do, I'm not at their level, and they know it."

"Nonsense. You're Sir Ronald Bainbridge's niece. If that doesn't open doors here in London, little else will." He stopped unrolling the sleeve and looked at me, a crease connecting his brows. "You do know that, don't you?"

I gave a small shrug of my shoulder, but wasn't really listening. I couldn't see how mentioning my uncle's name was going to encourage Lord Wrexham to talk to me about his illness. I'd barely got him to talk about his relationship with Pearl. Syphilis was a subject too far.

I left Mr. Armitage's office feeling less assured of myself than when I'd arrived. He was right. I had no proof. Even worse, I didn't know how to get it.

The investigation was at a dead end. It was time to tell Lord Rumford that I was giving up, that I couldn't say definitively whether Pearl killed herself or not. I wasn't looking forward to letting him down.

But what I really wasn't looking forward to was telling him that his lover not only had a child by another man, but she quite possibly had syphilis too, and may have given it to him.

CHAPTER 13

Mr. Hobart suggested I use his office to speak to Lord Rumford. He then discreetly left us alone and promised we wouldn't be disturbed. I sat in Mr. Hobart's chair and regarded Lord Rumford across the desk. I think he knew from my face that I didn't have good news.

"You're giving up, aren't you?" he asked.

"I'm afraid I have no choice. The people I need to speak to won't talk to me."

"And who are these people?"

I clasped my hands on the desk and sat forward. "Before I tell you that, I want you to know that I agree with your assessment of Pearl's death. By all accounts, she was happy, so it's unlikely she killed herself."

"I hope you learned more than that, Miss Fox."

I clasped my hands tighter and drew in a fortifying breath. "I learned that Pearl had a baby, four years ago this March."

His lips parted. He hadn't known.

"Mr. and Mrs. Larsen are raising the child as their own," I went on. "Did Pearl ever mention that her niece might be her own daughter?"

"She never mentioned the niece at all, except once, in passing."

"From what I can gather, Pearl didn't want the child. However, it's possible she changed her mind recently."

He shook his head. "She would have mentioned it to me if that were the case."

I doubted that, but didn't say. "It's possible she asked Lord Wrexham for money to support Millie."

There was no surprise on his face at the mention of Pearl's former benefactor. He'd already quickly calculated Millie's age and realized who'd fathered her. "You forget that Pearl did ask me for money too."

"*After* Wrexham refused her. But I don't think that's why Pearl was killed. I think it has to do with a disease she either caught from Wrexham or gave to him."

This time his expression left nothing to guesswork. Disgust was written all over it. "Pearl wasn't diseased, Miss Fox, and your insinuation is abhorrent."

"Lord Wrexham has syphilis—"

He shot to his feet. "I've heard enough. Wrexham's medical situation is no business of mine. If he is ill, it's not Pearl's fault. She hasn't been near him for years."

"You can't know—"

"I *can,*" he ground out between gritted teeth. "Pearl wasn't with anyone else when she was with me."

"That's not true. While I cannot be certain if she was with Wrexham, I do know she had another lover, one she's had for years. He knew about you, and Wrexham."

His mouth and jaw worked, as if he couldn't decide what to say next. I couldn't imagine what was going through his mind. Jealousy? Anger? Was he picturing Pearl taking her other lover to the flat he'd paid for?

Finally he found his voice. "She was not with Wrexham. Nor did she have any diseases. Believe me, Miss Fox, I would know. The thing about Wrexham is that he likes to show off his lovers. He's not discreet. It's a well-known fact in some circles that Wrexham's most recent lover is a dancer. It's also well-known that she disappeared from the stage some months ago, and speculation is that she is ill. If anyone gave Wrexham syphilis, it's her."

I capitulated on the point. I'd been given no reason to believe Pearl and Wrexham had resumed their relationship. She'd not been seen with him, except for that one time, after Christmas, and there were no letters from him among her things. By all accounts, she was content with Lord Rumford and she'd be a fool to jeopardize that by taking up with Wrexham again. If they hadn't been together lately, she could not have given him syphilis. Wrexham would have known that, which meant there was no reason for him to kill her.

There was still Lady Wrexham, however. She might not be aware her husband had caught the disease from another woman.

Lord Rumford strode to the door, but before opening it, turned back to me. The gaze he settled on me was as cold as ice. "Mr. Hobart recommended you, and against my better judgement, I hired you. I should have gone with my instinct and sent you on your way. I knew this would be too difficult for a woman. Female private detectives are better left to trapping philandering husbands than murderers."

I watched him storm out of the office, biting on my tongue until it hurt. Despite the fact he kept a mistress, I had liked Lord Rumford. Well, perhaps that wasn't quite true. It's safer to say I didn't *dislike* him. Until now.

With a sigh, I left Mr. Hobart's office and returned to the foyer where Peter was busy with new guests checking in. Goliath stood by, waiting for instructions on which room to take up a trolley full of luggage, and gave me a discreet nod as I passed. Mr. Hobart was in deep conversation with two guests, and didn't notice me as I headed for the stairs.

"Miss Fox," said Frank from behind me. "There's a lad who wants to speak to you. He says he's Peter's brother."

I followed him outside where he directed me to the boy standing a few feet away, a pack slung over his shoulder and a stool in one hand.

"I know you," he said. "I saw you go into the house."

"My name is Cleo Fox." I put out my hand and he shook it, introducing himself as William. "Have you come to tell me you're giving up?"

"No, miss! I want to report in about the mistress of the house. She went out this morning and I followed her."

I stood a little straighter. "Go on."

"She went to a shop in Shoreditch. Real small place, tucked away in a court behind a pub. She was in there for a few minutes and came out with something in a paper bag. She went straight home again."

"What does the shop sell?"

"Potions, as near as I can tell. I reckon the shopkeeper's a witch." He pulled a face. "She sure looked like one."

He gave me the address on Sclater Street and I paid him for his trouble.

He squirreled the money away in his pocket. "Any time you need a house watched, I'm your man."

"I can see that. Thank you."

"Working in an office or a fancy hotel ain't for the likes of men like me. I'll leave that to Peter and folks like him."

I wasn't sure what that meant. I didn't think William even knew what he meant. He couldn't have been more than twelve years old. He winked at me and went on his way, whistling.

Smiling, I returned to the hotel to fetch my coat and an umbrella. Ten minutes later, I caught a hansom to Sclater Street, Shoreditch. The shop William had seen Lady Wrexham enter was difficult to find. Accessed through an arched walkway beside the pub that opened to a small court, it had a single, grimy window with the word HERBALIST painted across the top.

I could smell burning incense before I even opened the door. There were so many scents mingled together, it was difficult to discern individual ones. The shop looked like a Medieval apothecary's laboratory. Bunches of drying herbs, flowers and berries hung from the rafters, some so low they skimmed my hat as I passed beneath them. Behind the counter was a large cabinet with small drawers, while the counter itself was covered with small pots of lotions, as well as soaps and sachets. A set of brass scales stood at one end beside a basket filled with dried rabbit's feet.

I bent to inspect the contents of a collection of glass jars on a table only to reel back when a pair of dead eyes stared back at me. The jars were filled with severed animal heads and entire bodies of small creatures suspended in fluid to preserve them.

"They're not for sale," came a crackling voice from behind me.

The elderly woman must have come from the adjoining room, accessed through the door near the counter. She'd not made a sound. It was no wonder William referred to her as a witch. She had the classic storybook profile with the hooked nose, sharp chin, and beady eyes. All that was missing was a broomstick and pointed black hat.

"You don't have an appointment," she said.

"You take appointments?" I asked. "What for?"

She went behind the counter and pulled out a ledger from a lower shelf. "Private consultations. You tell me what ails you, and I tailor a treatment to your specific needs. The consultation is free and there's no obligation to purchase anything."

"And what do your treatments entail?"

"Tonics, creams, tisanes, emetics…it depends on the ailment."

"What sort of ailments can you treat?"

"Everything." She opened the ledger and scanned her finger down the page. "I'm expecting a client any moment, but I can fit you in after her in thirty minutes. Will that suffice?"

"How long does it take for the cure to work?"

"It varies." She eyed me narrowly. "I see you're a skeptic. That's understandable. Many people come to me despite having reservations. Usually I'm the last resort. I suspect that deep down, however, you believe modern medicine is failing us. Doctors scoff at the ancient science of herbalism, but it works." She tapped the lid of a nearby jar with a boney finger. "My cures are based on recipes passed down through the female line of my family over hundreds of years. They don't fail, as long as you come to me early enough."

It was a sales spiel if ever I heard one, but I could see how it would work on the desperate who'd tried everything else. Desperation and hope were powerful weapons in the charlatan's armory.

"Do your customers often return after their initial consultation?"

"Of course, when their supplies run low. No follow-up appointment is necessary, unless one is requested."

The door opened and a woman entered. One side of her

face was covered with a red rash which she tried to hide upon seeing me.

"Miss?" The herbalist indicated her appointment book. "Will you come back in thirty minutes?"

"Not today," I said.

I left, waited five minutes, then returned to the shop. There was no sign of the herbalist or her client. I quickly slipped behind the counter, pulled out the appointment book, and scanned the column of names. There was no mention of Lady Wrexham so she'd probably just returned to replenish her supply of the herbalist's cure.

I flipped back through the pages until I came to the fifteenth, the day of Pearl's death. Lady Wrexham's name appeared with the time of three-thirty written next to it. The exact time Pearl was pushed over the balcony at the Piccadilly Playhouse.

Lady Wrexham couldn't have killed her.

Something slapped the back of my head, pushing my hat forward over my forehead. I swung around and caught the broom before the bristles smacked me in the face. The herbalist pulled the broom free from my grip and aimed it at my chest like a shotgun.

Her face took on an even more witchy appearance with her sneer. "I knew there was something strange about you. Get out! Get out of my shop before I put a curse on you!"

Keeping the counter at my back, I slipped out of her reach and hurried from the shop. I raced to the street and didn't stop until I was safely inside a hansom, heading home.

While the ordeal hadn't been pleasant, I'd come away with a new appreciation for our kindly family doctor in Cambridge and a vital clue that eliminated Lady Wrexham from my list of suspects.

It wasn't much, but it was something.

But I'd given up the case, of course. Striking Lady Wrexham off my list didn't make me want to resume.

It bothered me leaving the matter unfinished, however. Lord Rumford was right to be upset with me for giving up. I just wished I could see a way forward.

"Cleo, there you are!" Flossy cried when she spotted me in

the hotel foyer. "I've had Harmony looking all over the hotel for you."

I shrugged out of my coat and slung it over my arm. "Why?"

"It's time to get ready for the Caldicotts' dinner, silly."

"Is that tonight?"

She gave me an exasperated look. "Yes! And we both need to get ready."

"But it's just gone five."

She grabbed my arm and dragged me to the lift. John the lift operator waited with a smile and took us up to level four.

The door to my suite was unlocked and Harmony was inside, arranging things on my dressing table.

"I found her," Flossy announced. "She was out."

They both scowled at me as if I were a naughty child who'd dodged her chores.

"Do your best with what time you have, Harmony."

I watched Flossy leave then turned to Harmony. "I don't know what all the fuss is about. We have over two hours before we have to leave."

"Miss Bainbridge wants me to wash, dry and arrange your hair. She told me to make sure you look your best tonight." She frowned. "Will there be gentlemen there?"

"I believe so."

"Then it's no wonder. We'd best get started."

"It takes hours to dry my hair completely in winter. We won't wash it tonight."

Harmony waited for me to bathe then helped me dress in a black evening gown with pearlescent beads arranged in swirls and clusters across the bust and down the front. It was very elegant and appropriate mourning-wear. Despite Flossy urging me to set aside my dark mourning clothes, I wasn't yet prepared to do so. My grandmother hadn't even been gone two months.

While Harmony curled my hair with the tongs, I told her what I'd learned about the Wrexhams and their illness, and about Lady Wrexham's visit to the herbalist.

Five minutes before I was due to meet the others in the foyer, there was a brisk knock on my door. I opened it to see my uncle, looking troubled. Harmony excused herself and slipped out.

"I'll just collect my cloak," I said to Uncle Ronald.

"I'm not here to escort you down." He entered my suite, closing the door. "I'm here to have a word about something very disturbing."

I suspected I knew what this was about, but gave him an innocent smile anyway. I would have to brazen my way through the scolding that was coming.

"You know we're very happy to have you here with us, Cleo."

"But?"

"But I've received a complaint about you from Lord Wrexham."

"I see."

"You've been bothering him and Lady Wrexham, it seems."

"I've been making inquiries as part of my investigation into the death of Lord Rumford's mistress."

"What do the Wrexhams have to do with it?"

"That's what I'm trying to find out."

He tugged on his cuffs as he waited for more. I merely waited too. "You must end that line of inquiry," he eventually said. "Wrexham is a powerful fellow. I don't like upsetting him."

"Of course. I have no evidence against him anyway, so if he did do it, he's going to get away with it."

He winced. "Let's assume he didn't do it. Now, to the other matter."

"There's another matter? Who else has complained about me?" In truth, there could be a number of people, from Mr. Culpepper to the Larsens, although I doubted they would approach my uncle.

"Mrs. Short says you've been associating with the maids."

I blinked at him, not quite sure how seriously to take him. He appeared quite serious, however. "Harmony is my personal maid. She does my hair and cleans my room. That's all. I don't keep her from her duties."

"Mrs. Short says you're becoming too friendly with the girl."

"Is that a problem?"

"I know things were different for you in Cambridge, and this is all new. But here, family do not become friends with the hotel staff. It's not wise." He gave me a sympathetic smile. "I see that notion upsets you."

"It confuses me. Why is it unwise?"

He took my hand in both of his and patted it. "You're a kind-hearted girl, so it's not surprising that it never occurred to you, but it's my duty to warn you about people who befriend you simply so they can gain something."

I snatched my hand away, bristling at his condescending tone and his sweeping assumption. "That isn't fair. Harmony hasn't asked any favors from me."

"She will. I don't blame her, of course. Her situation is such that, if presented with the opportunity to befriend her employer's niece, she'd be mad not to take it."

He reached out to pat my shoulder, but I shrugged him off.

His lips flattened. "I know you miss your friends in Cambridge. That's only natural for an amiable, intelligent girl such as yourself. You're like your mother, in that regard. She enjoyed having her friends around her. But there's no need to go searching for friends among the staff. You have Flossy, naturally, and all of her acquaintances too. Tonight will do you good. I hear Caldicott's sons are very upstanding young men and are at an age to move to the next phase of their lives."

My entire body deflated with a silent groan. He could only mean they were on the hunt for wives. And Flossy and I were being offered up like lambs to the slaughter.

Perhaps I was being overly dramatic, but after enduring such a trying conversation with my uncle, I was not inclined to be optimistic.

"As a thank you to your aunt and me, I would appreciate it if you put on your most charming manner tonight. This dinner is important."

"Why?"

"Sir Lawrence Caldicott is my banker." He didn't elaborate as to why he needed to curry favor with his banker. I knew the hotel business wasn't an easy one, but surely the hotel wasn't in dire financial straits.

Uncle Ronald escorted me down to the foyer via the lift. He fell into conversation with the night lift operator, and I tuned them out. Every part of me silently cursed the Caldicotts for inviting me to their infernal dinner party, as well as Lord Wrexham and Mrs. Short for their complaints. Lord Wrexham I could understand, but Mrs. Short had no right to interfere.

Why couldn't I be friends with whomever I wanted? It wasn't the nineteenth century anymore, and I wasn't a society debutante searching for a suitable husband. People moved across different social levels all the time nowadays. Pearl, for example, had risen so far above her station that she'd attended parties with princes and dukes.

It wasn't lost on me that Pearl had only been able to attend those parties because she was a gentleman's mistress.

I sighed. I was a fool to think this century was any different to the last. I was fortunate to have been sheltered from the worst of English snobbery, having parents from different backgrounds who'd defied society's so-called rules to marry. But here, in this most elite of settings, I was surrounded by that snobbery.

I put such thoughts from my mind, or tried to. I had a dinner party to endure and it required my full attention. If I so much as lowered my guard just a little, I might find myself engaged to one of Sir Lawrence Caldicott's "upstanding" sons.

It was clear from the beginning that I was to be matched with the younger son and Flossy with the elder, even though I was older than my cousin. The eldest must be in line to inherit something over his younger brother, hence Flossy was earmarked for him. As Uncle Ronald's niece, I was only entitled to second best.

I didn't particularly care which son I was seated next to at the dinner table. They were both fine young men, well-spoken and educated. If only they were interested in something other than finance, I might have enjoyed their company more.

Although they engaged Floyd in conversation about the

Stock Exchange and property transactions, I suspected even he grew tired of their conversation after a while. It continued over dinner too. My gaze met Flossy's across the table and I rolled my eyes. She pressed her lips together, but a giggle still escaped.

Mrs. Mannering, our host's married daughter, noticed. "Edward," she said pointedly to the younger brother sitting beside me, "I hear Miss Bainbridge and Miss Fox attended a show at the Piccadilly Playhouse the other night. You have an interest in the theater."

Edward politely turned to me, even though I suspected he wanted to continue to listen to his father tell Uncle Ronald about the new motoring venture he was considering investing in. "What are they showing at the Playhouse these days?"

"*Cat and Mouse*."

"Ah, the doomed production." He waggled his eyebrows in what he must think was a mysterious manner.

"Why doomed?"

"The lead actress died. Some say it's now cursed."

Mrs. Mannering leaned forward and lowered her voice. "I hear her ghost haunts the dress circle."

Flossy's eyes widened. "I didn't see her, and we were in one of the boxes."

"Those are excellent seats," Mrs. Mannering said. "Perhaps the ghost avoids the boxes."

Edward picked up his wine glass. "What did you think of the show, Miss Fox?"

He seemed to be only half listening as I gave him my review so I cut it short. "It was quite good, although I think a ghostly presence will add to it. I'm not sure if the actors would appreciate a phantom's presence, however."

"It'll need something sensational to improve ticket sales. I hear there was a flurry of interest after Miss Westwood died, but that's dwindling again. It's a shame. The show's season will end early."

"Will they put on something else?" Flossy asked.

"Will they be prepared with something else?" Mrs. Mannering countered. "It can't be easy having to pivot mid-season."

Edward sliced into his beef. "They'll need to do something

or risk closing the Playhouse's doors forever. Or at least until a new financial backer can be found."

I frowned. I was beginning to suspect his "interest" in the Playhouse, as Mrs. Mannering called it, was a financial one, not artistic. "It's in trouble?"

He nodded but I had to wait for him to finish chewing before he answered. "The manager banks with Father. He's mortgaged to the hilt. If *Cat and Mouse* ends early, and he can't put on something else, he'll have to walk away, having lost everything. He can't afford to stay when the rent is so high and there's no money coming in. He'll go bankrupt."

Poor Mr. Culpepper. It was no wonder Pearl hadn't asked him for money despite being in a relationship with him. She knew he didn't have any to spare.

The evening wore on, but it improved after Mrs. Mannering forced her brothers to talk about topics other than finance. Indeed, they proved to be quite good company and we talked about all sorts of things once the men rejoined the women in the drawing room after they'd finished smoking.

The clock on the mantelpiece struck one, just as I laughed at something Edward said. I caught sight of Uncle Ronald, Sir Lawrence and Lady Caldicott watching me, smiling curiously. Beside Lady Caldicott sat Aunt Lilian, staring into the middle distance. With her arms tucked into her sides and her fingers clasped together on her lap, she appeared to be holding herself together.

I sat on her other side. "Are you all right, Aunt?"

She touched her temple. "It's just one of my headaches."

I met my uncle's gaze. "Perhaps we should go."

"No," Aunt Lilian said. "You young ones are having such a lovely time. Don't worry about me. It's nothing." She offered a smile, but no one was convinced.

Uncle Ronald rose and put out his hand to his wife to assist her to her feet. "Cleo's right, we should go."

Lady Caldicott took my hand, trapping me on the sofa. "You look so much like your aunt when she was younger, although that's where the resemblance ends. You're not like her in character. She tells me you're a lot like your mother though."

"So I'm told."

She gave me a sympathetic smile. "Your uncle is very proud of you. He couldn't stop praising you. Apparently you speak Italian."

I laughed. "Good lord, no. Not fluently."

"Edward is going to Italy this year for his Grand Tour. Perhaps you can teach him a few words, and when he comes back, he can tell you all about his adventures."

Oh dear. The trap was opening up before me and I needed to do a quick sidestep to avoid it. Fortunately, I was saved by Floyd offering me his hand.

"Come along, Cleo."

In the hall, he assisted me into my cloak. With his hands on my shoulders and his mouth near my ear, I could smell the alcohol on his breath. "You're welcome," he whispered.

"I didn't need saving," I whispered back.

"Oh? So you're quite happy to have her as a mother-in-law?"

"I wouldn't let it get that far."

"Sweet, naïve, Cuz. You have no idea how quickly these things can escalate. It begins as an innocent meeting, as a result of politeness to one's hostess, and ends with a walk down the aisle. If you're as determined to avoid the matrimonial noose as you say you are, then you need to be alert when mothers are around. Trust me, I know."

Edward approached, frowning. "What are you two conspiring about?"

Floyd fussed over my cloak, smoothing his hand over the wrinkles at my shoulder. "I'm just giving Cleo some advice."

"Financial advice?" Edward took my hand and bowed over it. "Please feel free to come to me at any time if you require advice of that nature, Miss Fox. I'd be happy to guide you."

"Oh, er, thank you," I managed to say.

Floyd shook Edward's hand. "Very good of you to offer. Considering Cleo doesn't intend to marry, she'll probably value your advice. A woman alone needs to plan for her future. Isn't that right?"

Edward was rendered speechless, which I suspected was Floyd's intention.

My cousin steered me outside after my aunt and uncle. "Aren't you glad I rescued you now?"

He assisted me into the carriage then helped Flossy in too. Once we were all settled and the carriage on its way, Floyd released a deep sigh. "Thank God they eventually stopped talking about money and investing. I was beginning to think they lived and breathed the bank."

"Is there something wrong with that?" his father barked. "You could learn a thing or two from the Caldicott boys."

"Like how to bore a woman in five minutes?" Floyd snorted.

My aunt winced and closed her eyes.

My uncle's eyes flashed like cold steel in the lamplight. "Like how not to ruin your future."

* * *

EDWARD CALDICOTT'S opinion of the Piccadilly Playhouse's financial predicament was the first thing on my mind when I awoke the following morning. Even though I'd vowed I was giving up the investigation, it seemed I wanted to continue. I couldn't stop thinking about Mr. Culpepper's situation. If things were as dire as Edward claimed, then Mr. Culpepper was in no position to assist Pearl if she asked him for money. Did Pearl know and not bother to ask? Or did she go to her long-time lover first before calling on Lord Wrexham? But why would she go to Mr. Culpepper first if he wasn't the father of Millie?

Unless he was.

There was one easy way of finding out.

After breakfast, I asked Frank where the General Register Office was located. He hailed a cab for me, and I headed to Somerset House on The Strand where the records of the country's births, deaths and marriages were housed in the imposing building. After giving one of the many clerks stationed at the counter my request, it took over two hours before I finally got my hands on Millie's birth certificate.

Pearl was listed as the mother under her real name of Eleanor, as I expected. The father's name, however, had me re-thinking everything. It wasn't Lord Wrexham, but Mr. Culpepper, after all.

If Pearl was with both men at the time, she couldn't have been absolutely sure who'd fathered Millie, but it was telling that she chose to list Culpepper over Wrexham. The choice she'd made almost four years ago was one thing, but the choice she'd made recently was quite another. She'd chosen to tell Lord Wrexham that *he* was Millie's father in the hope he'd give her money.

But it seemed just as likely that she'd gone to Millie's father first.

Mr. Culpepper had lied to me. He *must* have known Millie was his daughter.

If he'd lied about that, what else had he lied about? Pushing Pearl over the balcony after discovering she'd kept Millie from him all these years? Or because he didn't want to pay her money for supporting the child? Or had he finally snapped out of sheer jealousy over her other lovers?

He had the motive *and* the opportunity. He'd arrived at the scene of her death quickly. After Pearl's deathly scream, he'd been seen emerging from the fire exit which gave direct access to the dress circle balcony.

I had to confront him, but I'd be a fool to do it alone.

CHAPTER 14

I found Mr. Armitage putting on a second coat of paint on the walls in his office. The cold air coming through the open window diluted the fumes, but it made the room feel like ice. I kept my coat on as I greeted him.

He descended the ladder and set down the paint tin and brush. "It seems you can't stay away, Miss Fox."

"Perhaps you should put another desk in here for me."

"And add your name to the door?"

"What an excellent idea."

He grunted and wiped his hands on the paint-splattered cloth slung over his shoulder. "What can I do for you?"

"I want to request your company to speak to a suspect."

He frowned. "A violent suspect?"

"He might turn violent when I accuse him of murder."

"If you're worried, perhaps you shouldn't go. Tell my father what you know and let the police handle it."

"You said I needed more evidence or there was no point going to the police."

He began removing his overalls, which I took as a sign he'd already made up his mind to join me. "And I assume you found that evidence."

"It's still just speculation." I told him about seeing Mr. Culpepper's name on Millie's birth certificate and how he'd lied to me about knowing of her existence. "I don't have any proof that he lied, but I do have a strong suspicion. And if he lied about that, what else has he lied about?"

"It's quite a leap to go from lying to murder."

"That's why I want to confront him. I need answers, and, quite frankly, I can think of no one else who will provide them at this juncture. I've ruled out Lady Wrexham and am also quite sure Lord Wrexham didn't do it. She has an alibi and he was most likely elsewhere at the time of the murder too. Culpepper is my only suspect. So will you come with me?"

"I wouldn't be a gentleman if I ignored the request of a lady."

I tried to think of a retort but got distracted by his forearms again. They really were quite muscular. And the way his shirt fitted across his shoulders was also something of a revelation. I knew they were broad but without a waistcoat or jacket, I was able to see just how broad.

He suddenly looked up and I had to pretend to be studying something on the desk. Unfortunately, there was nothing on the desk within easy reach except a pencil. I picked it up, gave it the once over, and put it down again.

He plucked his waistcoat and tie off the stand then grabbed his jacket. Before putting it on, he removed a leather holster and gun from the bottom desk drawer.

I gasped.

"Why the surprise?" he asked as he strapped the holster on. "You've asked me along because you suspect Culpepper could pose a threat." He picked up the gun and loaded bullets into the barrel. "This is just in case you're right."

"I assumed you'd use your fists against him."

"I'm not super-human, Miss Fox. If he pulls a gun on us, my fists won't be of use."

He was right, but that didn't ease my mind. "Do you have another for me?"

"Thankfully no."

"'Thankfully?' I'd be very responsible, and only use it if absolutely necessary."

"Have you ever fired a gun before?" At the shake of my head, he thrust the gun into the holster. "Then let's leave the shooting to me."

"Does your father know you have that?"

He led the way outside and locked the door. "Who do you think gave it to me when I started this business?"

"Does your mother know?"

"Do you think I'm mad?" He followed me down the stairs, but instead of opening the front door, he reached past me and put his hand to the doorknob to stop me from grabbing it. "Don't tell her."

"Your secret is safe with me."

A short walk later, we found Mr. Culpepper at his desk at the Playhouse. He looked up from the ledger he was studying then, seeing me, quickly closed it. I introduced Mr. Armitage and Mr. Culpepper invited us both to sit. I did, but Mr. Armitage remained standing by my side. I was very aware of the gun in his holster. He'd left his jacket unbuttoned so he could access it quickly, but I was rather relieved to see Mr. Culpepper's hands remain where I could see them, on the desk.

"How may I help you, Miss Fox?" he asked.

"You lied to me." It was a gamble to accuse him when I wasn't absolutely certain, but the gamble paid off when he did not look surprised.

"What about?" he asked rather calmly.

"You knew Millie was your daughter all along."

He sat back, lowering his hands to his lap, out of sight. I hoped Mr. Armitage could see them from his higher vantage point.

"Why did you lie to me?"

"Because I panicked and fell back on instinct," he said. "I've been lying about being a father for years, and it comes naturally now. I knew how it would look if you knew that I knew about Millie, and that you'd accuse me of killing Pearl for keeping my daughter from me."

"So Pearl came to you around Christmas and asked for money to support Millie. Why then? Did she plan on taking Millie back and raising her as her own?"

He shook his head and sat forward again. "She never asked me, nor did she tell me about her plans for the girl. As far as I am aware, she was content to leave her with the Larsens."

"Did you never offer to marry Pearl and raise Millie together?"

He scoffed. "Of course I offered, when I found out she was with child. But Pearl wasn't interested in either marriage or motherhood. That's why I don't believe she wanted the girl back to raise her. Pearl and I would have made terrible parents. We're both too selfish and, to be quite honest, disinterested in children."

I wasn't sure whether that made me feel better about him or worse. On the one hand, it was good that a person could identify selfishness within themselves and give their child to a couple better suited to the task of parenting, but on the other hand, how did he know he'd be a terrible parent until he tried? He might have fallen in love with his daughter if he'd spent some time with her.

"If Pearl wasn't planning to raise Millie as her own, why did she need money?" I asked.

"I don't know. As I said, she didn't come to me. I wasn't lying about that."

"She knew you were in financial trouble, didn't she?"

Mr. Culpepper glanced at Mr. Armitage. He gave a small nod.

"So she went to Lord Wrexham and thought if she told him Millie was his, he'd be inclined to give her money." I was talking through my thoughts, now, hoping inspiration would strike. I didn't expect answers. "But he didn't care and refused. The question is, why did she need money *now*?"

"Her sister blamed Pearl for forgetting about the child."

I blinked back at him. "How could she forget about her own child?"

He heaved a sigh and rubbed his jaw. "I don't want you thinking badly of Pearl. It's not that she deliberately didn't think about Millie, but…" He shrugged. "She just wasn't part of her world. Out of sight, out of mind, as the saying goes."

"How do you know Mrs. Larsen blamed Pearl for forgetting about Millie? Did Pearl tell you that?"

He shook his head. "I overheard them arguing. I couldn't hear much, but I did hear that before they moved out of earshot. I know Pearl sent a little money to her sister each month for Millie's upkeep, so she probably just forgot that month."

"But they saw each other on Christmas Day. She would have confronted Pearl then about non-payment." I rubbed my forehead, annoyed by my mistake in assuming this man had killed the woman he loved.

"When did they argue?" Mr. Armitage asked.

Mr. Culpepper twisted his mouth to the side as he thought. "I can't quite recall. Mrs. Larsen came to the theater one day—"

"What?" I lowered my hand and stared at him. "Are you sure she came here?"

"Yes. She'd never been before and seemed in awe of the place. She asked Pearl to give her a tour."

When I first met Mrs. Larsen, she told me she'd never been to the Playhouse. She'd lied. And the only reason for her to lie was because her presence at the theater implicated her in the murder.

"What day did Mrs. Larsen visit?" I asked.

"I told you, I can't recall."

"Was it the day of Pearl's death?"

He shrugged. "It might have been." He clicked his fingers. "Perry might know. He has a good memory for these things. He's excellent at remembering everyone's lines, not just his own."

He led the way out of his office and down the corridor where we found Perry Alcott helping Dotty Clare's understudy with her lines. When Mr. Armitage realized we'd walked into the actresses' dressing room, he stepped back out again, although the understudy was the only woman present and she was fully clothed.

Mr. Alcott confirmed that he'd seen Mrs. Larsen in the theater, being shown around by Pearl. "It was the day before Pearl died."

"Are you sure?" I asked. "Not the day of?"

"Definitely the day before."

"Do you know what they argued about?"

He shook his head. "I was on stage and could see them in the dress circle, but I couldn't hear them. It seemed heated, but Mrs. Larsen appeared to be doing all of the talking. Poor Pearl just stood there and allowed her sister to bully her."

We thanked them and left the theater. Mr. Armitage hailed a hansom and I gave the driver directions to the Larsens' residence. The more I thought about it, the more I knew Mrs. Larsen had lied to throw me off course. She'd told me she'd never been to the Playhouse. She'd never admitted that Millie was Pearl's daughter. And she'd tried to blame Pearl's murder on a jealous lover.

We alighted at the entrance to the courtyard, but Mr. Armitage caught my arm and held me back. He nodded at the abandoned cart where Mr. Larsen stood beside Millie, his back to us. Millie sat on the cart, her little legs swinging in the air. He seemed to be talking to her while she simply stared straight ahead. It was impossible to tell if she was listening or not.

"Does his work allow him to have Saturdays off?" Mr. Armitage asked.

I wasn't sure. Now that I thought about it, Mr. Larsen had been home when I'd called last time too, and that had been a Wednesday. He'd also been repairing his own boots and Mrs. Larsen had been baking, perhaps to make ends meet if her husband was out of work. If they were in financial difficulty, it would explain why they needed money from Pearl.

"He seems devoted to Millie," Mr. Armitage said.

Yes, he did. Where Mrs. Larsen had no patience for her daughter, Mr. Larsen had it in abundance. He adored her. So if he thought Pearl was going to take Millie away from him, he might have done whatever was necessary to stop her.

I felt sick to my stomach.

Mr. Armitage led the way, his strides long and purposeful. I dragged my feet, but ended up at the same destination. I introduced the two men. By the end, my mouth was dry.

"Have you ever been to the Piccadilly Playhouse?" Mr. Armitage asked.

Mr. Larsen lifted Millie off the cart and put her on the ground. "No. Why?"

"Why aren't you at work today?"

Mr. Larsen's jaw set. "I don't see how that's any business of yours."

"Just answer the question."

Mr. Larsen took Millie's hand and led her away.

I stepped in front of him. "I need to speak to you, but I don't think Millie should overhear what I have to say."

"Then don't say it."

"I have to, and I will say it right here if you don't step away."

He glanced down at the girl. "Stay here, Millie. You understand? Don't move."

I walked a few feet away and he followed. Mr. Armitage joined us. "We know Millie is not your child. She's Pearl's, and Mr. Culpepper is the father."

Mr. Larsen rubbed the back of his neck and his shoulders slumped. He was a deflated, defeated man. "She's as good as ours. We've raised her. No one knows that she's not ours, only Pearl, Culpepper and now you." He shrugged. "What of it?"

"Was Pearl going to take her back?"

"No!"

"Did you need more money for Millie's upkeep?"

"I can provide for my family," he ground out. "She's just a little girl. She doesn't cost much."

"But you've lost your job, haven't you?" I pressed. "Have you taken in boarders? Is that why your parlor is closed off, because you're sleeping in there while your boarders rent your bedroom?"

"I don't have anything to say to you. Good day."

"Then I'll speak to your wife."

"She's not in."

"We know she confronted Pearl about money at the Playhouse, and lied to me about it. Indeed, she told me she'd never been there. I think she learned the layout of the theater then went back the following day and lured Pearl up to the dress circle on some pretext or other then pushed her over the balcony."

He shook his head, but his gaze did not meet mine.

"Mrs. Larsen hated her sister, didn't she? She hated her for being more beautiful, more popular, more talented. She hated that she wouldn't take responsibility for her child. A child that your wife isn't particularly fond of. A child she calls simple."

He stepped forward, his hands curled into fists. He bared his teeth in a growl. "She's not simple."

Mr. Armitage grabbed his arm and jerked him back, away from me.

"No, she's not." I looked at the girl, taking a tentative step forward, one hand extended in front of her. "She's quite musically talented. Unfortunately, your wife couldn't see it, and nor could Pearl. But you saw it. You love her and want to nurture her talent. But that requires money."

"She can develop her music ability here, without instruments or a teacher. She's content enough and there's time later for her to have proper lessons. I'll pay for them when I get a new job. You'll see. I'll pay for her music lessons if I have to work my fingers to the bone. We didn't need help from Pearl."

He was right. Millie was young. They had time. So why did they need the money now? It was clear he adored his daughter, although his wife wasn't quite so loving. To her, Millie was not quite right. But it was clear to me she wasn't so simple that she couldn't function in society. With some love and patience, she could grow up to be like other girls.

Millie took another tentative step forward. "Papa?"

Mr. Larsen spun around. "Millie, wait!" He raced to her and took her hand then led her back to the cart.

I followed them, watching as Millie felt around, her hands skimming over her surroundings, before settling down. "She's blind," I murmured.

Mr. Larsen made sure she had one hand grasping the cart's edge before he let her go. "Aye. Has been since birth, although we didn't know for months."

A woman like Mrs. Larsen, somewhat selfish herself and certainly impatient, would consider a blind child a burden. Particularly if she didn't love the girl as a daughter in the first place. Lady Wrexham had called Millie "damaged", so I suspected Pearl had told Lord Wrexham about Millie's blindness and his wife had overheard. Lady Wrexham and Mrs. Larsen were of like-mind in their view of blindness. To Lady

Wrexham, Millie was a social burden. To Mrs. Larsen, she was a financial one.

Mrs. Larsen had demanded Pearl give her money for Millie on Christmas Day, and I suspected it was more than the usual monthly amount. And I knew why.

"There's a school for the blind you want to send Millie to. She alluded to it when I was here. But it costs money, doesn't it?"

Mr. Larsen leaned back against the cart with a heavy sigh. "The school itself isn't costly, but it requires us to move to a more expensive area. We can't afford it, right now. Not until I find work."

"And your wife did not want the financial burden to fall on you both, so she asked Pearl to fund your move. When Pearl didn't pay straight away, Mrs. Larsen sought her out at the theater and they argued. Perhaps Pearl told her then that she was trying to get the money. But your wife ran out of patience and returned the next day. Do you know if it was an accident? Or did Mrs. Larsen push her over the balcony on purpose?"

Mr. Larsen dragged a hand over his face. When it came away, his skin was ashen. "She's my wife. The mother of my child. I can't tell you what happened. I *won't*."

I stepped closer, but Mr. Armitage put his arm out, blocking me. He shook his head in warning. "Is that the woman you want raising Millie?" I asked. "A woman capable of murdering her own sister and showing no remorse?"

He squeezed his eyes shut and buried his face in his hands.

"Tell me what happened on the day Pearl died," I said gently.

Footsteps pounded on the cobbles behind me. I swung around to see Mrs. Larsen wielding a glass bottle above her head. I stumbled back, arms up to protect myself, as she brought it down.

Mr. Armitage caught her wrist, the bottle just inches from my head.

She screamed in frustration, like a starving hawk denied her prey. "Stop talking to them!"

Mr. Larsen stood in front of Millie, his hands at the ready

to capture his wife if she got free of Mr. Armitage. But Mr. Armitage held her firmly. He wrenched the bottle from her and gave it to me then forced both her hands behind her back. She spat and snarled, cursing us and her sister.

A neighbor must have heard the commotion and emerged from her house. Mr. Armitage asked her to fetch a constable. She raced out through the arch, past the basket Mrs. Larsen had set down on the ground.

"Nellie deserved to die!" Mrs. Larsen shouted. "She was the most selfish, inconsiderate person you'd ever meet. She didn't care about her daughter. She'd forget to pay us for her upkeep some months."

"We didn't need the money," Mr. Larsen said. He sounded exhausted, but not surprised or angry. He'd known all along that his wife killed Pearl.

"You lost your job! It was left to me to bake pies just to make enough to put food on the table. We would have starved if it weren't for me. Nellie didn't care. And then you went and mentioned that bloody school to Millie. Once she got the idea into her head, it was all she spoke about, when the idiot of a girl did speak. Over and over, every day. It was driving me mad!"

"She's not an idiot."

She scoffed. "I wish Nellie had wanted her back. I'd have gladly got rid of her."

"You don't mean that." He picked up Millie and cuddled her, but the girl seemed unaware of the events unfolding around her.

"You admit you did it?" Mr. Armitage asked. "You pushed her over the balcony?"

Mrs. Larsen tried to wrench free of his grip, but it was useless. She growled in frustration and kicked out at me, standing directly in front of her. I dodged her foot and kicked back, hitting her in the shin with the toe of my boot. She howled in pain. It was the only way to stop her from doing it again.

"I don't regret it," she snarled. "Nellie got every advantage in life. It all came so easily to her. From the time she was born, our parents doted on her, their beautiful little girl. They gave her whatever she wanted, let her do what she wanted.

And she repaid them by bringing shame to them when she took to the stage. The world is better off without her, and I will *not* apologize for that."

Two sisters, both so different, yet one was wildly jealous of the other to the point where it consumed her, and turned her into something unrecognizable. Was that how my mother and Aunt Lilian were before my mother left to marry my father? Aunt Lilian told me she'd been jealous of my mother's easy, friendly nature, her natural poise and intelligence. If she thought my mother had been given every advantage, could she too have become consumed by hatred if my mother had never left?

But my aunt wasn't like Mrs. Larsen. She had a good heart and she admitted that she regretted her jealousy. Nor was my mother as selfish as Pearl. The two sets of sisters couldn't be compared.

The neighbor returned, bringing two constables with her. Mr. Armitage gave them a brief account as he handed Mrs. Larsen over to them. They handcuffed her and wrote down our details then took her away.

Mr. Larsen watched them go, his gaze unblinking. He looked pale and his hands shook as he set Millie down on the ground.

She started humming, rousing him from his stupor. "What happens now?" he muttered.

"A Scotland Yard detective will come and talk to you," Mr. Armitage said. "Be honest with him and you'll have nothing to worry about."

"Yes, but…what happens now?" He looked down at Millie, holding his hand and humming quietly to herself. "I have no work and Nellie is no longer alive to give us money every month. And the school…I can't afford to move closer."

"What about the things your wife took from Pearl's flat?"

"Already sold to pay off debts."

I clasped his arm, but nothing I could say would help. He was in shock. He'd lost his wife today. I felt sorry for him yet all I could give was empty assurances that all would be well, somehow.

I left with Mr. Armitage, happy that he offered to escort me to the hotel. I was also in shock. I hadn't liked Mrs.

Larsen, but I'd not thought her capable of murdering her own sister.

Mr. Armitage helped me up the step into the hansom, one hand at the small of my back, the other cradling my elbow. "Thank you," I said as he joined me on the seat. "I'm glad I brought you along."

He opened the hatch above our heads to give the driver instructions then closed it again. "You did it all, Miss Fox. You worked it out."

"But you stopped Mrs. Larsen from braining me with that bottle of cordial."

"It would have made quite a mess."

I laughed softly, despite my heavy heart.

I settled in for the journey home, our arms touching in the close proximity of the small hansom. His presence was a comfort, but I could never admit that to him.

Once I was back at the hotel, and Mr. Armitage went on his way, I told Frank, Goliath and Peter that I wanted to see them in the staff parlor during their afternoon break. One of them sent word to Harmony and Victor, so that we all met in the parlor at three-thirty.

Over cups of tea, I told them how the investigation had ended. "Thanks to your help, Pearl's murderer has been arrested."

"We didn't do anything," Peter said. "It was all you, Miss Fox."

"It was a little bit us," Goliath admitted.

"Quite a lot actually." Harmony gave Victor a sideways glance. "Some contributed more than others, however."

Victor stretched out his legs and crossed them at the ankles. "That we did."

She opened her mouth to retort, so I cut in before she could rise to his bait. "Does anyone know if Lord Rumford is in his suite? I ought to give him the news."

"He checked out this morning," Peter said.

"I thought he was staying until tomorrow."

Peter shrugged. "He checked out at around ten."

I slumped into the chair. There went any possibility of getting paid for all our hard work.

CHAPTER 15

With the investigation and its conclusion still playing on my mind, I had difficulty sleeping. I ordered a cup of hot chocolate through the speaking tube at three AM, but when it didn't arrive, I put on my dressing gown and headed down to the kitchen.

My candle flickered in the drafts swirling through the stairwell, creating dancing shadows on the wall. I clutched the dressing gown tightly at my throat, but it did little to block out the cold. I should have stayed in bed.

As my foot stepped onto the second floor landing, a figure emerged from the corridor. We both stopped and stared at the other. By the light of her candle, I could see her ruby red lips, her pink cheeks and painted eyes. Her shawl hung loosely around her bare shoulders, revealing an extremely low-cut dress and ample cleavage.

She wasn't one of the elegant mistresses I'd seen on the arms of gentlemen guests, treated as though she were his wife. This woman was not of the same quality, and her benefactor was treating her like a whore, making her leave in the middle of the night. She wasn't the sort of woman my uncle would want coming and going from the hotel.

She pressed a finger to her lips and giggled, then passed me and rushed down the stairs. I followed at a distance and waited at the base of the stairwell as she crossed the foyer. There was no beak-nosed man there tonight, no Mr. Hirst, only James, the night porter. He opened the door for the woman and she left without a backward glance.

I checked the vicinity then approached him. He swallowed heavily upon seeing me then he too, glanced around. I suspected he was looking for an escape, or someone to come to his rescue.

"Good evening, Miss Fox," he said, a nervous hitch in his voice.

"Good evening, James. Who was that?"

"What?"

"The woman who just left. Who was she?"

"A, er, a guest."

"A guest leaving on her own at this hour? Come now, James, I'm not a fool. I saw her in the stairwell. She is not a guest."

He blinked rapidly, his mouth working, but no sound coming out.

"I know what she is and why she's here," I went on. "She and the other women have not been discreet, and I suspect that will bother my uncle more than their actual presence in the hotel."

"You're going to tell him?" he squeaked.

"I have to. I can't turn the other cheek to something that affects the hotel's reputation. Uncle Ronald would never forgive me if he found out that I knew and never said a word. But I can spare you the worst, if you tell me who is orchestrating the comings and goings of those girls."

Even in the dim light, I could see his face blanch. "I can't. They'll punish me if I tell."

As much as James needed to take responsibility for his actions, I couldn't think too harshly of him. It was likely he was given no choice. He would have been threatened if he *didn't* do as ordered.

"Then we have to catch those responsible in the act so that you can't be blamed for tattling. Do you know where Mr. Hirst and that other fellow are now?"

He sucked in his lower lip and nibbled it. He finally released it with a nod of his head. "His name is Tucket. The girls belong to him."

"Belong?"

He shrugged. "That's what he says. They're in the hotel, upstairs. There was some trouble with one of the girls in room one-twenty-four and they went to appease the guest who ordered her company."

I had to hope they'd be there a little longer. If this was to work, I had to catch them in the act. But I couldn't do it alone.

I raced up the staircase so quickly my candle flame extinguished. I was out of breath by the time I knocked lightly on the door to my uncle and aunt's suite. My tap was so soft that I worried Uncle Ronald wouldn't hear it, but he opened the door a moment later, blinking blearily back at me.

"Cleo? Something wrong?"

"Get dressed, and hurry. We have to catch Mr. Hirst and a man known as Tucket in the act."

"The act of what?"

"Of procuring whores and smuggling them into the hotel."

If I were my uncle, I would have pressed for more details then and there, but thankfully he didn't question me. He trusted me.

A few minutes later, he joined me in the corridor as he threw on a velvet smoking jacket over his shirt and trousers. We raced down the stairs to level one. Instead of knocking on the door to room one-twenty-four, we waited. I could just make out raised voices coming from inside, a higher pitched female one and lower male ones.

When the door suddenly opened and a woman stormed out, followed by Mr. Hirst and the beak-nosed man, Uncle Ronald and I remained in the shadows until the door closed behind them. As much as we needed to catch them in the act, we could not embarrass the guest. I expected Uncle Ronald would discreetly inform him in the morning that the Mayfair didn't condone the presence of common whores. The hypocrisy of not allowing those sort of women yet turning the other cheek when a mistress arrived on the arm of her benefactor wasn't lost on me, but it wasn't my hotel or my rules.

When Mr. Hirst and Tucket passed us, Uncle Ronald stepped out of the shadows. "Come with me. Both of you."

The man named Tucket darted off, his footsteps thundering down the stairs. I suspected we wouldn't see him or his women again after tonight. Mr. Hirst, however, couldn't disappear as easily.

"I'll escort you to your room," Uncle Ronald told the assistant manager. "You will gather your things and leave immediately."

Mr. Hirst's nostrils flared. "Will I receive a reference, sir?"

"You have the gall to ask me that? You're lucky I'm not going to tell the police."

Mr. Hirst's eyes hardened in the light of his lantern. "You wouldn't do that, sir. You don't want the police here so soon after the murder. The hotel's reputation is everything." Haughty confidence dripped from every word. He knew he was right. He turned to me and I shivered beneath his ice-cold glare. "Speaking of reputations, do you know that Miss Fox is undertaking an investigation?"

"Yes, and what has that got to do with anything?" Uncle Ronald demanded.

"Do you know she's conducting that investigation with Harry Armitage? They've been seen together, looking *very* comfortable in one another's company." He strode off, a twisted smile on his lips.

My uncle shot me a speaking look that warned me we would be having words later, then he followed Mr. Hirst down the stairs. I headed up to my suite and didn't sleep a wink for the rest of the night.

* * *

Despite my reassurances to James, he was dismissed too. In hindsight, it was inevitable his participation in the scheme would be discovered by my uncle. Without his agreement, it couldn't have gone ahead. According to Harmony, who'd heard it from one of the footmen, James had at least been promised a reference by Mr. Hobart, who'd overseen his dismissal when he arrived for work in the morning.

I told her what had transpired overnight but asked her not to tell anyone else. The reason for the dismissals should remain a secret. "Did you hear how Mr. Hirst took it?" I asked as she sat across from me at breakfast. "Did he say something as he left?"

"He was gone before even the maids arrived. No one saw him go but Sir Ronald."

It didn't matter, I supposed. He'd already said enough to damage my reputation in my uncle's eyes. Uncle Ronald didn't like Mr. Armitage, and he'd already made it clear he didn't want him here, let alone want me associating with him.

That was not his decision to make, however, and I was determined to tell him as much when he confronted me about it. I could be friends with whomever I pleased. I only hoped it would not cause a rift between us.

Later that morning, I spent some time with Detective Inspector Hobart and his sergeant in Mr. Hobart's office. He had already spoken with Mr. Armitage but needed to hear my version of the events that unfolded at the Larsens' house. When I finished, the detective rose.

"Harry tells me you were quite extraordinary, Miss Fox."

"Hardly. I gave up the investigation more than once."

"But resumed each time. You were determined, and determination and persistence are nine-tenths of detective work."

"I couldn't have done it without Mr. Armitage's assistance."

"You make a good team."

"I'm only sorry I can't compensate him for his trouble. Lord Rumford never promised to pay me, and he has checked out of the hotel anyway. I'll write to him today to inform him of events, but I doubt I'll hear back. We didn't part on good terms when last we met. I'm afraid I was somewhat judgmental of his choice to keep a mistress."

He gave me a flat smile. "Harry wouldn't accept compensation for helping you anyway." He extended his hand and I shook it. "Good day, Miss Fox. I hope to see you again soon."

I watched him go, feeling somewhat restless. It was disappointing that I couldn't compensate Mr. Armitage for his time. He deserved something, but I had nothing to give. I was about to return upstairs, to write a letter to Lord Rumford, when Goliath signaled for me to join him by one of the large vases.

"I heard from my friend at the Savoy," he said. "The one who overheard a guest mention seeing Lady Rumford at the opera."

"It no longer matters now that the case is over. Lady Rumford's reason for being in London has nothing to do with Pearl's murder."

"I know, but don't you want to know why she didn't tell anyone she was here?" He wiggled his eyebrows suggestively. "It's a little scandalous."

"Then I'm all ears."

"According to that same lady that my friend overheard the first time, Lady Rumford has been seen with a man, several times."

"She has a gentleman friend?"

"It seems so, but I don't think he's a gentleman. Apparently no one knows who he is. That's what's got all the ladies gossiping."

"Meaning he isn't from their set." Perhaps Lady Rumford was doing the very same thing as her husband—paying a companion to be with her. I hoped so. If Lord Rumford could enjoy himself with women like Pearl, why couldn't his wife find her own satisfaction along a similar path? I dearly hoped she could weather the gossip that was about to engulf her.

I wrote the letter to Lord Rumford and gave it to Terence at the post desk. Instead of heading back up to my suite, I instead walked to Pearl's flat. I still had her key and I wanted to return the photograph I'd borrowed of her, Mr. Culpepper and the leading actor.

I inserted the key into the lock and my heart almost burst from my chest when the door suddenly opened. Upon seeing Lord Rumford, I pressed a hand to my stomach and breathed a sigh of relief.

"You gave me a fright."

"And you me." He frowned. "What are you doing here?"

I showed him the photograph. "Returning this. I borrowed it as part of the investigation. May I come in and talk to you? There has been an arrest."

He released a shuddery breath and closed his eyes. "My God. That is wonderful news. Wonderful news, indeed. Thank you, Miss Fox." He grasped my hand and shook it ferociously. "Thank you for persisting, even after our little disagreement." He drew me inside and shut the door. "I hope you can forgive me for that. I was in a bit of a state that day, and I took it out on you."

I blinked back my surprise. This man confounded me at every turn. Just when I'd made up my mind not to like him, I found that I wanted to forgive him. He'd been dealt a blow recently, and it was understandable that his gentlemanly manners slipped from time to time. We're all prone to outbursts on occasion.

We sat in Pearl's parlor, surrounded by images of her at every turn. It was impossible not to feel a connection with her here, among her things, even though I'd never met her. Yet I felt as though I'd come to know her, in a way. She was a flawed person, certainly, and not someone whose decisions I liked, particularly when it came to Millie, but she was aware of her flaws and tried to do as little harm to those around her as possible. Perhaps Millie was better off with Mr. Larsen than she would have been with parents who didn't want her. He adored her.

Lord Rumford listened to my account of how I'd solved the case and of Mrs. Larsen's arrest. He went a little pale when he learned that Pearl's own sister had killed her.

"And all for money, you say," he murmured. "Dear lord, if only I'd known what would transpire, I'd have given Pearl the money immediately. To think, I could have averted all this."

"Don't blame yourself. Mrs. Larsen was a little mad, I think. If this hadn't set her off, it would have been something else. She was jealous of Pearl, and angry at her, too. As she saw it, Pearl breezed through life, whereas she felt she had nothing but burdens and troubles." I shook my head sadly. "If you ask me, she had far more than Pearl. She had a lovely little girl to call her own and a supportive husband who was on her side until the end. If only she could see that her life was as full as Pearl's, only different."

Lord Rumford picked up a photograph of himself and Pearl, staring at the camera. He blinked back tears as he stroked his thumb over Pearl's image. "She was so lively and so lovely. She didn't deserve to have her life ended that way." He released a shuddery breath. "Now she will be forever young, forever beautiful. Forever in my heart." He kissed the photograph then returned it to the table.

I sat there, wondering how to broach the subject of payment. People of his ilk didn't like discussing money, but people like me couldn't afford not to mention it. "I am sorry to bring this up, my lord, but there's the matter of my fee. I know we didn't settle on a sum before this began, and that is entirely my fault, but I've had expenses, you see."

"Of course, of course." He pulled out a leather wallet from his inside jacket pocket and fished out some bank notes. "Will this be enough?"

I smiled, thanked him, and tucked the money into my purse. I gave him the flat key in exchange. "Thank you for trusting me with this investigation." I rose and he stood too. I put out my hand and he shook it.

"Thank *you*, Miss Fox. You have been a revelation." He followed me to the door, but I could see something else was on his mind. Finally, he got to the point. "Where can I find Pearl's brother-in-law?"

* * *

After dividing a third of Lord Rumford's payment among Harmony, Victor, Goliath, Frank and Peter over a cup of tea in the staff parlor, I headed out to the office of Armitage and Associates. I walked in on Mr. Armitage with his feet on the desk, crossed at the ankles, a newspaper in hand. One of Luigi's coffee cups sat empty on the desk.

Mr. Armitage lowered his feet and put down the paper. "You no longer feel the need to knock?"

"I think we've gone beyond knocking." I sat on the guest chair. "I'm practically a member of staff."

"No, you're not."

I opened my purse and passed him a bank note.

He frowned. "What's this?"

"A third of Lord Rumford's fee."

He pushed the money back. "Keep it."

I slid the note forward again. "You're entitled to it for all the help you gave me."

He picked up the note and rounded the desk. He opened

my purse and thrust the note inside before handing me the purse. "If you try to give it to me again, I'll be insulted. I helped you because I wanted to, not because I expected compensation." Before I could protest, he continued. "So Rumford came through?"

"He did. He's not such a bad sort. He loved Pearl very much, although I'm not sure she deserved it. They were both selfish, in their way, and inconsiderate of others. She of Millie and Mr. Culpepper, and he of his wife."

"I feel sorry for her."

"Don't worry about Lady Rumford." I smiled slyly. "She seems to have found a way to comfort herself."

"Oh?"

"I hear he's quite handsome, and young."

Mr. Armitage laughed softly, not at all shocked. As assistant manager at the Mayfair, I wondered if he'd witnessed similar arrangements between wealthy women and young men. I'm sure those were conducted discreetly, unlike the events of the previous night.

"Your old position has become vacant again," I told him. "Mr. Hirst was dismissed for endangering the reputation of the hotel." At his frown, I added, "He had an arrangement with the procurer of whores that allowed the girls to come and go in the night, with a percentage of their fee going to Mr. Hirst and James."

He sat on the edge of the desk and huffed a humorless laugh. "That explains why he was eager to leave his previous employment."

"Pardon?"

"Uncle Alfred wondered why Mr. Hirst wanted to leave a perfectly good position where he would one day take over as manager. It seemed odd that he would go to another position that was exactly the same, not a step up. His references were good, however, and his previous employer spoke highly of him, so Uncle Alfred and Sir Ronald saw no reason not to hire him."

"But his previous employer left out the fact he was forced to leave," I finished. "Most likely because they discovered he had an arrangement with the man known as Tucket to smuggle in his girls. The hotel probably wanted to keep the scandal out of the newspapers so gave him a reference to stop him talking."

"Hopefully Hirst won't stir up trouble for the Mayfair."

Mr. Hirst might not go to the newspapers, but he had already stirred up trouble for me with my uncle. I wouldn't worry Mr. Armitage with that, however. I didn't want him to feel compelled to change the nature of our friendship.

Mr. Armitage crossed his arms and ankles. "Two crimes solved. What a day you had yesterday."

"It was a most satisfying day." I rose and put out my hand. "Thank you again, although I wish you'd accept some payment for your trouble."

He shook my hand. The pressure was firm but not hard, and I could still feel it after he let go. "Goodbye, Miss Fox."

"Good day, not goodbye. I'm sure we'll see one another soon."

"I don't see why, unless you know something I don't."

I simply smiled and gave him a little wave as I left.

* * *

I MADE one more stop on the way home, via Fleet Street, then spent the rest of the day avoiding my uncle. While I knew the lecture was coming, I wanted to delay it as long as possible.

The following morning, Harmony brought in my breakfast tray with a copy of the newspaper I'd requested. A letter sat on the top of the folded paper. She poured coffee from the pot while I read it.

"It's from Mr. Larsen. How lovely of him to write." I scanned the untidy scrawl but struggled to see the end of it through my tears. "Oh. I shall never say a bad word about Lord Rumford again."

Harmony accepted the letter from me and read it. She gasped when she reached the part that had brought tears to my eyes.

Lord Rumford had called on Mr. Larsen and Millie the afternoon before. He'd given Mr. Larsen a sum to pay for his relocation closer to the school for blind children. Millie would attend all day classes there while Mr. Larsen worked in his new job as a foreman at a factory. Lord Rumford, as an investor in the factory, had obtained the job for him.

Harmony blinked back tears as she folded the letter up. "I still don't like that he kept a mistress. But I can forgive him a little."

"I think we should. It seems like he loved Pearl. Anyway, by all accounts, his wife is enjoying herself with her lover. If Lord and Lady Rumford's arrangement works for them, who are we to judge them harshly?"

She handed me a cup of coffee then sat back, blowing on hers to cool it. "I suppose not everyone is wholly bad."

"True. Even Mrs. Larsen had her good points. I think she did want Millie to attend that school or she wouldn't have asked her sister for the money."

Harmony didn't seem quite so convinced, however. "I reckon she only wanted her to go so she wouldn't have Millie around all day. It was a way to get rid of her. You know, I've noticed that about you."

"Noticed what?"

"That you tend to see the good in people." She lifted the lid on the platter of breakfast, which was enough for both of us. The kitchen staff knew to add more, now, and not let their superiors find out. "You might want to stop that if you wish to make a go of the detective business. You ought to think everyone's guilty and wait for them to prove otherwise. It'll make the task of investigating easier."

I pulled a face. "No thanks. I prefer my way."

I picked up the newspaper and was pleased to see the solving of Pearl's murder had made the front page. I quickly scanned the words for names, then re-read it to make sure mine didn't appear anywhere. It did not. But one did.

I smiled into my cup as I sipped but Harmony noticed.

"You don't happen to know who told the journalist that Armitage and Associates helped the police solve the case, do you?" she asked, oh-so-innocently.

I sipped so I couldn't answer.

"Odd that the only newspaper that mentions Armitage and Associates in relation to the case is this one. The same one you requested to see this morning."

"Mr. Armitage refused payment for helping me, so I had

to get creative. It wasn't right that he received nothing for his efforts. This way, I get his portion of the fee as well as my own, and he receives free advertising."

"I wager the mention in the paper will ultimately be more beneficial to him than his portion of Lord Rumford's fee."

I grinned. "I hope so."

She passed me a plate and cutlery. "He'll feel like he owes you."

"His thanks will be more than enough. However, if he does feel the need to thank me in other ways, I'll suggest he paints my name on his office door. Armitage and Fox Detective Agency sounds very professional, don't you think?"

Harmony did something rare—she tipped her head back and laughed.

Available 7th December 2021:
MURDER IN THE DRAWING ROOM
The 3rd Cleopatra Fox Mystery

A MESSAGE FROM THE AUTHOR

I hope you enjoyed reading MURDER AT THE PICCADILLY PLAYHOUSE as much as I enjoyed writing it. As an independent author, getting the word out about my book is vital to its success, so if you liked this book please consider telling your friends and writing a review at the store where you purchased it. If you would like to be contacted when I release a new book, subscribe to my newsletter at http://cjarcher.com/contact-cj/newsletter/. You will only be contacted when I have a new book out.

ALSO BY C.J. ARCHER

SERIES WITH 2 OR MORE BOOKS

Cleopatra Fox Mysteries

After The Rift

Glass and Steele

The Ministry of Curiosities Series

The Emily Chambers Spirit Medium Trilogy

The 1st Freak House Trilogy

The 2nd Freak House Trilogy

The 3rd Freak House Trilogy

The Assassins Guild Series

Lord Hawkesbury's Players Series

Witch Born

SINGLE TITLES NOT IN A SERIES

Courting His Countess

Surrender

Redemption

The Mercenary's Price

ABOUT THE AUTHOR

C.J. Archer has loved history and books for as long as she can remember and feels fortunate that she found a way to combine the two. She spent her early childhood in the dramatic beauty of outback Queensland, Australia, but now lives in suburban Melbourne with her husband, two children and a mischievous black & white cat named Coco.

Subscribe to C.J.'s newsletter through her website to be notified when she releases a new book, as well as get access to exclusive content and subscriber-only giveaways. Her website also contains up to date details on all her books: http://cjarcher.com She loves to hear from readers. You can contact her through email cj@cjarcher.com or follow her on social media to get the latest updates on her books:

facebook.com/CJArcherAuthorPage
twitter.com/cj_archer
instagram.com/authorcjarcher
pinterest.com/cjarcher
bookbub.com/authors/c-j-archer

www.ingramcontent.com/pod-product-compliance
Lightning Source LLC
Chambersburg PA
CBHW030334310726
48979CB00001B/23

9781922554703